DARK
DIVERSIONS

DARK DIVERSIONS

a traveler's tale

JOHN RALSTON SAUL

PINTAIL

PINTAIL
a member of Penguin Group (USA)

Published by the Penguin Group
Penguin Group (Canada)
90 Eglinton Avenue East, Suite 700, Toronto, Ontario, Canada M4P 2Y3
(a division of Pearson Canada Inc.)

Penguin Group (USA) Inc., 375 Hudson Street, New York, New York 10014, U.S.A.
Penguin Books Ltd, 80 Strand, London WC2R 0RL, England
Penguin Ireland, 25 St Stephen's Green, Dublin 2, Ireland
    (a division of Penguin Books Ltd)
Penguin Group (Australia), 707 Collins Street, Melbourne, Victoria 3008, Australia
    (a division of Pearson Australia Group Pty Ltd)
Penguin Books India Pvt Ltd, 11 Community Centre, Panchsheel Park,
    New Delhi – 110 017, India
Penguin Group (NZ), 67 Apollo Drive, Rosedale, Auckland 0632, New Zealand
    (a division of Pearson New Zealand Ltd)
Penguin Books (South Africa) (Pty) Ltd, 24 Sturdee Avenue, Rosebank,
    Johannesburg 2196, South Africa

Penguin Books Ltd, Registered Offices: 80 Strand, London WC2R 0RL, England

First published in English in Viking hardcover by Penguin Canada, a division of
Pearson Canada Inc., 2012. Previously published in France as *De si bons Américains*
by Éditions Payot & Rivages, 1996.
Published in this edition, 2013.

1 2 3 4 5 6 7 8 9 10   (RRD)

Copyright © John Ralston Saul, 2012

Author representation: Westwood Creative Artists
94 Harbord Street, Toronto, Ontario M5S 1G6

Manufactured in the U.S.A.

ISBN: 978-0-14-318750-9

Visit the Penguin US website at **www.penguin.com**

for

ÉMILE MARTEL

Money is a protection, and those who are protected should extend their arms to enfold others. Not fewer private elevators, but more people in them.

— ELEANOR BURTON

I
MONEY, MINDS
AND LOOKS

MRS. REVERE TOOK THE STEPS one at a time, down from the hotel to the terrace, mauve hair floating above her in a baroque cloud. Only the Holy Ghost and a host of angels were lacking. Her fingers, two stones on each hand, gathered up the painted *gandura* lest it catch in the gold of her sandals. Italian sun overlit the way, casting shadows beneath each line on her face and reflecting off the stones.

"What a surprise, dear! What a surprise." It was the voice of a trumpeter swan, not without vibrations of sexual warmth. "But what in God's name are you doing here?" The words seemed to be a comment on the guests at the other tables. The hotel was considered by some to be the finest in Italy.

I rose to give the old woman an affectionate kiss. There was something in the way, a second later, she both ignored the waiter, who manoeuvred a chair to meet her descending backside, and yet accepted the wicker with enough pleasure to imply gratitude that revealed beneath her Upper East Side exterior the hint of origins not unlike his own.

"I was passing this way. A friend mentioned you were staying here."

"Oh, you're always passing, dear boy. Always on the way somewhere. What friend? That pretty girl staying with the Franklins, I suppose." She tidied the floating cloth about her. "But then, why stop? Better to pass on by. You're so young, you can afford to. So long as you stay lean." She ran a hand over my thigh with feeling, then twisted up to the waiter. "*Portami un bicchiere de Prosecco, caro. Freddissimo!*" And back to me. "What's her name?"

"You don't know?"

She was momentarily caught out.

"The love of my life," I added.

"Ha!" Her hand went back to my thigh. "How many loves of your life are you up to?"

I shrugged.

"Tell me about her."

I shrugged again. "She has everything."

"Everything. What's everything?"

"Poreless skin, eggshell colour. Small wrists and feet. Likes writers. Speaks French but isn't impressed by the French. Shivers when I touch her."

"You're fantasizing. Men are always fantasizing. I promise you, dear, it's very tiring for girls. We hate men's expectations."

"As to passing by ..." There I stopped. I was on my way to Somalia via Rome to slip into the Eritrean war from the side, although it was beginning to look as if I might have to switch and fly to Addis in order to reach the Somali war. If the confusion increased, I could simply fly to Nairobi and head north to one of the other disaster zones. It was my story for the year, taken on to maintain my press card. The result would be time wasted while I was being escorted around the official part of the war. I'd try to get an interview with the president, a Marxist general who seemed to be caught in a nihilistic time warp. Of course, it wouldn't really be an interview. I'd ask questions. He'd make statements. You don't have conversations with dictators. There would be words, atmosphere, impressions. Then with a bit of luck I'd be able to get away from the political commissars and play at that vaguest of things – the writer nosing about for reflections of other people's reality.

If I had stopped in mid-sentence with Mrs. Revere, well, Eritrea, it occurred to me, wasn't a subject she would care to hear about.

"I used to come here in June," she volunteered. "Ercole is much quieter then. The whole coast is." Her eyes wandered along the cliff line to the sea, where speedboats marred the blue. "But, you know, I found it depressing. Only the rich are here in June. They're so ugly, dear. Emaciated. So many diets. So many paunches. Such meagre conversation ... and all those scars." She folded forward a lobe to prove that she herself had none and laughed. "So you see, I've gone back to the busy months of my youth." She adjusted her chair to avoid a ray of sun squeezing past the umbrella. "Of course, it is a bit hot. But I like the heat." Mrs. Revere picked the napkin up from her plate, looked down to the side of her chair as if avoiding a painful scene while she spread the cloth over her knees, her mouth puckered as if with concentrated effort. "It's such a pity that looks don't come with money."

"They don't need to," I offered. "Money can always buy looks."

An awkward silence fell. Why does the heat dull my sensibility? Her Prosecco arrived and she emptied half the glass with a thirsty little swallow. A swallow so full of life, of something that made her different from the others. Mrs. Revere giggled. She was a very young eighty. She had been a very young seventy when I first met her in Bhutan, where she had been a guest of the king.

"Of course it can, dear. It bought me ... I don't know much genetics. I don't really know what it is, but there's a rule nobody ever writes about: when it comes to the rich, one generation is enough to breed out the looks. So I guess ugly genes are dominant, provided they've got money." She shifted her chair again and looked distracted. Distressed. I suppose she was thinking of her own children and grandchildren and great-grandchildren – all of them apparently of another race. "It's the money, dear. Not the genes. The power's in the money. I figured it out. They start by buying looks. Wonderful looks, if they can afford it. Mine, dear! Mine were wonderful. Ten years later it's all gone. Age doesn't matter. The destructive decade. That's what I call it. Mr. Revere elevated me at seventeen – in the social sense only, I can assure you. As a family they were all sweet of tooth and slack of haunch. And stolid in the sack, dear, though I can only speak for Mr. Revere on that account. My looks were gone at twenty-seven. Oh yes, dear. Ten years of decorating myself like every day was Christmas ... after a while it got to be a masquerade. That's all, dear. Just the trappings of beauty hung out on good bone structure. So now I come here in August and go to the public beach once a day," she hesitated, then finished with a joking air, "to be part of the real flesh."

"Come on. There are as many paunches there as anywhere. It's no worse up here."

"It's not that we're worse, dear. It's just that our money doesn't seem to make us look any better. If you should be better and you aren't, well, then you're worse. That's all." She put a finger to her lips. "Never knock an American dream." She said "knock" with a little electric jolt. "Money is on the side of good. That's why they want it. To complete the Holy Trinity. Them in the centre, moral value on the left, cash value on the right. That's all there is to it. You should know, dear, with your profession."

Mrs. Revere still believed the professions to be the ultimate masculine role and so intended a compliment when she spoke of writing in that way. I felt a little stab at my self-esteem. What I did or didn't do and whether it was worth my life were doubts that lurked in the background. Mrs. Revere's compliment brought them out dancing.

"I say, dump the Trinity!" She ignored the stares from the next table. "What we're really talking about, dear, is a weigh scale. Now, looks are a moral quality, like everything on the surface. What you do with them shows what you've got inside. Look!" She stared baldly around at the other guests. "All they ever talk about is Maseratis and good hotels. Always the last hotel and the next one. Never where they're staying." She started, "There's Nicola."

I glanced up to see a young man peering about from the top of the steps. His haunches weren't slack. The profile was Renaissance. Mrs. Revere turned away from him.

"He'll find me. I don't worry about Nicola's looks. He won't get a decade out of me. Oh, no, dear. The bone structure will be bones by then. He is what you find on the public beach in August." She gave a snort of pleasure, then turned to me seriously. "Now look. Fifty years I've been one of them, playing my role, listening to their conversation, and," she leaned forward, her voice dropped, "I still don't understand. There's nothing in it. Nothing. You know them. It's your job to observe. I've seen you watching. But what do you see? That's what I'd like to know."

"I'm just the court fool."

"Well, the fool sees best. So you tell me. What have you ever seen or heard that makes them stand out? What? I'd like to know."

"*Ciao*, Paula." The voice sang out from behind us.

"*Ciao*, Nicola."

"*Ottima!*" he exclaimed, pointing to her sandals, and pulled up a chair close by her side.

"What?" She turned back to me. "I'm waiting."

It was close to five weeks before I got out of Eritrea and back to Rome. There I found the love of my life, who seemed less pleased to see me than I had been imagining she would be. Of course, thirty-five days of dirty clothes, political commissars, unfriendly heat and the company of men does swell delusions about women. I think she had difficulty understanding my disappearance while she was on holiday and available. In another two days she was flying back to New York. I also had the feeling there was a male shadow hanging over our evening; not mine.

To avoid talking about us, she spent most of the time telling me about Mrs. Revere, to whom I'd introduced her. A week after my visit to Porto Ercole, Mrs. Revere had flown home. "Driven by boredom, my dear," she had told someone. "At my age sex is so repetitive. A young man thinks it's all new. Thinks he's being original. The last new thing in sex, dear, was when human beings, or whatever we were, climbed out of the sea to live on land. Doing it dry, dear. Now that was new."

2
CONVERSATIONS
WITH DICTATORS I

THE KING'S COUSIN insisted that I have lunch with a couple of colonels. They weren't even Moroccan colonels. Why he was being so insistent wasn't clear to me. Perhaps it had to do with a Moroccan campaign to undermine Algeria by supporting the enemies of the officers who were then running Mauritania. Moulay Ahmed – the King's cousin – was probably hoping I would write something about the evils of Algeria. My attitude is that I don't refuse lunch with people who want to influence me. You never know when you're going to be surprised, and whoever ends up paying the bill, you still own your digestion.

I met Salem and Kader at the Rabat Hilton poolside restaurant. A cheery place. A holiday place, filled with flowers and large umbrellas. Colonel Salem was the ex-vice-president of Mauritania. Recently ex. He had fled three weeks before our lunch. Colonel Kader had been out for three months. He was the ex–minister of communications. They both wore seersucker jackets, Kader's bright green, Salem's light blue. Very festive. With assorted ties.

They resembled foreign graduates of some Ivy League school, which it turned out they weren't. They were also physically assorted – Salem tall, pale, relaxed; probably a Northerner, a dissident R'gibat. Kader was short and dark; probably a Southerner. That was where the blacks and the Arabs had intermarried. He whispered like a stage plotter. Of course, we were sitting in public in a country addicted to conspiracy. And they were indeed plotting the overthrow of the colonels – the other colonels – who had deprived them of power.

In summary, the colonels currently in office were left-wing and pro-Algerian. My hosts were right-wing and pro-Moroccan. What left-wing and right-wing actually meant in a country populated by nomads and marginal farmers wasn't terribly clear. Tribal and regional differences were probably the real source of rivalry, and Mauritania had the added complexity of being a non-country, invented abruptly by the French as a separate colony for the sole purpose of holding on to an iron ore mine out in the middle of the desert. Then the Empire came to an end and the colonels made their entry.

Once we'd got the political talk out of the way we had a nice lunch. We laughed a lot, which made us stand out less from the tourists and diplomats at the other tables. A waiter brought around a tray of fresh fish. I ordered red snapper. They did the same, and a dry white wine. Not Moroccan, if I remember correctly.

All three of us had studied in France, so we talked

about that. In fact we had overlapped one year, although in different residences, at the Cité Universitaire on the south edge of Paris. We'd never met, and I suppose we were escaping from different things. I spent a lot of time lying about in the park reading and talking about Proust with other students. Kader and Salem had been amazed to find themselves in that cool, wet, urban world and couldn't get enough of the streets. Like northerners with the sun, they were drawn to the tepid humidity. None of us had any money, so we'd eaten in the same student halls the same bad food. Lentils were served like a crusted milkshake. Pieces of horsemeat dark and dry, as if from some unnamed animal. But it was all cheap. It hadn't killed us. And we'd had a good time. Doing what, was no longer clear, but it had been an indolent time in a city where everyone except the university students seems to work very hard. That indolence is the key to Paris's reputation as a student's city. Kader paid for lunch with cash which I suppose had been supplied by the King's cousin.

About six months later I was picking my way through the racks of a newsstand in Paris – the one just in behind the Odéon. A headline on the cover of *Jeune Afrique* caught my eye: "Coup Failure in Mauritania." I flipped through the magazine. It was a two-page spread in the centre, half taken up by an amateurish snapshot of Kader and Salem. The camera hadn't even been held straight. The two colonels had their hands half held up in a disordered sort of way. Salem's head was roughly bandaged.

It was a black-and-white photo, which made it seem out of time and place. But you could see they were unshaven and filthy. You could also see, or rather sense, that they were terrified – not really standing but crouching, as if trying to spirit themselves away by force of will or fear. The cutline under the photo said it had been taken just as an emergency firing squad had taken aim.

Apparently the two had swum across the Senegal River to the southern edge of Mauritania and raised about five hundred men from among Kader's old friends. They got all the way up to Nouakchott, the capital, undetected and in time to surround the Presidential Palace during the weekly Cabinet meeting, cut all the telephone and electrical lines, then attack. Except that there was no Cabinet meeting that day. Why? No particular reason. Government troops soon surrounded and overwhelmed them. The two colonels were executed on the spot, in the ditch that ran around the palace. That explained part of the disoriented aura in the photo. They were standing on a rough incline staring up at the summary firing squad. How would you keep your balance in those circum-stances? And where would the various parts of your mind be – part on death, part on the basic mechanism of keeping a dignified stance? It must have been a fluke that someone had a camera handy. I began to retch. Speckles of vomit spattered onto the magazines – the Automobile section, just above International Politics.

But that isn't the point of what I am telling you. I had

been sent off to lunch with them by the King's cousin in order to distract me from my persistent requests for a meeting with General Dlimi, the King's strongman. According to most stories, it was Dlimi who had wrestled General Oufkir, the preceding strongman, to the floor in the Rabat palace throne room in the middle of the night and held him there so that the King could put several bullets through his head. It was publicly described as a suicide. Humorists had it that the general had committed suicide by shooting himself three times in the head. Dlimi was seen more as a loyal servant, less as the grand inquisitor and backstage manipulator that his predecessor had been. But then Oufkir had spent the second half of his career serving what was then a young and inexperienced King. Dlimi inherited a wily, scarred monarch.

So when I saw the King's cousin the next day, I thanked him for setting me up with his charming Mauritanian rebels. Then I brought up the matter of Dlimi. The problem was the war in the Sahara. It wasn't going well. Dlimi was in charge and therefore preoccupied. One of his difficulties was that – court politics being what they are – he had to stick close to the King and the King was in Marrakesh at the moment. Were he to leave Marrakesh and head farther south to command his army, one of the other courtiers might get to the King. In fact, the more battles he lost, the less Dlimi could afford to leave the King's side. It was an awkward way to fight a war. The

King's cousin was driving to Marrakesh the next day and offered to take me along on the off chance that Dlimi might find a free moment. We had reached that peculiar stage in the relationship between a fixer and a supplicant when the fixer's inability to deliver diminishes his reputation in his own eyes. No doubt that was why he came right to the Mamounia with me and strode in to make certain I was given a room on the garden. He had a curious way of moving in his *djellabah*, as if he might suddenly break into a run. The speed was in part to discourage citizens from grabbing his hand and kissing it as he passed. He did a lot of shouting at the front desk; that was his way. It was all quite good-natured. People liked being shouted at by a descendant of the Prophet and a cousin of the King. It was proof that they had been noticed.

Abruptly he turned and shouted across the lobby – "Ben Ali!" A sleek young man glided up to us. He was fixed into one of those French suits that are worn like armour – the style relentlessly deforming the man. Moulay Ahmed introduced him as one of Dlimi's aides – a major I believe – then dragged him away to insist privately that I be given an interview.

Ben Ali called at nine the next morning to say he'd pick me up in an hour. We rode in the back of a black Peugeot. The major was in uniform. It was beautifully cut, although he had only a single short row of ribbons. He'd been with Dlimi for six months, and for the preceding five years he'd been military attaché in Brussels. He was a concrete example of the rumour in the streets – that well-born officers were able to avoid the war zone.

The major couldn't remember how to get to Dlimi's villa. It was new and lay out in a district called La Palmeraie, where the rich were building their winter residences. Ben Ali had been there once and the driver never. There were no signs on the winding dirt tracks. Periodically there would be a grand gateway, then more brush and palm groves. No houses were visible. It was all very discreet.

Discretion was a complex business in Morocco. It was part of a mediaeval tradition, but then so was splendid generosity. The key point was to have as good a time as possible without attracting the King's attention. If he focused on someone's opulence he might think they had stolen too much and so abruptly strip them of everything.

The major was getting nervous by the time he recognized an unfinished archway off a dirt track to the right. He'd given up his easy military-attaché banter and so we bumped under the arch in silence and wound on for perhaps two hundred metres to the villa. It was clearly only just finished. Apart from a zigzag pattern of glazed blue-and-white tiles as a walkway, the grounds hadn't been touched. Inside there were boxes strewn about, half unpacked. We trailed from the small hall through a series of ordinary rooms. It was a big place, but with a suburban feel about it. There was none of the finesse or style of the ruling class. But then Dlimi was the King's man precisely because he had risen out of the lower middle class and had no friends in the elites. It followed that he had no powerful friends to help him betray the King.

Although little furniture had been brought in, there were ornaments – trinkets really – laid out on glass shelves here and there. They were the objects senior officers are given or pick up as they move around the world graduating from academies, visiting regiments, attending foreign staff colleges and, of course, consulting with the commanders of friendly armies. Silver tankards, inscribed. Painted porcelain statuettes of soldiers. Miniature drums with mottoes. That sort of thing.

We came to a room where three staff officers were hanging about. They looked very hot. The air conditioning wasn't yet hooked up and Dlimi's villa had been built in the modern mode so that no allowance had been made for natural cooling by means of high ceilings and cross drafts between windows. Ben Ali nodded towards the next door. One of the staff officers nodded back and we went on in. There were four steel-and-white-leather armchairs in a conventional modern style; ashtrays on glass tables; a door open onto the palmeraie. Dlimi was talking to another officer. The moment he saw me, he sent the man out and stood waiting where he was until I came across the room to shake his hand. It was very soft. The fingernails were carefully trimmed and shone.

"Alors, vous vouliez absolument me parler."

How was I to respond? I thanked him for taking the time at such a difficult moment in the war. He waved a hand – the one holding a cigarette – as if to say don't worry, then sat on the edge of the leather chair closest to the door opened to the outside. He gestured again, indicating the other chairs. Ben Ali perched on the one farthest away from his boss. Dlimi was tall. You could see he had once been fit. Now he carried an evenly distributed layer of fat, even on his face. He had a closely clipped policeman's moustache and was tanned in a manner looked down upon by the ruling class. In spite of the heat he wore a grey silk suit, white silk shirt and polka-dot tie. It was already about thirty-five degrees in the room and there was a film of sweat on his forehead.

I questioned him about the war, then about himself and finally about the old Ben Barka assassination business. It was in the 1960s, when there was still a lot of cooperation between the French and Moroccan secret services. Most of the individuals involved had served together in the colonial days. Ben Barka, the Moroccan opposition leader, had been kidnapped coming out of the Brasserie Lipp on Boulevard Saint-Germain in Paris and reportedly killed. Actually, his body never turned up. Then information began to leak out indicating high-level collusion between the Moroccan and French governments. The only way to stop the growing political damage to both the King and General de Gaulle was to offer up a sacrificial victim. Dlimi was at that point number two to the King's strongman. He volunteered himself and flew over to surrender to the French authorities. They kept him for eight months in La

Santé Prison. There was a hint of self-satisfaction in the way Dlimi pointed out that he had been given the cell of General Salan, the leader of the military rebels during the Algerian War. An historic cell. It was a sort of honour, I suppose. In any case, the end result was that he had proved his loyalty to the King, and the French justice system was prevailed upon to find him innocent.

From my point of view, there was the sheer delight of hearing him go through the whole scandal with such caring detail. It was a story he had told dozens of times – the protestation of innocence; the unfortunate coincidences of time and place which led to suspicions. There is nothing like the recital of a big lie long after it has ceased to matter; there's something erotic about it. The more often it's repeated, the more it belongs to the titillating imaginary world of myth. The pornography of violence.

Dlimi chain-smoked. As he finished each cigarette, Ben Ali jumped up and lit him another. Altogether, he told me nothing of interest in the frankest possible way. There was a sense of careful – not thoughtful – consideration which enveloped the movements of his hand and his glances. Most of the time he avoided eye contact, then abruptly he would stare straight at me. It was perhaps an old police interrogation technique. The careful precision was at first surprising. But he had once been a man on the make; now he had made it. In the process he had been converted into a survivor. For every ambitious man in the kingdom Dlimi was the single obstacle between him and the King. We talked for about two hours. A patch of sweat appeared on his suit under each armpit and gradually spread in a great circle. I was increasingly ill at ease. Why didn't a man who was losing a war, had public order to keep and a King to humour just throw me out? Eventually it was Ben Ali who interrupted us.

The general appeared surprised, as if he had expected to talk to me all day. I suppose, given the insistence of the King's cousin, that Dlimi had imagined the King himself was involved and that in some unexplained way I mattered. However, he took me by the arm and we walked back through the house. On the tiled walkway outside we posed for a photo. Ben Ali took it. I looked at it the other day and it remains a curious image. We're staring at each other as if something serious had happened. In fact he must have been bored out of his mind and I was trying to concentrate on him – looking for any interesting detail. In most cases after an innocuous meeting with power I would walk away with a few meaningless glimpses of the way it was held and presented. The effects it has on people are reasonably predictable. The general, for example, was entering into the comfort stage – a little fat, a little too much property, silk suits. On the surface there wasn't much evidence of the talents that had got him where he was and that kept the army in order and the prisons full. In the car Ben Ali said his boss would never have ended the meeting. He was far too polite.

Two years later Dlimi was run over. Apparently he had just come from a meeting with the King. They were again in Marrakesh. As he came out of the palace he met a businessman who was close to the royal family and who was also waiting for his car. The businessman said he wanted to talk over some project with the general. They rode out together to Dlimi's house with the business-man's car following. Just before they arrived at the villa, a truck came careening down the track out of control. Dlimi threw himself from the car to avoid the collision and the truck ran over him. I had difficulty imagining a truck getting up enough speed to careen on that winding dirt track.

It was only a matter of hours before more detailed reports began to leak out. People living in the area had heard heavy machine-gun fire and explosions. It seems that there was an ambush. Dlimi made a run for it, perhaps hoping that if he could get into the brush he could make it to his house, where there would be loyal soldiers. It must have been one of those moments when a layer of fat and a silk suit were not helpful. But in a physical crisis the state of mind is usually more important than the body. Dlimi's state of mind had always been one of careful consideration; the slow consideration of the interrogator and torturer. Had there been something wild and desperate about him he might have survived. I don't think Dlimi was genetically conceived to make a break for it. He was an exotic manager. His character was focused on being there, not on running away. Apparently they shot him so many times that he was almost unrecognizable. Then they doused him with gasoline and burnt the body to simulate the effects of the exploding runaway truck, but also to disguise the bullet wounds.

His family was not allowed to see the body. The coffin arrived at the official funeral with the lid screwed down and under guard. Most of his staff were arrested, a number of them executed – I'm not sure about Ben Ali. The King's businessman friend went on an extended holiday. Rumour had it that the whole thing was caused by a helicopter deal in which Dlimi was taking too large a rake-off. But my guess is that the King, with his superior sense of self-preservation, simply felt that it was time for a change.

SUNNY AND DAVID SPENSER spend a good part of each year at Cuernavaca. In general they choose the winter, when the weather is perfect; that leaves Paris for both the spring and the fall and California for the crack between fall and winter. Only summer remains, which always presents a problem. Most places are too hot and too crowded. The others are too cold and too empty. Their tendency, as the years have eased by, has been to embrace facility – to hide away in Cuernavaca and summon friends one or two at a time to provide private signs of life.

As for myself, I have always accepted the summons. Little sacrifice is involved. They are a perfectly happy couple. They both have one unfortunate marriage behind them. Children were produced in each case, none since. The children have come of age and gone their way without great disaster. And both of my friends brought to their second contract approximately equal amounts of money and taste. Their house is precisely what money can buy if reasonably spent: no bright colours; no imitation or, for that matter, real pieces of furniture; no sense of longing for other cultures or standards. Merely a number on a street, a discreet wall stuccoed in aged peach hiding a large, simple, old house and a much larger garden; all of which is filled with enough servants to make it effortless.

The only difference between Sunny and David is that she has always liked a bit of what she calls "life," while he is quite happy to read or doze or paddle up and down his pool between meals and Scotches. She invariably seems younger than the youngest person present, thanks to her optimism added to her good bones added to good care. He, on the other hand, is quite content to look sixty-odd; a healthy, plump, pink figure.

Last June I was hiding away in a village in Corsica, writing. On the twenty-fifth or -sixth the telephone broke a week's silence. It had taken Sunny eight calls to track me down and the urgency of this search was confirmed by the urgency of her invitation. There was a certain imperative, defenceless tone to her voice. She needed me to come. To come immediately. Why was not clear, which meant she was bored, and saving friends from boredom is at the heart of friendship. That was what Sunny always said.

I left two days later. Cuernavaca was as good a place as any to hide away. David left me alone and Sunny's need for "life" never took up more than two hours a day of good-humoured gossip over meals. The rest of the time I placed myself deep in the garden under a jacaranda tree and reminded the boy that he wasn't to bring me a beer before noon and then after 5:30 every ninety minutes until dinner was served.

On the night of the Fourth of July, Sunny gathered up the least objectionable of the other Americans in hiding and put on what she called a "typical Yankee dinner" – a corn soufflé, hot dogs stuffed with wild duck meat and tied together to make little dogs with legs and heads. The teeth and eyes and sexual parts had been put in with bits of vegetable. When Sunny saw an uncomfortable look on David's face, she leaned across the table, ran her palm along his cheek and half-whispered, "Poor darling. I know it's in bad taste. It's meant to be." And laughed. As long as the intent was clear, David didn't mind, so he chose the biggest one for himself and cut off its head. There was a blueberry charlotte after that and a particularly heavy Californian wine as liquid. Its production was so small that you needed an introduction to buy. We drank a great deal and stayed up until the air was cool.

The next morning I staggered down to find breakfast waiting in the shade beside the pool, the servants looking a little weary and David swathed in white towelling, his skin more yellow than pink, hung low over a plate of poached eggs as if he himself had been poached and really didn't mind.

"Good morning," I said, dropping into a seated position.

"Hey, Ding Dong." He attempted a smile, then slumped back to his eggs.

I heard the phone ring. David stirred with agitation, leaning forward from within his egg-white to say out loud, "Filth of July."

"What?"

"Filth of July." It was said with resignation. "Same every year."

I poured myself some coffee and emptied the cup before glancing back at David. His eyes were frozen on the open door leading into the house, not more than twenty feet away. I heard Sunny's steps clicking towards us from within.

"Wait," David whispered.

The pitch of her voice was enthusiastic, perhaps a little forced. "I have the most wonderful surprise. David, do you remember Patty ... Patty ... oh, you remember, she came to dinner in Paris at Diane's. Pretty, blond. A clever little thing."

David had been listening with a negative cast to his face. "No."

"You must."

"I don't."

She wiped this away with a quick smile. "Well, I do. She's just called from Acapulco. She's been staying there with her husband."

"The malarial plains. The heat. They happened to think of us." His pink colour had surged back.

"They're coming for a few nights."

"No."

"David!"

"I don't remember her and I've never met him. No."

Sunny adopted a momentary quizzical expression. "Well, it's too late. I've sent the driver down to pick them up. He's gone." David reverted to yellow. "I had no choice. She's got some problem with him. She had to bring him down to Mexico. Had to get him away from Los Angeles and at the wrong time of year."

"There or here?"

She ignored him. "And they were going crazy in Acapulco."

"In the heat."

"In the heat. So I really had to –"

"Get them up here to find out what their problem is."

I looked away and caught a servant's attention. "Coffee. In five minutes, down in the garden."

I MISSED LUNCH and didn't stir from under my tree until nearly six. My own name, repeated in a plaintive way by the voice of Sunny, broke the spell. I found her waiting on the edge of the garden, as if the plants were not to be trusted.

"They're here and David's upstairs asleep, so you must come and help me. Now don't worry about family names."

I put an arm around her. "Because you can't remember theirs?"

She laughed and pinched me. At which point the Pattys appeared on the terrace. She was indeed a blonde, in a California way – with careful, even rigorous, abandon. And not so little as Sunny had suggested. She was leggy, almost elegant, with just a hint of the stringiness to come in future years. But there was definitely something more to her than the Pacific standard model. A light shone through her eyes, though it was partially obscured by a wild look. At first I thought it was just uncertainty after forcing an invitation. But no, there was something else. There was also a small cast on her right ankle. A vision materialized beside her. He was six-three or -four; six-eight if you included the powder-blue Stetson on his head. Below that, a large, solid, once-muscular body was tightly sheathed in a powder-blue shirt with metal buttons. Powder-blue trousers in the form of a second skin were tucked into a pair of powder-blue snakeskin cowboy boots with rider's heels. His eyes were shaded by two mirrors. Behind him was a huge pile of matching luggage and the driver, exhausted after the eight-hour round trip.

Even Sunny was astounded. The silence was broken by the man in blue.

"Hi." The voice was intriguingly husky. "I'm Jack."

Sunny was shocked back into action. I knew immediately what was going through her mind. She had to get the man in blue out of those clothes before David wandered downstairs.

"A swim is what you need!" It was said in a tense of her own invention – the social imperative. "Introductions later." I felt myself being pushed forward. "Go on, lazy, help these hot people up with their luggage."

When I came back downstairs, David was swimming slowly in the pool. Sunny was sitting in the shade as if nothing had happened. She looked at me with a smile.

"Well, what do you think of Mr. Blue Boots?" We both laughed until coughing from the pool stopped us. We turned to see David trying to retch out a mouthful of water. His eyes were on the house door. We turned again. Patty was limping towards us, the two small straps which constituted her suit confirming everything I had imagined of her body, the cast on one leg only emphasizing the sweet curve of the other. Behind was Mr. Blue Boots. He was wearing a pink cowboy hat, a pink robe of metallic allure and what looked like soft space boots, also pink.

The afternoon was reasonably uncomplicated – nobody had to talk. Dinner was another matter. Mr. Blue Boots wore a mauve ensemble which made ingenious use of checks. He talked a great deal, in the monologue way, which at least laid out for us who he was – an oil man. Pipelining was his business and he did very well at it. Then he let us know what he thought of the government, of the deregulation of oil prices, then of gas prices; then he told us what he thought of California. He was from Arizona. His tone was extremely manful. Through all of this his wife looked wild-eyed and David emptied glass after glass.

At last, halfway through dessert, the monologue came to an end and he looked around as if seeing us for the first time. When he wasn't talking he appeared a little less sure of himself. His eyes never met Patty's. Hers, on the other hand, were fixed on him.

He snatched up his fork and using it with the force of a knife cut a piece from the slice of tart before him as if it were a slab of thick meat, then bent forward, opened his mouth to a size twice that of the piece cut and just before pushing the food in turned his head sideways; all done as a boy might eat a large hot dog in a bun, fully expecting the mustard to run out and down the side of his cheek. It was in itself of no consequence, being a not-uncommon trait in American men. I've seen them do it all over the world, with everything from minute pieces of foie gras to green grapes. But his was such a studied gesture that we all watched with fascination. Never have I seen so much trouble being taken to get such a small bit of food into such a large mouth.

"Well," he began again, "this is a quiet little house you've got here." The "is" was emphasized.

"That was the idea," David said mournfully.

Mr. Blue Boots looked hard at him through the candle-light, unsure of the meaning. "Was it now?"

I could see David leaning forward, ready to take up the point. But before he could begin the attack, Sunny was on her feet and pulling me to mine.

"Now, Jack." With these words she virtually summoned Mr. Blue Boots to his feet. "What you need is a walk. Patty's hardly in shape to join you, and we're too old." As she said it, she looked seventeen, and David had the expression of a young boxer entering the ring. "So, I'm sending you out in good hands." She shoved me forward. "You'll find him a very good listener, because he's a writer."

"Is he, now?" Jack began.

"Yes," she insisted, pushing us both.

By magic locomotion we were out the door. The street was cool and empty, the stars remarkably clear. Jack stood on the curb, luminous, and looked around, shrinking somehow with every second. When his eyes had finished their evasive tour and rested on me, they had the tentativeness of a little boy.

"I guess I didn't do too well in there."

"No … But it doesn't matter. Let's go find a drink." I put a hand on his shoulder and led him down the hill.

At first he said nothing, just plodded along, oblivious to the sweet scents rising up with the night air. I could feel something happening next to me but couldn't bring myself to look. Then quite abruptly he stopped – we were halfway down the hill – and stared at me tearfully.

"She's not my wife."

"No, I'm sure she isn't."

"She told you."

"I worked it out."

He seemed to accept that. I suppose he supposed that writers are able to work things out. We walked on a few paces before he stopped again.

"I'll tell you what I did, if you promise not to tell."

"I promise."

He was surprised by this quick acquiescence and looked carefully at me. There was a momentary return of his majestic manner. "Do you, now?"

I stared back at him. "Why shouldn't I?"

He became a child again and walked on of his own accord. The bar I took him to was empty and hot. He prepaid a bottle of decent tequila, a jug of sangria and four glasses, outside. We sat outside where he emptied three shots before saying a word.

"I love my wife, but that's nothing up against what I feel for Patty. I've got the money, so what does it matter, one woman or two? I can afford both. And," there was a boyish leer, "I can keep 'em both happy. So I met Patty maybe five years ago. And she's got something. You know?" I nodded. "Something that I need. So I got her to quit her job. It wasn't much, but she's smart. And I took care of her. I like buying her things. I bought her a house, then I bought her a nicer house. Up in the hills behind LA. You should see it. Boy, what a view. And I bought her a great car, an Alfa, you know. And did you see that ring she's wearing?" I had noticed the diamond village her second finger was supporting. "I bought her that, and, you know, I think she loves me. She doesn't do it for the money."

I was getting a bit tired of this, so I interrupted. "What's the problem then?"

He gave another of his shocked but careful glances. "I don't know." That absence of an idea seemed to roll around in his head for thirty seconds, producing an odd, vacant expression, and then he repeated it. "I don't know. But I can't take it anymore. I can't give her anything else and ... and I want it all back."

"You just said you needed her."

"I do. But I can't anymore. I mean, how do I know she needs me; I mean, except for the money?" He sneaked a glance to see how this had gone over and found no expression on my face. "But that's not it. I don't know. It's not right."

We fell into silence until I forced myself to shove on. "What isn't?"

"Two weeks ago we were in the car after I'd been visiting her. We'd been fucking all afternoon, so we went out for a drive up into the hills. We went in my car, and when we got up high to a really grand spot, Patty said she wanted to get out to look at the view. She got out and walked to the edge of the road. There was a big cliff there. And I stayed in the car. And when she turned to come back, I gunned the engine and ran her over. You know, if she'd gone over that cliff she'd be dead." He said this as if he'd failed to draw an ace in cards. It was almost charming.

"But?"

"I missed. Well, not exactly. That's how she sprained her ankle. And, you know, she saw I was trying to kill her. She saw it. Then she made me come to Mexico. She said I needed a holiday." He thought about that. "I told her my foot slipped, but she knows it didn't. She knows. But she didn't say a word."

"Maybe it's because she loves you."

He took a long, slow look at me, filled with suspicion. "Maybe. Do you think I love her? I mean, I don't need her."

"You said you did."

"Maybe. But I don't."

Without the tequila, which certainly simplified my reasoning, the conversation might have stopped there. "In any case, you shouldn't kill her." He followed my words very closely. "You don't need to. That's the point. Unless you are an idiot, don't kill her."

When we got back to Sunny's house I went straight to my room and dropped onto the bed without either stripping or washing. I was tired and drunk. There was a knock on the door, which opened. It was Sunny.

"They're not married."

I nodded.

"And there's a wife."

"Is that all, Sunny?"

"Isn't that enough?"

She seemed to have guessed that there was more. I didn't answer. My eyes were closed.

When I came down the next morning, late, Patty and Mr. Blue Boots were gone. Apparently the pipeline business had called him. A week later I went back to my Corsican village.

OVER THE NEXT FIVE MONTHS I had only fleeting glimpses of Sunny and David. It was easy to keep track of them. Their names were on the lists of the sort of charity balls, birthday parties and auctions that the international press cover in their society pages, or more exactly in their celebrity gossip section. On planes or in waiting rooms I would pick up a *Gala* or *Paris Match* and there they would be, pink and bejewelled at a Luxembourg duchess's eightieth birthday, or at the Prix de l'Arc de Triomphe with the owner of the winning horse, or a gala at the Met for AIDS research. Somehow these were the right events in the right places at the right time. I was usually on my way through a week later. It wasn't till early December that Sunny called me in my New York apartment with one of her invitations. She was back in Cuernavaca. Patty was there. Did I remember Patty? In a terrible state. I asked if Mr. Blue Boots was with her. No. That was just it, but she couldn't get any sense out of the poor girl. Something terrible had happened.

I was surprised that Sunny felt I should and could talk to the girl, and indeed that Sunny herself had failed. Women are supposed to be good at talking to each other. The secrets are between the sexes. I suppose Patty was one of those women who had reserved all her talking for the man in her life and in his absence only another man would do. Sunny, being smart, had picked this up, and having done so there weren't many men to choose from. David was not a great talker. I was the only other male who had been party to whatever was going on. I suppose it was vicarious and even opportunistic of me to go, but there was certainly a story to be finished. I arrived the next day to find that Patty had hardly come out of her room. She ate her meals there. None of this bothered David, but Sunny was a warm-hearted soul and couldn't bear anyone to suffer alone. She hardly let me put down my case before pushing me upstairs with dinner on a tray.

The air was filled with an oppressive mixture of perfumes and powders. Patty was lying on the bed in a silk dressing gown. She had arrived without a suitcase, so it was Sunny's. Even in the half-light I could see that the expression on her face was as confused as it was unhappy. The effect was to wipe away the last trace of her California plastic mould, leaving only herself and revealing a new level of beauty.

I opened a window and shutter, letting in the musk of the garden air. In the light I saw that her left hand was bandaged. Her diamond ring had been moved to the right hand, where it seemed even larger than before – more a town of important houses than a village. I sat on the windowsill.

At first she didn't recognize me. I reminded her of my walk with Jack and told her what he had told me. Her eyes stretched open. I suppose she had assumed that Jack had even more reason to be close-mouthed about it. A perfectly rational assumption.

"Why would he tell you that?"

"I don't know. We were drunk. He didn't know me. He didn't know why he'd done it. He was asking himself out loud."

"Why didn't you tell me?" She moved her body for the first time, as if that might help to clear the confusion. "Why didn't you do something?"

"Me? You knew. Why didn't you do something yourself?" That wasn't exactly what I was thinking. Why don't people take preventive action when they know something is going to happen? They don't. They sit on the tracks and wait for the train thundering down upon them. Why? Because they have their own reasons. Or because they are pessimists. Or optimists. Whatever.

She sat up. "You thought it was a momentary fit?"

I smiled in vague agreement. "What happened?"

She threw herself back on the pillows and stared at the ceiling. "Oh, nothing. We went home from here and everything kept on the way it had before. We had some good times. The way we always did." She looked up at me dubiously, fearful that I might be making a face. "You don't know him. He's a good guy. Really."

"All right. He's a good guy who wears strange clothes."

Hearing it in someone else's mouth made her sit up again. I moved across to the bed long enough to put some pillows behind her back.

"A good guy," she repeated. "He doesn't go on holidays. He works. He isn't great about social behaviour. I don't know, he was pretty confused. Maybe he thought dressing up made him seem like a fun guy."

"Fair enough."

She looked carefully at me, then plunged. "Well, a couple of weeks ago, just after lunch, two men arrived at my house. I wouldn't have let them in except they said Jack had sent them. They were supposed to meet him at my place. I was expecting him for the afternoon. He'd done that a couple of times before, you know, stuck a business meeting into one of our personal get-togethers, and they looked okay. Youngish guys. Big. Good-looking. In nice grey suits." She giggled. "Not like Jack. More like the people who work for him. Anyway, Jack was already late so I thought he'd be there pretty soon, so I asked them if they'd like a drink. They had gin and we sat down in my sitting room. It's got a great view, really." I had no reason to disagree. "You should see. There isn't another house in sight. Anyway, my air conditioning wasn't working that day and it was hot, so I suggested they take off their jackets. One of them was wearing a gun holster. I guess he forgot. And the other guy seemed upset about that, though he didn't say much, just flushed and stared. So the guy took off his holster as well. He had a big chest. You know, the holster was tight around the muscles. He was the older of the two, bigger.

"I guess I was surprised, but what do I know about these things. They emptied their glasses and I gave them two more big drinks. They seemed to need it. Still Jack didn't come. I was beginning to wonder. I mean, they didn't seem to want to telephone him. But you could see they were waiting for something. They didn't talk much. They just stared at me, then looked fast at each other, then stared at me.

"I don't know, suddenly I got it. It didn't scare me at first. I had a clear mind for the first time in months. I guess I'd been living in a fog, waiting for a gust of wind to clear the air. I looked at the bigger one. He had a friendly sort of face. Really short hair, baseball style. You don't see that much anymore except on fags, and pretty good teeth. I said, 'So he sent you?'

"The guy was pretty surprised, but he saw I understood and that made it easier. He nodded.

"I said, 'He sent you to kill me?'

"Neither of them said anything. Then the younger one – he wasn't so good-looking, but he had nice eyes – said to his friend, 'Hey, come on. She's got a right to know.' He nodded at me. 'That's right.' It was kind of cute the way he said it. Boyish, you know.

"I said, 'Is there a message?'

"That surprised them too. 'No,' the younger one said, 'no message.'

"'Oh.' That was all I could think to say. I jumped to

my feet. 'You guys need another drink.' And I got the gin bottle again. They drank that pretty quick, and I had one too. Then I asked them about themselves. You should always ask people about themselves. They like that. And so they told me. They used to work for this man, a gangster I guess you'd say. That was when they first met Jack. Now they were more or less out on their own. Free enterprise. They did a lot of little jobs, mostly collections, threats, knees nailed to the floor."

She saw my eyes pop a little and looked at me with an unexpected expression: impatience.

"Hey. I read about it just like you. Don't you believe what you read?" She took little notice of my slight flush. "They did that kind of thing. Not many killings. And they'd never done a woman before. Mostly other gangsters. Professional stuff. So I asked them what the deal was. They didn't like to talk about that, but I encouraged them. They said it was fifty thousand, plus they had to bring my ring back," she flashed it at me, "on my finger, as proof, you see.

"Well, that shocked me a bit. I've always had nice hands. So I kind of laughed and said, 'In that case, gin isn't good enough. If I'm going to die, I want champagne.' They followed me into the kitchen and I got a bottle out of the fridge. It was Mumm's. Jack's favourite kind. I gave it to the big guy to open and got some glasses. We drank half of it and I kept asking them questions about themselves. They were more relaxed by now. That was kind of dangerous. They were relaxed either way, so I said, 'Listen, are you guys any good in bed?' There aren't many men who won't answer that. They got to, you know. It doesn't matter how lousy they are. I didn't give them time to think about it. 'If I'm going to die,' I said, 'the least you can do is give me a little pleasure first.' They looked at each other, kind of rivals already.

"'Both of you,' I said, and I got to my feet and led them to the bedroom. I brought the champagne. Well, I've got a pretty sexy bedroom. A big bed, lots of mirrors. Jack likes all that stuff. He says it helps me. So I started taking my clothes off the best way I know how, which got their attention. After that I helped them do the same. Then I made sure they had a good time. First the big one, then the younger guy. And you know," she blushed a little, "I kind of enjoyed myself. I guess it was sort of an occasion. They noticed, too. A man can tell when you're really enjoying it and not just acting, if he wants to. And I think they said to themselves, 'Hey, she's quite a girl, enjoying herself when we're about to kill her.'"

She continued to ignore my embarrassment, but then she hadn't been able to tell anyone, and this must have been the hardest part of what she'd been through.

"After that I told them the story about how the smaller men's penises were, the more ambitious they turned out to be. And how that explained why Jack had an oil company and they were just gunmen. They laughed, because they were both a good size and men like to know you noticed.

They like to think they're better than the other guys, especially when it's the guy who's paying them. Then I asked, 'Do you want to do it again?'

"The younger guy said, 'In a minute maybe.'

"'I don't mind waiting,' I said. That made them laugh pretty hard. When they'd finished the champagne, I said, 'Listen, guys, I'll do a deal with you. If you don't kill me, I'll give you twice what Jack's offering. Cash.' Jack always gave me money in cash, and I had about a hundred thousand in my safe. I could see these guys were honest in their own slow way, so I could risk telling them I had the cash. Anyway, there wasn't much choice.

"They looked doubtful, but interested. The big guy said, 'What would we tell him?'

"By then I could see they were ready for another session, and besides, it would give me time to think. So we did that. Then I said, 'Look, you can have my money and his money and you won't have to kill me, plus I'll get him off the streets so you don't have to worry about what he'll do.' They liked the sound of that. We got dressed and I gave them my car keys and then we went around the house and pulled out all the telephone lines, ending up in the kitchen. I got another bottle of champagne out of the fridge, a bowl of ice, my meat cleaver and chopping board, a towel and some giant-sized bandages and plaster tape." She made it sound like a shopping list. "I made the big guy sharpen the cleaver. We sat down in the sitting room and drank the champagne. I drank a good part of it myself, while I kept my hand in the ice. Then I stretched the finger with the ring on it out along the chopping board. You know, those two guys were so soft I almost had to cut if off myself. Men are like that once things get personal. I was so hyped up I hardly felt it happen. There was quite a bit of blood, but we got the bandages on really quick and wrapped the finger in one of my guest towels. It was a nice set, you know, with flowers embroidered on linen. Anyway, I still have five. Then I gave them the combination to the safe and they took the money. They were still kind of unsure, but I kept myself going and got them out the door. 'You go fast to Jack,' I said. 'Give him the finger and then get out and telephone for an ambulance. Don't worry. I didn't see you. You knocked me out. I'll look after everything.'

"The younger one, just before he got in the car, shouted at me, 'You're a great lay, Patty.' Shit. And me standing there without a finger, ready to faint. I managed to get to a chair before I kind of passed out. The next thing I know the ambulance is there. I'm half crazy by then and the pain is terrible, but not too crazy. First thing I do is say it was Jack. They radio the police." She paused to look right at me. For the first time there was a glint of pleasure in her eyes. "You know what? They found Jack in his study at home, drunk, looking at my finger floating in a bowl of ice water. He was staring at it. Ha! Crazy. Crazy, eh?"

I could hardly disagree with her. But she wasn't finished.

"I told the police that these masked men had broken in and had wanted to kill me. I told the whole story, about how it was Jack who hired them and how I did the deal with them. Everything except the part about the sex." She blushed. I think for a moment she regretted having told me. "But when they asked me to describe the two guys, I went hysterical, like it was too much of a trauma. I stuck to my part of the deal. I didn't want them coming back. That left Jack on the line one hundred percent. After that I just sat around in my house for ten days, in a coma sort of. I took a lot of Librium to keep calm. I mean, anything might have happened next. I mean, Jack might have hired some other guys, and there I was in this big house with no money. Then last week I got a letter from Jack. It was in a fat brown envelope. He got his lawyer to deliver it. Unbelievable. It's a love letter. Twelve pages of gooey puke. Only the letter is just a wrapper. In the middle there's six hundred one-thousand-dollar bills. And the lawyer watches me read the letter and count the bills. Then he asks me if I'll drop my story. Christ! 'What about the finger?' I said. 'Once he's out I'd just lose the others.' The lawyer says to me we'll work something out. Christ! I say I'll think about it. Two days later, there's another love letter. I don't know who brought it, because it was pushed through the mail slot in the middle of the night. There was another three hundred thousand in it.

"Well, I couldn't take it. So I bought a ticket and came running down here. Sunny doesn't know anything, but she's a good person." Patty paused to give me one of those honest, penetrating looks. "What did I know myself until this happened? And this morning Sunny gets a phone call. It's from Jack's wife. She knows I'm here and she's in town, coming to see me tonight. God. I mean, it's my money, isn't it? It's cash. They don't know where it is."

I got off the window ledge and took her unbandaged hand and squeezed it. "It's your money, Patty. We'll see what his wife has to say."

Jack's wife appeared a good hour later. That gave me enough time to tell Sunny the bare bones of the story and to have a bath. The wife looked like an ex-starlet gone family. That's unfair, because I'm sure she'd had a lot to put up with. She made us all fully conscious that she was the wife and a respectable one at that, in a blue-and-orange outfit from Neiman Marcus, forty percent polyester, uncreased. What else could she do, with her husband in jail for trying to murder his mistress? She was blond, leggy, in fact very much like Patty, but minus the character. The eyes were flat, burnt out. She must have begun life as the sort of girl a young man would choose. What she did have, however, was a very clear mind. *Reader's Digest* with edge. Sunny had sent David to bed, and having heard a bit of the story he went willingly. The three women and I sat out in the garden. Drinks were not offered.

The wife's name was Linda. I think she realized that she and Patty looked alike, because I caught her staring several times with a hint of recognition. Linda didn't seem to know how to begin, so Sunny played hostess.

"I believe you wanted to see Patty. We are her friends." As there was another pause, she added, "What do you want?"

That jolted the wife into words. She spoke slowly, as if reading out loud. In fact she had probably memorized every word.

"My husband is a fool. That I love him is my problem." She looked up at Patty kindly. "You, I fully accept, loved him also, but I am certain that recent events have ended whatever you felt. I have learnt that he is sending you money. Please understand that I do not mind. Really I don't." She made a gesture with her right hand as if to refuse an egg-salad sandwich on white bread, crusts off. "We can afford it and he owes you. Perhaps I do, too. After all, I must have failed him or none of this would have happened. And so I want to ask you not to withdraw your charges for the moment. Make sure he gives you enough money for your happiness for the rest of your life. I want you to be happy. I know how much we have. We can certainly afford two million ... perhaps that will be enough. Perhaps after that you might consider dropping ..." She hesitated, there were tears in her eyes. "I promise that he will not try to harm you again. I shall make sure he is happy and that he is mine."

The speech, because it was a speech, in the old-fashioned sense (one that might have been given from the auditorium stage in Grade Twelve; had she been standing, the hands would have been clasped), brought the other two women to the edge of tears. I was astounded. I'd never heard anyone actually talk like that. It put my fundamental rejection of romanticism into question. I brushed away an insect that was irritating one of my eyes.

Patty leaned forward to grasp the wife awkwardly. "Of course I'll withdraw them. Of course I will." She was now in tears.

Linda accepted the embrace and broke into full weeping, through which she managed to stutter in words broken with emotion, "Make him pay first. Make him pay."

CALIFORNIA IS NOT my favourite state; however, I found myself on my way there in the spring. I came via Paris, where I dined with Sunny.

She had had a confused letter from Patty a month before. Apparently Jack had gone on sending money in fits and starts, along with love letters and increasingly desperate pleas for her to drop her charges. When she had close to two million, the letters and the money abruptly stopped coming. Patty waited a month without hearing another word, then decided that one million, eight hundred and seventy-five thousand was enough and called the police officer who was handling things. She said she wanted to revise her story. He said not to worry about it. They would call her if necessary. She telephoned Jack's wife, but Linda wasn't around and didn't call her back. Meanwhile, Jack was still in jail awaiting his trial.

When I got to LA, I tried to telephone Patty. There was no reply. I tried several times over the next week without success. Then I looked up Jack's home number, hoping to get his wife. The family had moved and the line had been disconnected, probably replaced with an unlisted number. The publicity can't have done their family much good. I tried the police, only to be told that what I wanted to know wasn't public information, apart from the name of the jail where Jack was being held.

I have visited a few jails, but never such a pleasant one. It was new and what they call a model prison (the meaning of which deserves investigation). It had been designed in a clever way so that starkness became clean lines. There was a great deal of cream and tile and glass (unbreakable without looking unbreakable). The entrance was cheerful and full of cheerful men in neat uniforms. It might have been one of the better Holiday Inns. I was carefully searched and put through a machine, as if flying somewhere, before being taken into a room got up as a studio apartment. There was a sitting area at one end and a bed at the other. The furniture was all done in white-on-cream stripes. One wall was broken by a charming theatre effect: a picture window, lit as if by sunlight, but not transparent. I suppose a brick wall lay beyond it. There was a tasselled fringe around the bedspread and this theme was picked up around the base of the chairs.

I chose the most comfortable and had sunk into foam only a moment before Jack was introduced through the equivalent of a stage door. The first thing I noticed was that he looked extremely happy. The second was that his prison uniform was perfectly assorted to the room.

"Hello, Mr. Blue Boots," I said.

He seemed confused, then laughed in his full, deep voice. "I was expecting someone else."

"Ah," I said, but he offered nothing more. "Well, have you got a minute?" The question sounded bizarre the moment I asked it, but Jack liked the idea.

"Of course I've got a minute. Shit, I've got nothing but." He sauntered over and sprawled in a chair.

"Well, what's going on? I tried to contact your wife and Patty, but they've both disappeared."

He looked at me. Evasive. Sharp. A little boy. "I guess you heard about what I did?"

"Every detail. Some even you don't know."

"Is that so? Did you hear what my wife's done for me?" I kept a blank look. I didn't know how much she had told him. "So you didn't? Hey, this is too good to miss. I've been sending Patty some money. You know, I've been really sorry for what happened, and I still feel the same way about her. I really love that girl. I just can't get her out of my system. So I sent this cash, you know, a few hundred thousand at a time. I had to get my lawyer to sell off some shares and things like that, quietly. Anyway, I guess I sent her near on two million and maybe hoped she would forgive me."

"And forget her story?"

He looked at me brightly. "Sure. Hell, why not? If she loved me. She always used to say she loved me. She could have proved it. Hey, I did a lot for her. Anyway, I've been having my doubts about all that. I didn't hear a word from her. I mean, I sent her all these nice letters along with the money, but silence was all I got. And Linda, my wife, has been great. She comes to see me. We've got conjugal rights here. And I think that's decent of her, considering what I've done. Anyway, we've been having a good time together. It's quiet here and they leave you alone for your two hours. No telephone calls, nothing. That's great for sex. Then about a month ago she comes in all upset. She says she's just found out that I've been sending money to Patty and now Patty's putting the touch on her for more. You get it. If Patty told the police I'd been trying to buy her off, that wouldn't be good." He said this with sincerity.

"Patty wouldn't do that," I protested.

"Hey, listen to me. I'm the one in here. I'm the one telling the story. I'm the one with all the money. I'm the one people want to touch. And there's more. The company is getting into trouble without me there and everyone worrying what will happen if I'm convicted. So Linda says she can help me if I'll let her. So we work out a deal. I turn all my shares and belongings over to her. That means I'm not a mark for Patty anymore or for anyone else. Shows I'm a good family man, too. And it takes the pressure off the company. Simple and neat. I wrote out a little paper right then and there and signed it. We had just enough time left for a little go on the bed." He indicated the other end of the room. "She always did like to have it regular. That was the last I heard of her."

"Patty?"

"No, Linda. Except that she's suing me for divorce."

"Oh."

"And I hear from my lawyer that she's making efforts to encourage the law in their job – i.e., put me away good and proper. It's a real complicated case. There's some evidence but not many witnesses. I may be here for years before they even figure out how to try me. Pretty dumb," he said, as if it didn't matter.

"Pretty dumb," I agreed. "Why do you look so happy?"

He smiled his boyish smile. "I like things simple. Everything is simple again. I got rid of a wife who didn't love me. She had me fooled, you know. And I got rid of all that money. I can always make it back when I get out of here. That's not a big deal."

"No. I suppose it isn't."

A guard came in and said, with kindness, that there was someone else to see him. I jumped up to leave and wished him luck. What else was there to offer?

I was halfway across the Holiday Inn lobby when I noticed Patty sitting on a sofa, waiting. She was surprised to see me. The bandage was off her hand and a black silk glove had taken its place. One of the fingers was folded back and neatly sown in place.

"What are you doing here?" A stupid question.

She laughed. Well, I suppose it was a laugh, a little awkward, a little defensive. "I'm here to see Jack. Did you hear about his wife? What a dirty trick. I wrote him to say I was coming. I just hope he wants to see me."

"What about you? You're the one minus a finger."

"Oh," she said. "I got two million out of it. And he has nothing. Now he needs me. Besides, I'm pretty safe in this place. She drew closer and whispered, "They've got conjugal rights here."

"So I hear."

She drew away, revealing a determined look. "I'll get him back."

I gave her a little kiss on the cheek. Then, as she began to walk away, a thought came to me. "Did you talk to anyone about all this? I mean, what to do now you're rich? Your parents, for example?"

She shook her head. "They're in Minnesota."

"Minnesota?"

She nodded. "Eden Bluffs. My dad's got the drugstore."

I nodded. At the front door of the prison they searched all my pockets before they let me out.

4
THE CITIZEN

GEORGE MARKHAM WAS SOMEONE I first met in Paris but came to know in New York. His manner suggested a split personality. He had finished his education in France and had married French, but was American and earned his money in the States.

This made him a rare sort of lawyer. He lacked the locked-in focus of someone who is convinced that the law ends at a border, that a case may be lost through argument or ignorance but at least the geographical parameters are fixed. George had a permanent nervous edge, because each solution in France was a question in New York, and every judgement in New York might have been an appeal in Paris.

This edge was buried under the protective ease with which he chose to address the world. He was tall, even for an American, and he bent his soft form down towards other people's levels. When I say soft, I mean there was neither anything angular about him nor mushy. He appeared slight, but relaxed. And his face was reassuring, although finely cut.

I was in Paris to launch a book and ran into him at a dinner. It was a surprise. He had appeared from some recess of our host's apartment just as we sat down at the table. Although George was often in France on business for American clients, his evenings were invariably swallowed up by his wife's family – a series of interrelated tentacles without interest, except to themselves.

I was seated one away from him and leaned back to say in English behind the aging countess who separated us, "What are you doing out in the world? Where are the aunts-in-law?"

He smiled with his nervous softness and pointed to a woman on the other side of the table at the far end. "A niece of sorts. And a client."

I looked across the massed Napoleon III china and candelabra jumbled up with other bits of our host's heritage and saw a young woman in a simple black dress. She was a little plump and alluring in that self-willed Paris way, a bit like George's wife. The woman caught us staring at her. I could see she hadn't assumed a compliment. She gave George a stare, along with a hurt expression. Her lips suggested the slightest of pouts, as if she were injured. There was something inadvertently seductive that held my eye. I looked away.

"Et vous, messieurs, vous êtes parisiens en ce moment?" The countess between us reinserted herself, the fingers of one hand twisted around her single strand of pearls, the fingers of the other carefully in view on the tablecloth, her head turning from one of us to the other.

"Oui, madame," I sat up, and she released her pearls.

I was looking forward to meeting George's niece, but as the dinner ended, our hostess manoeuvred me onto a sofa with a young diplomat just posted to New York. My payment for the dinner was obviously to look after him there. A few words between us confirmed how expensive the evening had been. When George got up to leave, I followed.

"I'll come with you."

We were headed towards the door before I realized that the young woman wasn't moving. We made our way across the shadowy entrance hall; mediocre Gobelins tapestries covering walls that needed painting.

Downstairs, I asked, "Why did you leave your wife's niece behind?"

"She's staying there. I've been with her since three. I went to talk business and they kept me on for dinner. Enough. My god ..."

We were strolling down rue de l'Université. He looked at me, his annoyance clear even in the street light. Then he laughed, because I usually teased him about his wife's octopus-like family and I suppose he thought one of my onslaughts was coming.

"There was something interesting about her," I said, meaning unlike the rest of the family. "She had a pathetic look on her face, just enough to break the lacquer. It seemed to me there was a raw edge showing through. Not exactly passion. What does she need you for?" I didn't expect an answer. I assumed it was privileged information.

"She's wonderful. It's the others who do me in. She isn't like them. We've always been great friends. Normally I wouldn't take on a relative, but my correspondent lawyer in Paris is also her lawyer and he insisted."

"Do I know him?"

"Pierre de Foret. He was there tonight, sitting on her right."

I remembered a man in a blazer and grey flannels. He had pasty skin, as if he had never been outside. A Parisian look. In this case it was visually shocking, because his hair was thick and perfectly black.

"He's been a great support to her."

"In what cause?"

"Her husband died last month. Peter Roberts."

"The tire company?"

"Son of the tire company. One hundred million worth of tires in New Jersey. I was the one who introduced them. That's the other reason we get on. Christ, she married an American. Most French wouldn't dream of –"

I interrupted. "Your wife did."

"That's different. I have character. Now Peter was nice enough, but money was his big plus. They'd been married three years, during which they lived on airplanes, because

Marie-Louise wanted to live here and he wanted to live there. He was a nervous flyer, and the doctors had warned him that he shouldn't overdo it. Last month he had a heart attack on Concorde and died over the Atlantic. She came to me because she's pregnant."

I looked at him, confused. "Poor girl."

He looked back at me as we walked. "It's worse than tragic. There was a pre-nuptial contract. The rest of his family own a percentage of the tires and insisted. Only his children can inherit. They were worried about control of the company falling to a French woman who wants to live in France. Problem is, there isn't a child."

"But she's pregnant!" Suddenly I understood her wounded look.

"Four months," George added. "There's nothing in the marriage contract about that."

"Surely the family ..." We were talking about solid American stock.

"The family doesn't want the company controlled by an infant who is in the hands of a French mother in France. They're insisting on the letter of the contract."

"That's ridiculous, George. I mean, what does that girl want with running a tire company? There's enough money to make everyone happy."

"That's why my French lawyer friend called me in. Marie-Louise says they've insulted her and the memory of her husband. Peter's family says the same about her. Now we have the lunacy of a family feud."

There was emotion in his voice. I could see he felt committed to the case beyond any question of law. By then we had reached St. Germain. I suggested a brandy at the Flore.

Six weeks later I was home in New York. George telephoned.

"Are you free today?" he asked.

"Should I be?"

"Yes. You remember Marie-Louise?"

Her face reconstituted in my mind as in an electronic flash. That surprised me. I hadn't thought of her since seeing George in Paris, but she had obviously made an impact.

"Look, Marie-Louise is in town. My wife's away. Couldn't you amuse her for the day? She doesn't remember you, but I've told her where you met and that you're on her side, so she's pretending to remember."

I needed little prompting. She was staying at the Sherry. I picked her up there, gave her lunch and then she suggested we go for a walk. She had filled out with the baby in the last six weeks until the child had become part of her attraction. She carried it high, as if it were something that had always been there. I found her radiant. The seductive air I remembered now had a clearly sexual edge, as so often with pregnant women. I guessed that the promise of childbirth had pushed her husband's death out of her mind.

The only awkward part of her pregnancy seemed to be that she had to stop walking when she wanted to talk.

We were on our way up Madison when she came to a halt for the third time. "George has told you about my case?"

I didn't know how much I was supposed to know, so I just said, "I'm sorry about it all."

"They've been terrible. They want to disinherit Peter's child. I couldn't let that happen. You knew Peter?"

"Not well."

"I couldn't forgive myself if I were weak now."

I didn't know what to say, so I gave in to sentiment. "Surely something can be worked out."

"George and I saw them yesterday. They said the child could have the money if I agree to bring it up in the United States and if they could be custodians of its inheritance until it was eighteen. Otherwise they'll insist on the letter of the contract."

"I can't believe that contract would stand. Of course, I know nothing about law."

"In any case," Marie-Louise said in a determined way, "I'll drag them through the courts. If they're going to be immoral, I'll make certain the world and their friends see them for what they are." Her courage was a form of beauty in itself.

A week later I ran into George outside his house on the East Side. He was triumphant. He dragged me off the street into his drawing room. "They gave in."

I understood immediately. "How did you do it?"

"It was Marie-Louise. She was right. They couldn't face the courts. Marie-Louise had to make a few concessions.

She agreed not to sell the shares without their agreement. She also agreed to have the child partially educated in the States. And its final inheritance rests on opting for American citizenship when it becomes a major. Marie-Louise is beside herself. She's upstairs phoning de Foret. He's been such a support."

Marie-Louise appeared on the stairs. When she saw me, she ran down with unexpected agility, threw her arms around my neck and kissed me. I was surprised, but she was obviously bubbling over with happiness.

"George has been wonderful." She went over and gave him a hug. "I talked to Pierre. He's so happy."

George had never liked public emotion. "Then we're all happy," was all he said.

I try to spend at least part of May in Paris, and three months after that conversation I found myself there. I asked friends about Marie-Louise. They said she was about to give birth. Apparently there had been a bit of a row because George had wanted the child to be born in New York, to simplify the citizenship question, and she had refused to leave Paris. I tracked George down and he asked me to meet him that afternoon at a private clinic on the rue Mabillon. It was one of those expensive clinics where the nurses are badly paid for the privilege of looking after well-born people. Marie-Louise had given birth the day before and was ready to see friends.

We arrived in the main lobby at the same time and were processed through by a collection of unsmiling nurses.

Marie-Louise looked wonderful. She was not alone. At first I didn't recognize the man, then I remembered his dark hair and pale skin. It was Pierre de Foret.

George was annoyed. But he recovered quickly. "Where's the boy? Let's see him."

"They're bringing him now," Marie-Louise replied with uncomplicated pleasure.

A moment later the door opened and a nurse brought the child in. We all took turns leaning over and admiring him in her arms. There isn't actually a great deal that can be said about a baby. This one did have a surprisingly thick head of hair, so we focused on that for our compliments.

De Foret bent over the baby last, and I don't know what it was, but Marie-Louise, George and I were suddenly frozen by the sight of the two of them together. The black hair, the pale skin. Marie-Louise exclaimed, "Du thé!" and rang for a nurse. George was so taken aback that I thought he would burst out with something. His eyes went from the child to de Foret to Marie-Louise, and there his stare held. Then she broke into chatter, which fell into a vacuum. We all left soon after. In the street de Foret asked which way we were going and said he was going the other.

Five days later I was woken by a call from George. He was on his way to pick me up and would explain later. He sounded distraught. When I climbed into the rented Renault there was no word of greeting. We drove south across Paris in an uncomfortable silence. When we were on the autoroute he abruptly said, "The child's dead."

"What child?" But I understood.

He didn't seem to have heard me. "My God, Marie-Louise left the clinic two days ago. Everything was normal. She insisted on going to her country place outside Fontainebleau to recover. She said the country would be good for the baby and herself. A maid went along.

"At six this morning I got a call from de Foret. He was out there. He said he had arrived the night before. Marie-Louise had called him because the child was dead."

"But of what?"

"Suffocated or something. I said I was coming straight out. He said not to. Said Marie-Louise couldn't face anyone. What do they expect me to do? I don't under-stand." He looked at me as he drove. It was one of those magical Ile-de-France spring mornings. Soft greens in the fields and on the trees, pale wildflowers, mist here and there over the low parcels of land. There is a particular mystical atmosphere to the light in the forests around Fontainebleau. That was part of what had attracted the Barbizon school of painters in the early nineteenth century. George and I said nothing more until we arrived.

The house was one of those mock François I hunting lodges. The maid answered the door and led us to a sitting room where we waited five minutes. Then the local doctor appeared from somewhere farther inside the house. He was rather creaky, in a heavy black wool suit – very much the provincial official. The child had been buried that morning. He informed us that Marie-Louise had insisted. She couldn't bear to wait.

"Surely that's not possible. The regulations –"

The doctor turned to leave, speaking over his shoulder. "Oh, in the country, you know –"

"But –"

"At least" – he turned back to us with a reassuring tone – "the child had been christened. That was done the day after she arrived." I suppose he realized that George understood he'd broken the rules.

I don't know what made me ask, "Who were the godparents?"

The doctor looked at me quizzically. Such an irrelevant question. "M. de Foret drove down for the morning with one of Marie-Louise's cousins. I don't remember her name. And myself. I am an old friend of the family."

We asked to see Marie-Louise. He said it was impossible. She could see no one. And de Foret had already left for Paris. We must have passed him on the road. George insisted, but the doctor was adamant. Voices rose, and then the doctor left saying he had other calls to make. We waited for an hour, during which not even the maid reappeared. Eventually we left, sheepishly.

I never heard George mention Marie-Louise again, and of course I never brought up the subject. But the tragedy drew us together. Whenever we were in Paris at the same time, we saw each other. From what he told me, he no longer had contact with his wife's family. He wasn't the same person as before. His soft, nervous edge had hardened into something brittle.

The other day I ran into George on rue Jacob. We decided on the spur of the moment to have lunch together and managed to get a table at a new restaurant everyone was talking about. It was on the edge of the Bois de Boulogne. A fifty-franc note got us a place at the window. We were eating and talking away with almost the old enthusiasm when I noticed a Rolls-Royce draw up outside. A well-dressed, slightly blowsy woman got out. Behind her came a man. I recognized Pierre de Foret. It was only when he took the woman by the arm that I realized it was Marie-Louise. I looked at George. He had seen them too.

They swept into the restaurant and were about to be seated two tables away from us when she saw us staring at her. Her skin was puffy, distorting her appeal. In truth there was none left, which even her thick application of makeup couldn't disguise. Her body was like an empty shell. She turned away and said to the waiter that she didn't want a table near the windows.

George waited until they were seated out of hearing, then whispered, unnecessarily, "I haven't seen her since that day at the clinic. You know what happened?"

"What do you mean?"

"The child lived six days. So it inherited."

"But it hadn't opted for American citizenship. Hardly had the chance."

George cut me off. "That was merely a choice to be made at maturity. It inherited and it died. So its mother remained the child's only heir. Marie-Louise got the hundred million. And as the child wasn't American, there were no death duties. A year later she married de Foret. They fired her husband's relatives from the tire company and put in their own people. De Foret runs it from Paris."

We ate in silence. Eventually I mumbled, "Have they had any other children?"

"No."

5

CONVERSATIONS
WITH DICTATORS II

WE WERE READING the Saturday papers over breakfast on a cold Sunday morning in Toronto when I came across a reference to Ian Paisley preaching in the north of the city.

"Christ," I said to my hostess, "Paisley's preaching here this morning."

She replied rather sourly, "They shouldn't have let him in." That was the subject of the article. There'd been a move to deny him entry on the basis that he stirred up bigotry.

"We could still make it," I said.

At that, she and Robert looked up with what passed for early morning surprise. They both glanced around their big sunny kitchen as if something might have crept in.

"He's a hatemonger," was all my hostess replied. Robert was a trial lawyer. He said nothing and went back to reading.

"Exactly. Look, humour me. Demagogues, dictators, bigots, racists, populists. They're all the same: leadership through fear, the roots of hero-worship. These people may be evil, but they stir up crowds. To see an honest man stir up a crowd is sometimes moving. To watch a dishonest man do it is much more interesting. Then you can see the full spectrum of our weaknesses being played. Like an instrument. The inner fears we try to control are suddenly encouraged to blossom, and some of us let go. Suddenly normal citizens become monsters. If you haven't seen this happen – seen it, not read about it – then you can't understand what goes wrong in society." They were staring at me with wary distress. Some conversations are supposed to take place in the last third of the day, not the first. "The point is, these are perfectly ordinary citizens in whom something has abruptly gone wrong. Look, does anyone want to come?"

Robert said quietly and coolly, "I meet enough delusional people in the courts."

"Well, could you lend me a car and a map?" I hadn't been home to Toronto for some time.

It took about half an hour to find my way from the baroque Edwardian prosperity of the Annex to the Free Presbyterian Church of Ulster in a Scarborough suburb of postwar bungalows. A very clean suburb. In the summer these little houses would have been surrounded by severe flat surfaces of grass broken by thin rows of flowers in primary colours. It was at its bleakest in mid-January. Even the warm beauty of the snow had been blown into a smooth crust of metallic white, severed with mechanical regularity by the driveways of the stuccoed-box houses.

Toronto had once been an Orange town, but generation by generation the children had gradually separated themselves from the sectarian prejudices which had brought on Orange versus Catholic riots and meant that businesses wouldn't hire outside of their religion. Now the descendants of those right-thinking immigrants were often married to people from the more flexible branches of Christianity – the Anglican and the United Church, for a start. Some were even married to Catholics or to non-Anglos, or to new Canadians of other colours. Few of them cared one way or the other about the old truths, and the Anglos in general were now a minority in the city. This little Church of Ulster, fiercely neat and without charm, was a reduced bastion; a place for last stands.

I was late. They were on their feet, singing loudly without moving. I slid into the church and found a place on the side partway up. The congregation was about two-thirds older people. None of the women wore makeup or lipstick. Even the young women came plain – there was no sense of the succulent innocence ripening like a fruit which you could find, for example, in southern Italy. Monreale, just outside of Palermo, was the first image to pop into my mind as I took my place. Monreale with its Gothic madness and the girls somehow enveloped in an aura created by the heat. Here even the young looked tired. The fatigue of bitterness. And this in spite of rousing hymns. We sat. Paisley was up at the front in a large armchair facing us, just off centre, a bulky square of a man, immobile as he listened to the local rector, who went on for some time but struck no spark of life into the congregation until he referred to the Queen's invitation to the Pope to visit Britain.

There was audible moaning and shaking of heads. "This terrible thing called dialogue," the rector added, then turned to Paisley. "There are those who would say to our brother, stay out, but we would say, come in."

A roll of "Amen" went through the pews – the sort of response you'd have expected in a Southern Baptist church.

"'Thou shalt lead us to the sea of glass and the city that lies four-square.'" It wasn't clear whether this was a reference to God or to Paisley.

The reading was from Exodus. Chapter 3, and in particular verses 2, 8 and 20. The Jews were in captivity in Egypt, where Moses was a shepherd. On this particular day he was out with his flock in the desert.

And the Angel of the LORD appeared unto him in a flame of fire out of the midst of a bush: and he looked, and, behold, the bush burned with fire, and the bush was not consumed.

And I – the LORD – am come to deliver them out of the hand of the Egyptians, and to bring them up out of that land unto a good land and a large, unto a land flowing with milk and honey; unto the place of the Canaanites, and the Hittites and the Amorites, and the Perizzites, and the Hivites, and the Jebusites.

And I – the LORD – will stretch out my hand, and smite Egypt
with all my wonders which I will do in the midst thereof; and
after that he will let you go.

When Paisley rose he spent little time on verses 8
and 20. Their message was clear. God's reference to
the Jews was a symbolic reference to the Ulsterites. The
Canaanites, Hittites, etc., were the Catholics, probably
also the Anglicans, and indeed anyone not white and
indeed anyone not in agreement; myself, for example.
It isn't very pleasant to be the devil's representative,
stuck in a pew surrounded by God's people. The fact
that no one seemed to notice was, I suppose, a reminder
of the subtlety of the devil. He appears and is not seen.
The message in this particular reading was that God
encouraged the true believers to drive the pagans off
whatever lands they occupied. In fact, God offered active
support.

But the verse Paisley chose to read to us again was
centred on the burning bush. Unfortunately I was so
mesmerized by his argument that I took no notes. I do
remember the core of his argument. The holy people
need have no fear of burning. Their cause being just,
they couldn't be consumed by fire. Burning in hell for
having used violence against sinners was therefore not a
risk. Using violence was actually a good thing, because
it was the fire of God. He didn't actually mention the
bombs and the assassination squads. He didn't need to.

And that might have got him expelled. I looked about for the RCMP plainclothes officers who no doubt were there.

The odd thing was the mismatch between Paisley and the congregation. He was such a big man in this small church. Big bones. Big features on his face. A large mouth which moved in an exaggerated, almost disjointed, manner. His chest was out of proportion. After looking hard at the lines showing through his waistcoat I decided it was covering a bulletproof vest. And that was odd – the bulletproof vest in this little lower-middle-class church in Ontario. It seemed a clumsy reflection of the violence in their souls, which here no longer escaped into public disorder. To the contrary. These were people obsessed by public order. Above all it struck me that he didn't preach well. He didn't even incite with conviction. Perhaps he'd done it too often. Perhaps he was so used to the charged-up, dangerous atmosphere of Ulster that he didn't know how to gear down in order to communicate with these sad, shrinking people who lived so far away from the burning bush and were asphyxiating themselves with bitterness. They did, after all, live in a land jam-packed with Canaanites and Hittites, etc., etc. But it was not a bomb-throwing sort of place. He went on shouting great words all around them – above, below, down the aisle – his mouth like a cavernous machine manufacturing syllables laboriously behind the lips which then shot the words out as shells. And the congregation sat there immobile.

Perhaps living in a place where that bitterness could not be easily expressed in public only made it worse. Perhaps the bitterness turned instead into a self-destructive worm, twisting away in their guts. They had come to be moved, but he was too much for them – not the message, but the dramatic method.

He wound up his performance with some standard references. "The Pope can bring in his minions, but the church will be built." "Minions" was said as if it contained two extra syllables, and so this inflated word surged through the church hall like a storm of mytho-logical corruption. "You don't need a pastor, a priest or a prelate. What you need is Jesus Christ." Perhaps he was putting too much into each word. "Poupe. Caan. Brriing. Iinn. Hiss. Miiniioons." Only the definite article escaped being articulated as a free-standing subject. There was no cadence. It was all heavy artillery. Perhaps that barrage approach was what worked best in Ulster, in an atmos-phere of ongoing hatred and daily killings by both sides. Somewhere in the closing sentence he threw in that Rome was Babylon. They all knew that one, and it probably made them feel better, you know, just to hear it said. It was one of those touchstone phrases, like the meek shall inherit the earth.

Then he collapsed into his chair, the proverbial spent volcano, except that he was more like an aging classical actor who had been reduced to overplaying in provin-cial theatres. This morning he had been offering his most famous role. Indeed it was the volcano. The burning bush that will not burn, but flows like lava. Or something to that effect. Then the congregation pulled on their hats and mitts and went out quietly into the snow.

6
PRINCESS

WHEN I FIRST MET Mark Lang he was not so fat. That was ten years ago. Even then he did have porcine tendencies hidden under what still passed for the healthy sheen of youth. Yet when he pulled himself up to his piano under kind lighting, he sang away in a remarkably thin, even fragile, voice which denied the weight of the man.

Sometimes when I go to Chicago I manage to sneak quietly into town more or less unseen. But Elizabeth Pink has a sharp eye for all movement of social interest, and if she finds me out I am berated for not staying in her house, then swept up into a seamless web of entertainment.

Elizabeth is not an old friend. She discovered me, as she would see it, on one of my trips to her town, then made me hers whenever I reappeared. By hers I mean that Elizabeth lives by her force of social movement. There are those who maintain that kind of presence with mirrors or other people's money, their corporation's, for example. Elizabeth uses her own and, without protest, her husband's to create a wake like unto that created by a great ocean liner. Perhaps far behind her that wake disappears without trace into the calm of the sea. "But then, everybody disappears," she once said to me. "So it's just a question of choosing what you want to be transitory about. I choose the most ephemeral things, because that is the least pretentious way to live."

This was the sort of logic which had first endeared her to me. In fact I look forward to being swept up periodically in meaninglessness. I'm being unfair. Sometimes it was meaninglessness as understood by the absurdists.

The first time she took us – outings for individuals were unknown – to Mark Lang's Piano Bar was after a John Cage recital she had organized in her house in Lake Forest. The house was lost in just enough of a park that I never noticed the neighbours or the house itself, which was probably just as well. It was one of those sensible mountains that money built, not taste. Harry Pink had bought the place only a few years before and Elizabeth had a decorator stuff it full of things that had nothing to do with the house or with each other.

It was a benefit for a charity that supported poor music students, those who might make it to Juilliard or do something interesting. Cage was actually there. How she did it I don't know. It was one of his last outings away from New York, and he had to move carefully. The teenagers played one of his chance pieces involving texts from Walt Whitman. Those who had paid listened carefully. Chicago is a music town, and many of them not only paid, they believed. Cage said a few words to them, very few, but with humour, then devoted himself to the students. I was close enough to overhear him talking about his visit to Toronto to visit Marshall McLuhan, the guru of the spatial and the non-linear. Then he told them about Frank Zappa. Then described the sorry state of the world. Finally he began questioning them.

"Do you think everything is erotic?"

There was silence. They had been in awe; now they were in confusion. Then one of the girls laughed and asked, "You mean in music?"

"No, everything. If it isn't erotic it isn't interesting." He smiled at them and they smiled back, tentatively. "Well, then, is life serious?"

The same girl had her voice now. "What do you think? We haven't had a life yet."

"How should I know!" Cage laughed. "But you mustn't be serious. A serious person cannot have sex."

"Why not?"

"If you have to ask, you'll never know." He winked and they all laughed.

Then he was taken away by Elizabeth and his handler, with the music-worthies staring after. Cage didn't stay for the dinner.

After the fifty paying guests were gone, Elizabeth insisted that the house guests not go to bed but accompany her downtown, in spite of the distance. The three of us along with the Pinks ended up on Dearborn Street in Mark Lang's Piano Bar. She pushed in first, a solid form moving up through the narrow, deep bar towards the sound of the piano, people being swept aside by her reverberations. I had never thought of Elizabeth as being young. As I have already mentioned, she strikes me as more of a ship. An attractive, lively liner, but built of steel all the same. Harry, much loved and pampered, followed gracefully in the wake with the rest of us.

When Elizabeth reached the piano, Mark Lang broke off his song and stood to embrace her. Three medallions hung from gold chains around his neck. They were caught up in the thick chest hair and gave off an occasional glint of reflected light against the flesh exposed by unbuttoned buttons. A table was cleared for us beyond the piano at the far end of the bar and champagne was produced. We slouched down amidst the mirrors and black acrylic while Mark Lang squeezed back behind his piano and began forcing out unwilling notes. I had heard all the songs somewhere before but forgot them as he finished each.

The place was jammed with people who looked like hoods but probably sold property. The women had that look of reckless sexual abandon which can be applied after seven when the office is forgotten and the children are in bed.

Perhaps things were more exciting at the other end of the bar, near the door. There the clients who didn't merit a table were kept standing.

Elizabeth noticed none of this. She was satisfied to be awake and among the living and sat forward on her banquette, smiling at her friends and addressing to them comments that permitted no reply. She pointed out Mark Lang's wife, sitting on one of the stools around the piano, gazing at her husband with adoration. Apparently they had a number of charming children.

When we left, I said I had enjoyed myself and Elizabeth took me at my word, because the next time I was in Chicago she took me back. This tradition went on, and she began to call the place my treat. "We must go to Mark's. Our New York friend loves it." At which point someone would protest and Elizabeth would silence them. "I know it's gone down a bit, but we mustn't abandon our friends."

That it was in decline was obvious. There was no need to push your way in. There were always people, but not so many and not the curly haired men with their reckless women. Everyone was a bit neater, a bit straighter. I mean the hair. Everyone except Mark himself. Each time I saw him he seemed to have swelled a bit more, stretching out the skin in all directions so that he was exactly the same person, just bigger. The only exception was his chest, which began to fall like breasts onto his stomach, which in turn hung in a mammoth lump over his tight trousers. As his listeners became neater, he unbuttoned his shirt further, and by the time ten years had gone by only his belt held the shirt in place. The one thing that didn't change was his voice, which went on as thin as ever.

Last January, I telephoned Elizabeth from New York to say I was coming through. For the first time she said I couldn't stay with them but was to keep both nights open. "I have a special guest."

She had room for a lot more than one guest, so whoever it was somehow merited particularly special treatment. I arrived at my hotel to find a dinner invitation waiting. As usual there were about fifty people and as usual the men were in dinner jackets. Elizabeth was near the door when I arrived and more excited than I was used to seeing her. She took me across the room and introduced me to a tall, stiff young woman in a gold-and-white gown – it was unquestionably a gown. "Princess Helena." Nothing more. Beneath the stiffness she was actually quite beautiful. She had long hair, almost blond, and an old-fashioned, generous figure. But her face was marred by the lack of any expression. At first I thought she was playing at being grand, giving the plebes their money's worth. But on second glance I was sure that she was afraid. She didn't have much to say and I'm not much good at small talk, so I allowed someone else to take my place and dragged Elizabeth away with me.

"What's the big deal?"

She feigned surprised. "Helena is the daughter of the king of ..." and she named a European country.

"You mean the Nazi collaborator?"

I'm not quite sure how to describe the look Elizabeth gave me. Horror, perhaps. Or the fear of social shame.

"Surely you know. The one who abdicated fast after the war to avoid being put on trial."

"Don't say that. The poor girl. Don't you think that has been following her around all her life?"

"There shouldn't be anything poor about her. They had all those mines in Africa. Come on, Elizabeth. All those dead Africans. All that money. The family still has the throne. I'm sure they've all been looked after. What's she doing here?"

"I met her last winter in Courchevel. She's such a nice girl, but all people can do there is gossip. I thought this would do her good. These people," Elizabeth glanced around with a rare show of contempt, "know nothing about her, and we'll keep it that way. " She glared at me. "She is still the daughter of a king."

I looked over at the Princess. She was talking to a young man, taller than her, blonder, with a finer face and figure and better dressed than the other men. "Does he come with her?"

Elizabeth laughed. "That's Korma. He bought a house down the street a few months ago. The big stone one you can see from the road."

"He's too young to have made enough money for that," I said.

Elizabeth laughed again. "He uses the house as an art gallery. The whole place is filled with the most wonderful pictures." She pointed with pride to a bad Picasso on the wall behind us. "He sold me that."

I made no comment and nodded towards the Aryan couple. "She seems to be in his spell."

"My silly friend," Elizabeth took my arm, "everyone is in Korma's spell, but his interests don't tend towards women, which makes him the perfect extra male. He has a houseboy." She paused as if regretting that last remark. "The best part is that he brings the young man along with him to help out in the kitchen."

I found myself sitting at the same table as Korma, and he was as charming as Elizabeth had promised. His secret was a simplicity that left people feeling something important was being withheld. My eyes were drawn back to him continually, and suddenly I realized why. I had met him before. Where, I couldn't pinpoint. His voice was what had stuck. It was perfectly neutral, caught between the masculine and the feminine, with an edge that suggested a foreign accent but might merely have been something created for the benefit of his mystique.

It was clear from the conversation that a good number of the businessmen around the table or their wives had been to his parties and bought paintings. Abruptly I remembered and interjected, "You sold me a pair of shoes."

Our eyes met for a second. He looked away as if nothing had been said and began talking to the woman on his far side. I think the others assumed that I meant a pair of paintings by someone called Choos, perhaps, or Shous. Or perhaps it was an insider's nickname for Schnabel. They had all read about the broken plates on the wall, probably in *Time*. A few of them decided that I knew more about art than they did and began to probe for my views on the Impressionists, of which they all owned at least one.

I didn't say another word to Korma, not even after dinner, when the Pinks and the last six guests set off for Mark Lang's Piano Bar. We took two cars. The Princess rode with the Pinks while I slid onto the back seat of Korma's Rolls-Royce and sat quietly behind the silhouette of the houseboy driving us into the centre of the city.

The bar was almost empty and Lang was singing as hard as he could to fill the gap. The hair on his chest was matted down with sweat and tangled around the medallions. He broke off to greet us – he knew my name by then – and led us to a table at the back. When Princess Helena was introduced he automatically kissed her hand, his large mouth burying the small fingers, and said he would sing a song for her. He took a Tony Bennett tune about a beautiful woman and substituted Princess Helena for the woman's name. It was actually an improvement on the original, as he had sent the rhymes askew. The Princess's face came alive for the first time that evening.

Elizabeth had placed her against the wall in the centre of our group – which meant giving up what would have been her own place – but the Princess ignored our conversation and leaned forward to stare at the piano and Mark Lang. Eventually she said she couldn't hear the songs and wanted to sit on a stool at the piano. When she was gone, Elizabeth moaned in a low tone to all of us, "Poor girl. She's such an innocent. Two years ago she was still in a convent school and since then she's been in a gilded cage. Her title and her money alone were enough to do that. I knew it was a good idea to invite her here. Look, already she's beginning to have a good time."

The next morning Elizabeth got a phone call from a journalist at the *Sun-Times*. He had been in the piano bar the night before, had overheard the introductions and listened to Lang's song. He had asked around, found out about the Princess and wondered if she would give an interview. At first Elizabeth said no. He said he was writing a story anyway, so it was simply a question of whether they would be kind enough to save him the work of digging out her life story from press files. As Elizabeth put it to me, she had to compromise for the poor girl's sake. The Nazi king was forgotten by most, but not by the files. So she asked the journalist to join them for lunch.

That afternoon the last edition carried a picture of Elizabeth and her house guest beneath "King's Daughter Visits Chicago." The story included lots of colourful filler, her discovery of hoagies, her fascination with sliders, Chicago skyscrapers, Frank Lloyd Wright, no Nazis and a mention of her visit to Mark Lang's Piano Bar.

Later in the evening Elizabeth took a small party, including Korma and myself, to the symphony and on to dinner. The Princess insisted we finish up at the piano bar. Once there, she insisted on sitting at the piano's edge. There were a few more drinkers that evening and I noticed that a number of them were watching Helena. They were talking about her.

When we left Korma asked me if I would come back to his house for a last drink. He was a bit drunk and it was more than out of my way, but I'm not very good at refusing. We dropped a couple off before heading over to Lake Forest. The house appeared unfriendly, grey stone with small windows. Inside it was warm and informal – as informal as those enormous rooms could ever be. He had painted them light colours, used nothing but modern furniture, covered every table with large bouquets of flowers and hung a maximum of paintings, most of them third-rate by first-rate artists.

Korma's servant appeared with two cognacs. He was of the southern-Italian type. Dark with muscular thighs. When he was gone, I said to Korma, "Not only have I already met you, I've also seen your servant somewhere."

Korma wasn't bothered in the least. "Lang's bar. He was a waiter there when I discovered him." This was said in a friendly, ironical tone.

He then went on to tell me all about himself. Yes, I probably had bought a pair of shoes from him. His new life was truly new. What's more, it wasn't really his. He leased the Rolls-Royce. He rented the house. Most of the paintings were on consignment from people in other cities. All of this he explained with the seriousness of a little boy until I felt obliged to prick his bubble.

"And what about the flowers?" I waved at the dozens of lilies and orchids and roses.

"Oh!" he laughed. It was a child's laugh, and I realized his was a child's game. "I have a deal with a wholesale florist. I get their flowers when they are too far gone to sell. We pick them over, pull out the dead bits and take good care of them."

I found myself laughing with him. At first his confession had surprised me, but gradually I understood. There was nothing strange about him, except perhaps that he was too obvious. He wanted me to know everything. Above all, that he was honest – that he had not become a millionaire by questionable means. If his buyers began to think that, they might stop buying. He was far from being rich. He lived on the narrow margin between maintaining a vast public illusion and selling the odd Renoir that Renoir had meant to burn.

When he had finished, he stood up and went over to a small Degas sketch. "Do you like this?"

It was pretty ordinary, probably not even real. I politely admired it. He took it off the wall and handed it to me. "I would be grateful if you wouldn't repeat any of this."

I put out my hands in protest. "No. You keep it, Korma. I won't say a word."

Before leaving Chicago the next morning, I telephoned Elizabeth to thank her. She was agitated.

"Have you seen the *Tribune*? There's another article. They're following us around. I've had phone calls all morning from people I hardly know wanting us to come to dinner. Us. That means bring along Helena. And the governor just called. He's alright. We give him lots of money. But he wants Helena to open a bridge, then come to their country place next weekend."

I detected mixed emotions in Elizabeth's voice. "What's the matter with that?"

"I don't know." It wasn't her sort of phrase. "I just have a bad feeling."

A month later I was back in Chicago and discovered that she had buried her feelings and was diligently guiding Helena through Chicago society. As for the Princess, she had changed, at least on the surface. She appeared to have the measure of the place and had fallen back on the European class system, treating the rich with the kind of bearable contempt they seem unconsciously to desire. Above all, she had taken a liking to café life. Elizabeth and Harry Pink were kept busy discovering new restaurants and bars, befriending their owners and cooks and generally working hard at being mentioned in every gossip column, making and breaking the reputations of various establishments in the process. Where the Princess ate, the city ran to eat. I was amazed to discover when we all ended up at Mark Lang's late at night on my first day back in town that it was packed, the way it had been ten years before. Lang gave us a grateful welcome. But he also must have been nervous that we might change our minds and start going somewhere else. By we, I mean the Princess, who abandoned us the moment we arrived and was hanging over the piano. Elizabeth told me that Lang's bar was Helena's favourite place – and so had become Chicago's favourite.

I still couldn't make out what the fuss was about. She was a boring convent girl with no conversation, no experience, poor English and probably not many brains. And relaxation didn't suit her looks. She resembled someone off duty who only existed on duty. All the same, I was filled with admiration. She had created a court without any of the responsibilities of being queen. She was turning the great anti-monarchy town into a fiefdom.

About three weeks ago I had another Chicago excuse and telephoned Elizabeth to let her know I was coming. She sounded distraught. To be accurate, there was a bitter note in her voice.

"Helena has played me a trick and made a fool of herself."

"She's not smart enough to trick you, Elizabeth."

"The silly girl has been seeing Mark Lang on her own."

"You mean they're having an affair."

"No. You fool. The girl's a virgin. At least she was. She's been seeing him during the day. You know he has an apartment on Astor, around the corner from his bar?

Well, one of the papers printed a story about the Princess and her best friend – Mark Lang. They had been following her. Looking for a story. They timed her visits to his apartment. Timed them. You can imagine the –" she paused to find an appropriate word "– the difficulty." It was a rare moment of understatement. Elizabeth said it quietly. "I questioned her. I had to. And she admitted everything. That was only the beginning. There is an honorary consul in Chicago, you know, for her country." I loved the way Elizabeth never mentioned the country's name. At one level she seemed to feel it was protection against the Nazi story. At another level this somehow made Helena her personal responsibility. Elizabeth was her new, protective country. There was nothing unpleasant about this. It was my friend at her most endearing and complex. "Well, when he saw this article the consul sent off a report. You can imagine. And the next thing we knew two men arrived at the house. No notice. Ten thirty!" As if this were a bit early for calls. "I stayed with her. She asked me to. They tried to convince her to come home."

"Convince?"

"Exactly. They looked like policemen. At my house. Policemen. Foreign policemen! After about half an hour they left saying they would call again. Those were the words. 'We will call again tomorrow, ma'am.' Obsequious. Threatening. That's what I thought. The moment they were out the door Helena went crazy. She ran upstairs. Two minutes later she rushed down, weeping. I held her.

She just kept on, like a teenager. Then she rushed off. Took the little BMW. You know, the sports model. I'd been letting her use it. Well, I didn't know what to do. I cancelled my lunch. I don't know. Next thing I hear the maid who was ironing screaming my name. I could hear her across the house. I rushed down to the basement and there she was with the iron held out in front of her, pointing at the television. The five o'clock local news. A live report. Helena and Mark giving a press conference at his bar, demanding the protection of the Chicago police. They said they loved each other and wanted to be left alone. Helena said she was afraid her family would have her kidnapped rather than let her involve herself with an American entertainer."

"Good for her."

"Good? What's so good? Their ambassador flew in from Washington the next day. My reputation has been ruined. Not only is Mark a piano player, he has a divorce that means nothing to the Catholic Church, he has two children and he's Jewish."

I burst into uncontrollable laughter. She must have mistaken it for something else, because when I managed to ask her to go on, she did.

"I put all the pressure on her I could. The ambassador said he would have the Americans revoke her visa if she didn't cooperate. That was two days ago. So she and Mark flew to Mexico and got married."

"Married?"

"She's a fool."

It was ten days before I arrived in Chicago. Elizabeth had recovered, at least superficially, although I wasn't allowed to mention Helena's name. I was now free to stay there again. Korma had been included in the dinner that evening, and when it was over I suggested we go down to the piano bar. I don't know what I expected to find, but I felt it was an experience which couldn't be avoided. Elizabeth looked at me with a hurt expression before refusing to come. I smiled and dragged Korma off with me.

His houseboy appeared from Elizabeth's kitchen to drive us. On the way there I was filled in on the marriage. Now that she had Lang during the day, the Princess no longer felt obliged to go to the bar at night. Instead, she was working at cementing her social support, which Elizabeth was attempting to subvert. I was sorry to miss her. I had wanted to see the effects on her of marriage to such a large piano player.

The bar was jammed. Nevertheless, Lang found us a table and whispered to me that I should give his regards to Elizabeth. I wanted to ask him about everything, but that would have to wait until he took a break, and the crowd was so demanding that he played on and on, squeaking out sweet love while sweat poured down his exposed chest.

When at last he broke off, Lang shouted to us that he would be right back and headed off to his office down a corridor behind the bar. About five minutes later Korma pointed out the Princess pushing her way into the bar. Her passage caused quite a sensation. Apparently people came in the vain hope that she might make an appearance, which she hadn't done for five days. She was dressed for a dinner that must have just ended and wore an almost transparent dress which clung to her body. That was probably Lang's influence. For the first time, there was a little glint in her eyes. A hint of life. The convent would not have approved.

She waved hello and asked where her husband was. I said he had gone to his office. She was hardly out of sight before there was a sharp, prolonged scream. I leapt to my feet and down the corridor. Lang's office door was ajar and I flung it open. The Princess was frozen with her back to me, staring at her husband. He stood with his open shirt no longer kept in place by his belt. Nor was his mountainous stomach held up, as his belt lay around his ankles and Korma's houseboy was down on his knees in a position which could have been one of prayer.

The Princess collapsed in a nineteenth-century sort of way. I caught her and half-dragged her back along the corridor to our table, where I made her sit. No one said anything. She gulped down my glass of champagne and, focusing on Korma across the table, put out her hand.

"Get me away from here before he comes out."

Korma jumped to his feet and we each took Helena under one arm, literally lifting her down the full length of the room and out the door. When we were seated in the Rolls, all three of us in the front, Korma hesitated. He still didn't know what had happened.

Again she gave an order. "Take me to your place."

We were gone without another word. It was the middle of the night before Korma and I had finished comforting her and I was able to escape back to Elizabeth's. I had suggested the Princess come back with me, but she was afraid Elizabeth would turn her away. Korma wouldn't hear of her leaving. He said she could stay forever. He said it in an engaging, elegant way, and so I left the Princess behind. She was, after all, perfectly safe with Korma.

I had to leave town the next day. That was two weeks ago. Elizabeth phoned me yesterday. Apparently the Princess has sued for divorce, which has only increased the popularity of Lang's piano bar. And Korma had just given a large party to sell his new collection of paintings. Elizabeth didn't feel she could go, but heard from friends that the Princess was receiving at the front door as if she were Korma's wife and the Chicago rich turned out in droves to spend a record amount of money.

7

THE SWEET
TOOTH

THE BROWN PALACE is one of the few hotels left where
you feel you are in the United States of America, what
they used to call America, as opposed to the States – an
America that knew what it was, whatever that means.

I was in Denver for one night. A friend in New York
had given me an introduction. They were apparently
very nice people; American, like the Brown Palace.
He ran a local family business, and that made him just
rich enough to be independent by nature. My friend
had said vaguely that they used their independence to
take advantage of what Colorado is best at – country.
He thought I would enjoy hearing about that and had
written ahead.

I phoned the house on the morning I got into town,
expecting to get Mrs. Martin. Instead, it was a male
voice. Not very welcoming, that was my first impression.
It was clear and balanced, a voice with a good seat, but it
wasn't friendly.

I explained who I was. He thought about that for a

while. That's why I like Colorado. They take the time to think. They don't just fill the gaps with sound.

When he was ready, he said, "We received the letter. Al wrote us all about you." The voice was now polite, but distinctly put upon. "I'm Henry Martin. Look, we'd like to see you, like to entertain you, only I'm afraid something happened last week and my wife's just been allowed home this morning." From the tremor creeping into his voice, I began to think he was decent to be talking to me at all.

"Don't worry, Mr. Martin, we'll do it another –"

"No," he interrupted. "Listen, you come to dinner. No, no. If you don't mind I think it might do Katie some good. It'll give her something to do, you see." Suddenly he sounded pathetic. I could hardly protest. "She can organize a dinner for you. You can help me cheer her up. I mean, you're in the word business." This was meant as a little joke. A compliment of sorts.

I agreed to come at seven thirty. It was only after we'd hung up that I realized I'd no idea what disaster had struck them. I suppose he was so upset he hadn't noticed how little he had told me.

I'd originally looked forward to an interesting day – the main purpose of my visit to Denver was a conference on the situation in the Horn of Africa – but it went very slowly. Very academic. I was the eye witness – the entertainment. My contribution certainly wasn't up to what everyone was expecting. I wasn't entertaining enough.

You could see that in their eyes. I'm afraid my mind was on the Martins. It wasn't that I wanted to go and help cheer her up. It's just that there is something horribly compelling about human tragedy, and I could feel it was that. We are all – I'm no exception – drawn towards it, whenever it happens, with our eyes desperately shut, protesting that we hate it and want to look the other way.

I arrived sharp at seven thirty. If there were going to be other people, I wanted to get there first to find out what had happened.

The house was hidden behind a lot of pine trees that smelled of spring. It was on a sharp incline and had probably been built at what was then the edge of town. For the walls of the house they had used large pieces of stone put together in a maze as if they were rough slabs. The impression was of a generous, slumbering beast. Almost the first thing Martin told me was that his father had built it in the thirties, when he was making money and others weren't. He continued with a chuckle, "My father was a Democrat. He saw it as a personal contribution to Roosevelt's make-work projects."

Henry Martin was, as I expected, a nice tidy man. He was wearing an open-necked shirt – of the Egyptian cotton, button-down-collar variety – with an old brown jacket thrown over that. There was a paisley silk handkerchief stuffed into the breast pocket. He drew me through the front door into a large wooden gallery – a Western baronial hall. I'd have put him at forty-five. He had probably been a healthy, good-looking boy in school and now he was on the road of general expansion, which left him a bit flushed and out of stride with himself. All the same it was a healthy expansion, and at another time I'd have probably guessed that he was happy with his life and glad to be alive. Despite the tension under which he was clearly labouring, his smile was a broad white welcome.

"I hope you didn't mind me prevailing on you to come, but Katie has already pulled herself together enough to cook you something."

That seemed like the perfect moment to find out what had happened, but as I started to speak a door into the hall opened. The woman who stood in the doorway wasn't more than five feet four. I could imagine exactly what had attracted him to her. In her time she must have been one of those perfect little numbers. She wore a simple grey silk dress that followed her line and let you see she was still pretty perfect. But it all meant nothing, because even from a distance it was clear that the essence of life was being crushed out of her.

"Now don't stand out there gossiping. Bring him in." It was a girl's voice, yet surprisingly solid. As I began to say something she came forward, took my hand, shook it gently and said, "No apologies. Henry was quite right to make you come." I couldn't see the colour of her eyes. They were so withdrawn and misty. Her heavy makeup disguised nothing. "The last thing Henry and I want to do is sit here looking at each other."

The living room was all in wood, with beams. He got me a good strong Scotch, which I certainly needed, and then Katie began asking me about our friend in common in New York. Well, it was at least something to talk about and it seemed to cheer them up. They'd done a lot of travelling with Al, so we were still on the same subject when we went in to dinner. By then we were on to Al and his peculiarities, of which he has a number. Henry hunted with Al, went on whitewater canoe trips, and so they had shared cabins and tents. Al's snoring was legendary. We took turns telling stories about our friend and they listened attentively to each other, which isn't all that common among long-married couples.

The meal had a distracted feel to it – overcooked here, undercooked there – which was the least of my concerns. Even when all three of us were laughing, it was as if they were crying. The atmosphere was unbearable.

I asked them if Al often came out to visit them in Denver. At that Henry Martin began with great enthusiasm, "Denver, no! The ranch, yes! We can't keep him in this house. He'll only come out if we promise to keep him down on the ranch."

"What ranch?"

It was, he said, the love of their life. He hadn't really wanted to run the family company, but someone had to, and so as a compensation he bought himself what he'd really wanted – a good-sized working ranch. That was where they spent their weekends and sometimes up to three or four days of the week. It was clearly making him feel a great deal better to be talking away. "Normally," he said, "we'd have gone there this morning." As soon as the words were out he seemed to regret them.

"It's alright, Henry," his wife broke in. "We've got to start saying it. If Petie weren't dead we'd be going out there." Her voice drained away as she finished the sentence.

Henry began nodding methodically. "I think he loved the place more than we did."

"Look," I said. "I'm very sorry. Your husband didn't really explain to me this morning." They both looked at me, amazed that there was somebody who hadn't heard. Tragedies are always like that; those struck believe the whole world knows, as if by osmosis. "I'm afraid I don't know what has happened."

Martin kept looking at me while he considered what I'd said. Things having gone as far as they had, it was pretty difficult not to go on, even if it did upset his wife.

"I'm sorry. I guess I was so rattled when you rang that I thought … Petie was our boy. Our only child. He was fourteen. The kind of boy I guess most people dream they might produce. Lots of character. Spunk, I used to call it. And fast. Anyway, we both loved him too much. You shouldn't do that. Anyway, Petie died last week."

"He was killed! Say it, Henry!" The bitterness in her voice seemed to give her strength. "We can't start lying to ourselves."

"No, Katie. That's not right." He was bending across the table towards her, very quietly, slowly; appealing. "That isn't fair. We won't be able to live if we ..."

She began shaking her head from side to side and waved his words away. "He was killed! And I killed him. Those are the facts." He tried to interrupt, but she kept repeating, "Those are the facts."

"My wife," Henry said to me, trying to restore order to his voice, "has been having trouble the last few years. It happens to a lot of people. She just hasn't been able to get her picture of herself straight. She's had a lot of depression. So we've been doing all the right things and she has a very good analyst." He paused, as if to say, swallow that. "Well, she tried to kill herself last week. She tried to poison herself. Katie is a bit of a romantic. That was one of the first things I loved about her." He reached over and took his wife's hand as it fiddled with a fork. His eyes seemed mesmerized by the moving bit of metal. "And so she decided she would have one last happy meal with us and die in her sleep. She made some little lemon tarts on Wednesday evening – they're one of her specialties we all love. Not just any old lemon tarts. Katie's are decorated and everything. She made these tarts and put them in a cupboard for the next day." His voice had gradually become laboured. "Anyway, one of the tarts had poison in it. She knew which one from the decorating. She was going to eat it with us, and then, when I woke up in the morning, I'd just find her there dead. Only Petie ..." He looked up from his hands, which were clasped around his wife's, the fork fixed in place. His eyes had no focus. "I told you he had a lot of spunk. Well, he found the tarts that same evening. I guess we were reading or something. And he ate a couple. He had a really sweet tooth. I guess he inherited that from me. And in the morning Katie found him dead. She ... she just came back into our room where I was dressing. And I saw right away something was wrong." His voice had shrunk to a monotone. "There was no blood in her face. She looked like a dead person. She just went over to one of her drawers and pulled out this letter and gave it to me. It was her suicide note. She'd had it all prepared in advance. Well, I read it. Then she said, 'Petie's dead.' Just like that. Then she had a kind of fit and went unconscious. I thought she'd had a stroke. I didn't know what to do. I felt crazy. I checked that she was still breathing, then I ran to Petie's room, and there he was, all white."

"Stop it, Henry."

"No, honey. I want to say it all the way through. So he was dead. No doubt there. Then the doctor came and the police. They had to take Katie away. You see, technically she'd killed him. They couldn't see what else to do. Katie and I both went to school with the police officer. I'd played football with him. And there we were. They held her for six days, trying to figure out what to do. I got her out today. I mean, I know them all. They're all old friends of ours, the judges and the prosecutors. All of them." I suppose it had distracted him, made him feel useful to have something to do. "They understood. So I got her out and I don't think they're going to charge her in the end. I think that'll be alright."

He had been looking at me all the time, without seeing me. Now he looked away and got heavily to his feet. "I think I'll just go out and get a bit of air." As he went through the door, his shoulders were collapsing and shaking.

Mrs. Martin and I sat at the table in silence while his footsteps disappeared. Then without warning she pushed her chair back and opened her mouth wide as if to scream and began rocking in her chair. "Oh, my God! Oh, my God!"

I felt I should get up and put an arm around her. Any comfort. But then an ethereal whisper came out.

"It was for him!" She shook her hand towards the door through which her husband had disappeared. "It was for him! The poison was for him!"

I sat in a petrified silence. Her hand was still shaking in agitation at the door. Her mouth was stretching wider and wider as if she would explode. The words came out like escaping gas. "I hate him! I hate him! So much. I hate him so much."

If only to stop her, I tried to interrupt, "You could have just divorced him ..."

"And what? What? Become the ex–Mrs. Martin? 'He never should have married her,' they'd all say, 'she was never up to it.' And after all these years, what would

I have got? A settlement so I could live in some apartment down in that town. Do you think they would have given me this house? His father's house? His? It's mine! I suffered here for twenty years. Six of them alone with him, without even Petie." Then she came to a cold stop and examined me. "You don't see it. It wasn't the house or the money. It was what he was doing to Petie. Turning my child into a copy of himself. I couldn't allow him to do that. He didn't have the right. The only way to put a stop to it was to kill him. Then Petie would be free to become himself. Oh, God. Oh, God."

She wrapped her arms around herself and rocked maniacally.

"Surely," I began, "he can't be … He seems to be –"

"He's a monster! He's not human!" She was spitting through her tears. "There's nothing inside." She thumped herself. "Nothing inside."

"But surely –"

"What do you know?" She was staring at me, her eyes suddenly filled with hatred. "What do you know about us? About him? What makes you think you can come in here and know what makes a man inhuman? You know nothing!"

She was right. I knew nothing. Then she began rocking again and sobbing. At that point Henry Martin reappeared. I jumped up.

"You'd better call me a cab. I think your wife has been under enough strain for the day."

He saw the tears streaming down her face and went over and took her in his arms. "It's okay, baby. We'll think of something. It's okay." He went on comforting her for what seemed like an eternity. Then he insisted on driving me back to the Brown Palace. He said it would only take him twenty minutes there and back.

On the way there I almost told him what she'd said. What would that have done? My word against hers. No proof. Chances were she wouldn't try again. Nobody would believe a second accident. Besides, she would always fear that I might come forward. And if I did tell him? He was already broken. What would it do? Besides, I knew nothing of him. Nothing at all. I thought I might tell our mutual friend in New York and see what he thought.

8

CONVERSATIONS
WITH DICTATORS III

THERE IS A MACABRE SIDE to this business of collecting dictators. And I have an insatiable appetite to see them up close. Something about the face of the devil and the unlimited forms it can take. Something about the seduction of large groups of people, which is intimately linked to the murder of large groups of people. In other words, theatre. Theatre of the gods in the Homeric tradition.

Word was going around that the Haitian government wanted someone to come down to report on the damage done by Hurricane Sally. A newspaper phoned me. I called Georges Anglade, one of my Haitian writer friends, for advice. Like most of them, he lived in exile in Montreal. Georges is a burly guy, brilliant, funny, specialized in writing *lodyans* – fast, explosive, comic stories – a Haitian specialty. After some unprintable comments on the Duvaliers, he said I should go. Any opportunity to describe the Haitian reality should be seized. So I said yes, provided that the paper could get me an interview with Baby Doc, the current president for life and the son of

Doctor Duvalier. Most people on the plane were going to the Club Med. The couple sitting next to me had been once before. They said they loved it. Loved Haiti. Apparently the food was wonderful, and if you were lucky Petit Pierre, that character from the Graham Greene novel, would come out from Port-au-Prince to have dinner in the Club's compound while you were there. He was one of the rare Haitians allowed in, apart from those who came to clean up. No one seemed to remember his real name or what he'd been like before appearing in the novel, but now he went nowhere out of his white suit and without his elaborate walking stick. He had become his fictional self. The couple sitting beside me had seen him on their last holiday. He'd been only four chairs away at their table. They'd found it quite exciting. They'd had to wait until they got home to rush out to buy the novel and look through it for the bits with Petit Pierre. They had marked these and shown them to their friends. They were both lawyers. They played a lot of tennis, they said. If you got up early the courts at the Club weren't too hot. Anyway, they loved Haiti. The atmosphere, they said, was evocative.

A woman from the government was waiting for me at the foot of the boarding ramp. She took me straight through as if the passport and customs officers didn't exist, and we drove to a concrete hotel not far from the presidential palace. It was a very efficient hotel, she said. Her blouse and skirt were out of the basic Saint Laurent school. Her hair was combed up and back in a Jacqueline

Kennedy style. She was mulatto. The road into town had the feel that if you fall off the edge, you land in another place. So keep moving.

The next day Madame Boutellier – the government woman – picked me up at ten. She didn't say much. I guessed that Haiti wasn't the kind of dictatorship where flacks talked a lot. They were just glad to have some work.

She took me to the palace. It was white. Late colonial Versailles, several storeys high. More in the Petit Trianon category, with a wrought-iron fence around it and a formal garden inside. Lots of trimmed, decorative bushes. A few guards. Not too many. We drove through the gates fast and stopped at the main stairs, which were on the side. Monumental marble steps covered in white carpet. Thick wool. They cut straight up into the heart of the palace like a gigantic frozen erection. On the étage noble the stairs transformed themselves into a wide corridor running straight on down the centre to the other end of the building. Everything was white except for the secretary sitting behind his desk outside an office at the top of the stairs. There was a manual typewriter in front of him. He just sat there. There was no one else in sight.

"The president will be back soon," Mrs. Boutellier said and led me down the corridor to a large reception room. She left me there with the grand doors folded back. They were decorated with gold leaf. So were the walls. Apart from that the room was empty. Four ceiling-to-floor French windows were open to catch a breeze. It wasn't yet too hot. The curtains were tied back, heavy white silk; too heavy to move in less than a wind.

I walked across and hung over the balcony of the window on the right. This was the facade side and very much l'étage noble. You'd give a speech from one of these windows, or wave, if anyone were interested. I could see that the decorative bushes in the formal garden served to obscure machine-gun posts.

"Bonjour, monsieur."

The voice was rather pinched. I turned around. Across the room in the doorway there was a crowd. A large, fat man wearing a single-breasted black suit stood at the front in the middle. I walked towards him.

"Bonjour, Monsieur le Président."

He took on a childish smile. "Vous parlez français?"

"Eh, pourquoi pas?"

He giggled. The crowd laughed. I was now close enough to shake his hand. He moved it up slowly. The fingers were soft. The grip also. I gazed into his eyes, which were very small. Two of the smallest eyes I'd ever seen, sunk into a fat face. He wore a white shirt and a pale tie. Both these and the suit were silk.

"Venez."

The president turned and the crowd scattered, jostling each other. Twenty or so of them. Most were older. Overweight, not fat. Muscular men with paunches. Most wore an open shirt without a jacket and a pistol tucked into his belt at the front under the protruding belly. No holster. They were Tonton Macoute inherited from the president's father. A few were young soldiers, more or less in uniform. They had rifles and carried them as if out in the country shooting rabbits, barrels up or down in an indiscriminate way.

"Venez."

We went back up the hall and into an office on the other side. He was one of those fat men whose legs are glued together down to their knees when they walk. The male secretary sitting outside behind the manual type-writer didn't move. The president for life's office was empty except for an ornate desk with an Empire armchair behind it. A small Empire chair was placed in front for the visitor. There was an intercom on the desk, along with a photo of his wife and one of his father, small and accountant-like. Nothing else.

She was mulatto. Very pale. Everyone said she ran the country, she and her father. The mulattoes had all the businesses and the big money. The Duvaliers had the Tonton Macoutes and the kind of cash a determined dictatorship can bring in.

I asked him a few questions. He had memorized some formal multi-purpose answers of no interest. He was so simple – stupid would be a more accurate word – he said right out that he wanted me to report on the hurricane damage as a preliminary step towards him making an international request for emergency aid. People would believe a journalist, he said. He wanted two hundred million.

Everyone knew that cash aid to Haiti went straight into the Duvaliers' pockets. Or rather, into their foreign bank accounts. That's why most aid agencies sent seeds or hospital equipment. These of course could be sold off to bring in money, but at least the regime had to do some extra work. Curiously enough there were still people here and there – in Washington, for example – willing to send cash. Like most observers, my assumption was that those people were either as stupid as Baby Doc or had another agenda.

"Je vous envoie en hélicoptère. Il faut voir la tragédie, monsieur. C'est un catastrophe pour le peuple."

There were no roads to that end of the island and he wanted me to go immediately. In his personal helicopter. He leaned across the desk towards the intercom, his belly spreading out over the marquetry, like dough being rolled. The machine was on my side. He pushed some buttons, then spoke into it. Nothing happened. He pushed more buttons, with a growing, slow impatience. Then he levered himself back into his chair and onto his feet. As he crossed to the door he pulled his shirt and suit back into place. The men were milling about outside in the corridor, crowding it, an atypical claque of courtiers.

"L'hélicoptère!" he said, as if anything not memorized had to be limited to single words, and walked away through the crowd. They jostled each other to clear a path. Their rifles seemed somehow to be in the way, like awkward appendages.

"Ma femme m'attend," he said over his shoulder. I caught a glimpse of her coming down the stairs from above. She was extremely slim. A formal silhouette of beauty. Like ice. In something expensive but predictable, maybe Dior. Very First Lady. She was at a certain distance, but the ice I'm sure about. He didn't say goodbye or anything. The crowd ran down the erection staircase after the presidential couple. One man lingered behind just long enough to pull his pistol from his waist and point it at the seated male secretary.

"Un hélicoptère pour monsieur."

He wasn't threatening the man. I could see that. It was just his way of pointing when he wanted something.

The flack, Madame Boutellier, took me to the airport. There was an old helicopter waiting. I exaggerate. It was perhaps twenty years old. A troop carrier.

"The president's?" I asked her.

She looked away and said she'd be waiting to pick me up when I got back. I climbed up into the belly of the helicopter with a young guy who wore an army shirt and trousers. No belt. No shoes. He had a big rag in his right hand and smiled nicely. There was nothing else in the belly apart from a steel barrel sitting upright.

I stripped off my tie and jacket and handed them down to Madame Boutellier. "Gardez-les en souvenir de moi." She didn't smile. I sat on the floor. The soldier did the same. We took off with the side wide open, as if for an attack. This gave me a good view. After we'd dipped once and then hit an air pocket, I noticed there was nothing to hold on to. And the barrel was unattached and leaking generously. It was fuel, for the return trip I guess. The soldier got up and started to mop away at the spreading fuel with his rag, then squeezed it out the open door. Then mopped some more. That was his job. We went up over the mountains then curved in through a series of passes, sometimes above, sometimes below the scattered cloud. I looked back over at the barrel, the busy mopper and then around at the inside of the helicopter. It was a shit box. I thought about maintenance, looked at dust thickness on some of the rivets. Once a year perhaps. I tried not to think about maintenance. Fools die stupidly. I was glad I couldn't see the pilot's cabin up in front.

We flew about an hour, up over more jungle peaks, through more low cloud. It was very beautiful. I concentrated on that. Then we came down onto a coastal plain. I could see the people coming out of the woods all around as we neared the ground. By the time we landed there must have been a thousand of them. They surrounded the helicopter. Close. All in rags. Old shirts and trousers with broken zippers. Ripped skirts. Stained work shifts.

There was some shouting from the outside of the ring and the crowd broke apart on one side. Two men came through, one wearing a policeman's shirt and carrying a wooden club about a metre long. The other wore a straw hat with a very wide brim. He came to the front and announced that he was the mayor. He wore a pistol tucked into his trousers above the zipper. No paunch. He also wore shoes. The policeman did too, although without laces, but his zipper was broken and partially replaced by a safety pin. They seemed to own the only shoes in the village. The policeman turned to face the crowd and shouted.

"En arrière!"

They didn't move. Their curiosity held them there, staring at me, with my clean clothes, my functioning zipper, my shoes, my socks. The mayor had no socks.

At that, the policeman raised his club, as if to strike. The crowd leaned back, without moving their feet, as in a scene from a classical ballet. Or a scene between a master and his slave, both sides aware of the real limits. Authority threatened; the crowd reacted to the threat. You could see it was an established relationship. The policeman raised his stick a bit higher and began to bring it down. This time the crowd moved their feet, and the mayor drew his pistol, raised it, then pushed his way through with me close behind. A lot of the children I brushed by had red hair. I believe that means their mothers had been suffering from malnutrition at the time of giving birth, which apparently doesn't do much for the child's body or brains.

Anyway, the mayor took me around to inspect the hurricane damage. There were two small concrete buildings; more like two-car garages. They were the city hall and the jail. Their roofs had been blown off. The peasants lived in wooden shacks. They'd already put them back up. The mayor talked a lot about the damage and the human tragedy. We both agreed that a hurricane was a terrible thing. They were pretty old shoes he was wearing. I could see he had cut one lace in two to make do for the pair.

9
BEANS AND
RICE

IT HAD BEEN YEARS since I slept with Dorothy. Or Dorothy with me, depending on who wanted to claim responsibility. Dorothy Carrot, I used to call her, she being a vegetarian. Ours was a short number – more than one month, less than six, I can't remember – which hadn't been particularly exclusive. I was the one who ended it, because of her strong personality. Not in bed. There we had a good time, but the moment we got up I was faced by her drive, and, well, that was in my early New York days and I felt I had enough competition on the streets.

I cut it off, or perhaps she did. Memory is at its trickiest in love affairs. To our mutual surprise we became friends; the sort of friends who shout at each other. When I saw in the paper the other day that her ex-husband had died, of course I felt a shock and went to the funeral. She would have done the same had the roles been reversed. Patrick Russell was one of those people everyone knew and called a friend, although there was no rough edge or strong link between him and anyone. He was just a very agreeable,

I'd even say willing, type. And since he combined that with some money, good looks and an entertaining character, there wasn't much reason for people to treat him as other than a friend.

Patrick met Dorothy through me. It wasn't my fault. A casual introduction in a restaurant is hardly a binding contract. In fact I was amazed when he phoned me the next morning in search of her number. On the surface they appeared to have nothing in common, but then the surface has little to do with these things. Patrick and Dorothy disappeared from view the next day. I mean they dropped out of the recognized fabric of East Side life. They came to nobody's parties, were not chanced upon in the expected restaurants or at the required events – visual or oral – organized to satisfy the public orifices. I say "they," but at the time we merely noticed their separate absences.

Three months later, it was the spring of 1971, I found in my mail an invitation to their wedding. It was to be held out on Long Island, with the reception at his parents' house in Oyster Bay. I won't say that no one in those days had spectacular weddings. Most who could afford it, or felt they had to pretend they could afford it, went on with their massive rituals. But among the people I knew – those burdened by public doubts about the world or who at least pretended to be concerned – a certain vogue for simplicity had been accepted. The hair shirt of the moneyed class. What's more, Dorothy was one of the most concerned people I knew. She was constantly disappearing off to public and private meetings or protests, writing letters, organizing groups, I don't know, opposing the war in a hundred little ways.

My surprise was therefore great when I arrived to find the pseudo-Gothic Episcopalian tomb where they were to be married filled with five hundred people and several hundredweight of white flowers. The reception was equally unspoilt by the outside world.

The only strange thing was the food. It was magnificent looking. However, there was no sign of meat or fish or dairy products, not until you got down to a small table at one end of the marquee. We all knew that Dorothy was a vegetarian, but somehow we hadn't expected disguised chickpeas with the champagne. It all tasted quite good; it was just that Patrick's table, the one set up for carnivores at the end of the marquee, was mobbed and stripped. Only then was there a retreat back to the vegetables and fruits and purer forms of protein. Dorothy took the whole thing as a great joke. She enjoyed her own tricks. For myself, I eat little meat. All the same, there was something unsettling about spending an afternoon of celebration with five hundred hungry, dissatisfied people. When I got back to New York I went out and ate a steak for the first time in years.

As I sat in a bar on 3rd, chewing away in a determined, almost revivalist, way at this flesh, one image of the wedding came slipping back into my mind. It was Patrick, well-meaning and anxious, his healthy, meaty figure leaning over a table covered with vegetarian delights, trying to find something he really wanted to eat.

Given time for reflection, people agreed with Dorothy. It had all been a good joke. The new couple returned to New York, where they melted back into city life. I saw them more than most because of my affection for Dorothy, and I had little reason to regret my introduction. They seemed to grow happier and happier together. The only change I noticed was that Patrick began to eat less of all the things that Dorothy had forbidden herself.

Two months after their wedding I gave a dinner in their honour. Patrick refused milk for his coffee.

"But Patrick, you take milk."

"Not anymore, Dong," he said, with his innocent warmth.

I laughed and looked at Dorothy. "Bending to the will of others."

He smiled. "So long as it's good for me."

I knew Dorothy's will. She was an almost unconscious purveyor of what she believed in and therefore wanted. She used none of the common forms of cajolement. It was all of a subtlety that left the receiver with the impression nothing was wanted of him, that he had himself come up with a good idea which just happened to coincide with what Dorothy believed.

Meat was next. I noticed that he began to avoid anything red that required chewing. Chicken survived, then a year later that went too and he fell back on fish. New York being the seaside town that it is, he had taken refuge in a vast and delicious category. It wasn't until late in '75 that I began to watch more carefully. We had lunch together in the Oyster Bar under Grand Central Station, chosen to please him, and he ate nothing but a salad.

Interestingly enough, those five years of evolution had had a good effect on him. He had lost the ex-school-jock look and taken on a sleek litheness. He had the air of someone who belonged in Madrid or Milan. Nevertheless, I asked him, as he picked away at his leaves, "Don't tell me you've gone all the way, Patrick?"

His desire to please was still apparent in the look he gave me. "All the way. I was staring at Dorothy the other day. She looks wonderful. And at myself. Well, I look fine, but there's a certain clarity missing. So I thought I'd give it a try. There was only the fish and a bit of cheese left to give up. So why not?"

"How about pleasure? Who the hell wants to eat fried beans and rice for the rest of their life? I mean, you're reducing yourself to the diet of the starving millions who have no choice. Dorothy hasn't –"

He jumped before I could finish. "Dorothy has never said a word. It's my choice."

I stared at him as hard as I could manage, then went back to my bluefish.

"Dorothy's pregnant," he added. "That was what

decided me. I felt somehow that we should all live the same way."

"You mean the child is going to be brought up vegetarian?"

"Yes, if there are no complications."

I didn't see much of them over the next few months. Patrick's father died and they moved out to his house at Oyster Bay, trading with Patrick's mother, who wanted an apartment in town. Patrick was a lawyer and found he could commute quite easily. They quickly decided they preferred the more relaxed life of Oyster Bay, plus there was lots of room for the English nanny they hired the moment the boy was born.

The next time I saw Patrick was at the christening. They asked me to be the godfather and I accepted – my sixth and last. Patrick Thomas had the cross of water applied in the church where they had been married. Dorothy was as serene and self-confident as ever. The child was one of the plumpest, healthiest children I'd ever seen, as was the nanny. But Patrick had lost a good twenty pounds. He now looked thin and wan and out of place, none of which dampened his enthusiasm.

I got him alone for a moment later in the day.

"You look terrible. Are you still following Dorothy's diet?"

He laughed at me. "That's got nothing to do with it. I'd be worse if I were eating like you."

"Well, then, what's the matter with you?"

"I'm having some tests done. They're not certain yet."

What more could I say? Living as we do in an age when beliefs are dead among sophisticated people and food has become their new religion, with people spending more time in worship of it than their grandfathers ever did in their churches, more time comparing sauces than the scriptures were ever compared, I felt somehow bound not to doubt his word.

I didn't see much of them after that. There was no particular reason. They had simply disappeared out into the extremities of the city, and given my horror of the suburbs, expensive or not, meeting had become complicated. But each time we did meet, Patrick looked worse. We could have had lunch more often, I suppose, but I eat for pleasure. It would have been like fornicating while a puritan stood over the bed preaching. Whenever we did get together I tackled him on it, to no effect. The doctors had tried to isolate his problems, without managing to lay the blame on his diet, and were still doing endless tests. What's more, the baby was prospering on the same food. If anything, it was too plump. Patrick told me that his own health was actually a bit better since Dorothy had begun experimenting with new combinations of grains, cutting back on the lentils and increasing the soy beans. When he mentioned her name, I could see that he still loved her as he first had.

Frankly, I believed that was where the problem lay. The rest was as clear as it could be. He was blinding himself to his real problem. It was only when I saw him one day in the summer of '78, walking slowly down Madison with the help of a cane, that I decided something had to be done. I phoned Dorothy and asked myself out to lunch.

It was a delightful house, filled with air and space, with wonderfully strange paintings and modern furniture made by young designers for the rooms. The garden was equally original, with all the vegetables blended into the perennial beds, which were dominated by native species. I should say "gardens," because they were organized so that you flowed naturally as if from one room to another, as if each were a secret bower. Patrick and Dorothy had been following the initiatives along these lines of Frank Cabot near New York.

We sat outside overlooking the water and had a light lunch, a sort of vegetable couscous, everything grown from those beds. Dorothy was certainly good publicity for her own obsessions. She looked better than when I had first biblically known her.

I asked her about Patrick, after saying that I had seen him with a cane.

"So you've come to intercede." She looked at me, eyes wide open.

"That's right."

"I'm not forcing him. I've told him he must do whatever he wants. I'm not going to tell him it's the diet that is making him sick. I don't believe it is, and the doctors won't say it is. We've all come to believe that sickness is sudden, identifiable and either quickly curable or fatal. That's not so. Some diseases haul us back into the last century, when people suffered and suffered while doctors dithered around trying to discover what it was and what to do. I love Patrick. You don't know how much I love him. How much I need him. He is the most wonderful man ..." She trailed off in confusion and looked towards the gardens. I'd never seen her so uncertain about the nature of life. Then she made an effort and turned her eyes back to mine. "Why would I do anything to harm him? Why? I'm doing all I can to help. Part of our relationship from the beginning has been that we don't interfere with each other's beliefs. No matter how much I love him, he controls his own life. I've told him to follow his own instincts. To be honest, I've suggested several times that he go back to his old diet, just to see. He just goes into a funk, as if it's about failure. Patrick's face to the world is soft and easy. But I know him. He is a romantic and romantics are stubborn. What more can I do?" The last words were a plea. Perhaps she herself was out of her depths, dragged there initially by her own will, and she couldn't deal with the undertow.

Before I could answer, the nanny appeared. She was still a formidable size, as was the boy who followed her, a big, ruddy four-year-old. He reminded me already of the Patrick I had first known.

The child was prodded into some polite remarks and then taken away.

"Is he still a vegetarian?"

"Not only that," Dorothy said, "but you can see how much he resembles Patrick."

"The one you married," I said sharply.

She looked at me with a wounded expression. I felt she was about to do something I had never seen Dorothy do. I could sense the tears welling up. Tears of love? Of frustration? Of inner confusion? I found it impossible to judge. A few minutes later she stood up as a signal that I should go.

As to what followed, I heard about it through various people who stayed in touch. Patrick's sight was the next thing to go. He found it difficult to commute and began spending more time at his apartment in town. Early last year he went blind. At first he insisted that his mother move back out to Oyster Bay to help Dorothy while he stayed in New York. He also refused to let Dorothy spend much time looking after him. Instead, he hired a manservant. He loved Dorothy too much to destroy her life. That was the argument he used when he insisted a few months later that they divorce. She protested but he insisted.

He settled everything on her, keeping only the apartment in town and a small income for himself. In the end, she felt obliged to accept, if only to stop him from exciting himself. In fact it changed nothing in what was left of their relationship. She came to see him as often as he would allow her, which was less and less. The same was true of his boy, who was old enough to be of some company, but Patrick found it impossible to talk with him.

It was a ritual I later had described to me. When the boy arrived, Patrick would embrace him. The moment the frail blind man felt the healthy body of his son, he withdrew into silence and eventually the boy was taken away. As for Patrick's diet, he stuck to it.

All of that came to an end last week. The old gang dragged itself out to Long Island for the funeral. I don't know why. Perhaps it was just the scent of tragedy. Or our curious need for the final packaging of lives with which we've been involved. Faites vos paquets, the French say. Patrick had neatly tied up the packages of his life but left ours in disorder. I hung at the back of the church with David Spenser. Dorothy wouldn't see me there and I didn't intend to stay for the burial, but then I did. It was a beautiful day. June is a perfect month for any kind of ceremony. I could see that Dorothy was overwhelmed with grief. That indomitable will of hers seemed broken. There was to be no reception afterwards. She clutched at the hand of her son, who was crying more from osmosis than anything else. What could that boy have found to identify with in the father he had known? As opposed to the father he had not known?

Again, I stayed at the back. I found myself next to the nanny, who had a kind of grim Devon expression on her face. When she recognized me, she said, "You're the godfather."

I nodded.

She kept glancing my way, tentatively, uncertainly.

Then abruptly she whispered, "You're the one who argued with Mrs. Russell about the food." It was more an assertion than a whisper.

I was surprised that she knew. "Did Dorothy tell you?"

"I heard them talking that night. She said you blamed her."

I nodded, unable to think of what to reply. I suddenly realized she was crying in a self-controlled way that hid greater emotion.

"He was a nice man," she said with determination. "I wish I had been able to do more."

I looked at her stolid face. "What do you mean?"

She gave me a hard look. It was an evaluation, which finished in my favour. "In case Mrs. Russell ever sends me away," she said quietly, "someone should know what to do. I saved the boy, you see. I always gave him meat when she wasn't around."

I grabbed her arm without realizing it. She pushed my hand off with a firm shove.

"That was all I could do. I couldn't tell them. They would have fired me. I'll have to be very careful now."

She turned to meet my appalled stare. I felt the blood draining from my face.

"I saved the boy. You can't save everyone."

10
THE NARRATOR
PAUSES TO REFLECT

ODD. The nanny's face stayed with me for days. Square, plump. A pudding face. More precisely, it was the fierce, stubborn stare that remained. I dreamt of her. She would pop into my vision on an airplane or over dinner. And there around her in the background were Patrick and Dorothy and Patrick Thomas, my little godson. All four of them posed together as if for a portrait, reminiscent of the Holy Family, with the nanny included as the Virgin Mary gone wrong. They said nothing. Did nothing. Just made themselves felt. At first this disturbed me, the way a person's nervous tic can get to you, although it is their problem and not yours. After a few days I sensed that I was losing my composure. Why have I handed over their story? There was a choice, after all. Whether to write it or not. Why their story rather than another? For that matter, why choose Elizabeth Pink and Sunny Spenser? Why choose such comfortable individuals from among the people I know; people who seem to amuse or destroy themselves with equal commitment? Some might say they lead meaningless lives, whatever meaningless means. That is not something I would admit, even though late-twentieth-century postmodern fiction requires personal involvement from the narrator, even commitment. All around me there are narrators caught up in a wave of parabolising so severe and so general that they intervene continually in their stories. Everywhere today the narrator is to be seen disguised as Christ in full flight.

There was a time when the writer hid himself cannily within – not behind, but deep within – his characters. He gave the appearance of leaving his creations to act out their destinies, while all the time he was their secret heart. As for a narrator such as myself, he would be nothing more than the writer's strong arm. The lessons and parables were all there. But the reader was left to discover what they were, to take note of them in his own manner, to draw personal conclusions.

Now there are writers who draw your conclusions for you. The novel as parable. The short story as parable perfect. And every line carries opinion and direction. You dare not turn your head without permission, let alone have an independent thought about a character. As for feeling, they tell you exactly what the emotional state of every character is. Often they tell you little else. These are violations of the soul of both the character and the reader. What follows is a terrible confusion in the reader's mind as to where the writer ends and the narrator begins. Do not for a moment imagine that there is any confusion on these pages. A self-respecting writer does not lend himself and his private parts out as a narrator. And a narrator, well, he's not in the writing business, not if he does his job well.

None of which justifies my friends. What conclusions could you possibly draw from their actions? There isn't even the reassuring knowledge that I've invented these people. They are disguised, of course, with the odd one melded together out of this and that to avoid the risk of libel. Not that the risk is great. There is a way of telling a story so that no one sues. Anyway, people never recognize accurate portraits of themselves drawn by others, because they see themselves quite differently.

So there you are. I might have picked other friends, other acquaintances, other enemies. For that matter other experiences. More edifying experiences. So many important questions are waiting to be raised by serious narrators. And I'm certainly not ignorant of either meaning or significance. I could have dealt some out had I wanted to. Truly, I could have. Instead, I'm stuck here with the nanny's face interrupting me at unexpected hours. A Cheshire-cat invasion. The implication, I suppose, is that I could have done more. More for Patrick, for example. "After all, he didn't go blind and curl up to die overnight." That's what you're thinking. Well, forgive me, but your attitude assumes that because I know these people well enough to know their story, I should also interfere in some sort of definitive manner. You're wrong. That's not my role. I'm just the narrator.

"He's a bit of a shit." That's what you'd like to say, if only you could get yourself onto these pages. First you'd have to get yourself by the writer. Then by me. Or rather, by my prerogative. You're unlikely to get here if I don't want to narrate you. And if your attitude is so negative, why should I?

Of course, you may well be right. And while I'm in no position to ask favours, I'd prefer you didn't hate me. You needn't like me. We haven't even met. But don't hate me. I don't deserve that. It's true, I could have stopped Patrick. I could have found a way. But narration is not an existential business. My job is to observe. Anyway, what do you know about me? What call do you have on me? For a start, I might well be the author dissembling as the narrator. You can't be certain, and why should I remove any doubt? You noticed that the narrator doesn't have a name. "So!" you think. "He must be the author." Well, then, my name is Thomas Bell. Tom to my friends. Except my oldest friends, who call me Dong, as in ding dong, as in Bell. Teenage habits are always embarrassing. Where did that get you? Do you want my date of birth? I won't tell you. Why should I? Perhaps some family history would calm your curiosity. My mother, for example, grew up with Dalmatians. Of course, they were really German shepherds, but then my grandfather was a very complex person. I should add, in light of what follows, that my father refused on principle to set foot inside a church during his entire adult life. My mother didn't care one way or the other and went occasionally; most often to weddings, during which she dozed. Other people thought this was a form of ostentation. I am convinced it was true indifference.

Frankly, being stuck where I am, between the writer and you, is unpleasant and uncomfortable. I didn't ask for the job. It's not as if we were soulmates, the author and I. For one thing, he's tall and thin. He eats like a pig and never gains a pound. I'm medium and have to watch my weight. I do have certain advantages over him. He spent eight years in various universities and drags his learning around like an invisible third foot. I could do his job better if he'd leave me alone. I'll tell you this much – I write better than him and faster. But then I walked out of university after two years. They can't teach you how to read or how to write or how to get your meaning across. He'd have been better off starting as a sports reporter if he wanted to write fiction.

Apart from that I suppose the two of us aren't in great disagreement, except on French politics, which he follows and I find boring. Always the same questions and the same faces. What I like is the honestly sordid quality of American politics, which he can't stand. We don't have the same taste in women either, except for a shared admiration of ankles, wrists and necks, a sort of predilection for the fineness of the extremities. And we both enjoy grubbing about. That, I suppose, comes from a horror of belonging. If you're off in Africa talking to revolutionaries, you can't be nestling comfortably into an urban intellectual nest where everyone warms everyone else's eggs or breaks them.

None of which is relevant. I've told my friends' stories very carefully, as if their obsessions were worth recording. They are worth recording. That's my decision. It certainly isn't yours. By the nature of our functions, yours will be quite different: to believe me, to decide who I am, to burn the book, not to pick it up in the first place. I've buried these particular thoughts well into the middle pages so that with any luck you have already bought it. I owe the writer that much. Or stolen it, which would suggest a greater commitment. At any rate you have read this far.

Let me take you back to the question of choice. I could have told you about people you might have wanted to be. That might have ensured your liking me. I could have told you about two friends who are quite original in the nicest possible way. Every New Year's Eve since their marriage they have stayed home, gone to bed at 11 P.M. and aimed for an orgasm to begin on the first chime of midnight. There is an accurate church clock quite close to their apartment in New York. Their score is five on time, three early and four late.

For the oddest reason, churches, not just the New Year's Eve timekeeper, have been absolutely central to their lives. Their marriage functioned very close to perfection, which throws doubt on the mythological contradictory baggage of the marital contract, love and sex by which we have all been weighed down for half a millennium. Two centuries ago, Diderot summarized these beliefs perfectly. "Every day we sleep with women we don't love and we don't sleep with women we do love." In the eighteenth century perhaps. But I would say our problems today come from the fact that we sleep too much with the women we do love and not enough with the women we don't. Why? Well, I don't know. It's merely something I notice when I look at the disasters that strike people's lives. These friends I've begun to tell you about were an exception to this rule. They loved each other, were happy together and agreed on everything except religion. She was a basic Catholic – didn't care about Latin, thought saints were all right but didn't pay much attention to them, and she followed the rules when they suited her. That sort of Catholic. He was a High Church Episcopalian. Incense. The King James version. The Book of Common Prayer; i.e., more Catholic than the pope, as the cliché goes. Anyway, they went to church wherever they happened to be and in whatever church was handy, and they could rarely get out of the place before starting an argument. Often quite violent. Usually right in their pew over some point incomprehensible to anyone overhearing. Her style was all common sense, morals, faith, social stability. His was intellect, ethics, doubt, God before society. In one of those interesting contradictions which are a specialty of Christianity, he thought St. Augustine was a traitor to the cause and she, like so many Low Church Catholics, thought Augustine was the father of the working church, a conviction shared by most Protestants. He was equally down on St. Paul, about whom she preferred not to talk. She would admit, if pushed, that he was as responsible as St. Augustine for the creation of the working church. But Paul was too rigorous about it, too serious. He lacked the flexibility of a normal human or of a humanist saint.

Their tendency was to fall into Old Testament diction for the purposes of these arguments, which meant a very violent turn of phrase. The upside of it all, I suppose, was that such battles gave a weekly lift to their calm and devoted married life.

A few years ago they were in St. Patrick's when the priest brought up the subject of Mary of the Immaculate Conception. It had always been a sore point between them, because like most Catholics she hadn't realized, until my friend filled her in a month after their wedding, that this title referred to Mary's birth, not to Christ's. What's more, every time Mary's birth came up, the whole question of the pope's infallibility came up with it. She felt about this infallibility rather the way she felt about saints – it ought to be both accepted and ignored. He on the other hand was obsessed by it as a concrete flaw in the Church of Rome; a position I personally sympathize with. Infallibility, uniformity, perfection. Those are all nineteenth-century ideas and quite ridiculous. Like Marxism and capitalism and isms in general. We all know they don't exist. We all know that complete ideas are like unwritten plays. The curtain just never seems to go up. But this is crude narrator interference and you should ignore it.

The point is that some text read by the priest got my two friends going. They were seated back near the doors over on the right side, and in no time at all they were shouting whispers at each other. Then the shouts weren't enough and she gave him a shove on the shoulder. He shoved her right back. Well, she was so shocked she slapped him, not hard, but he gave her a little thump on the rear with his prayer book and she slapped him again. This went on, rather like a Charlie Chaplin routine, until they left, punctuating each good retort with a slap which the other would try to duck.

What they hadn't noticed was another worshipper, a woman, who had witnessed all of this with horror from two pews behind and felt obliged to follow them out of the cathedral and up the avenue. I suppose she was worried that the violence might get out of hand. She followed them all the way to their brownstone on 62nd, and as the row was still going on when they disappeared inside she called the police from a pay phone on the corner of Madison.

"Ha! He's at it again." That's what you're thinking. A house on the Upper East Side. Elitism, etc. ... But not at all. You're quite wrong. I am taking great care to describe none of that. Why? Because in this case it doesn't matter. What does matter is their remarkable relationship. I have not even mentioned their features (average; in fact, good average) or the way they dress. Nothing. I am concentrating on their moral and intellectual worth.

The police don't like to interfere between married people. Most legal codes give any husband more or less the right to beat his wife if he wants to, which is an interesting comment on something or other, although I don't think I'm up to dealing with that here and now, if only because it is quite a different problem from the one at hand. After all, this particular police precinct wasn't in a position to know that my friend is not a wife beater. Had they known, they might have taken the complaint more seriously. Instead, they sent a young officer to check it out. He had a university degree and I suppose the sergeant was getting even by giving him all the dirty jobs. The young officer was New York Irish; i.e., your basic Catholic.

He left the complainer at a safe distance, near the telephone booth, walked up the three steps to the front door of the brownstone and rang the bell. He heard steps and a raised voice, the handle turning, and then saw the back of a man's head – my friend's – not balding, curly, thick and dark brown, shouting away to someone lurking within. "A cheap political trick, that's all it was. A smart pope wouldn't have got himself into such a no-win corner. He'd already lost most of Italy and was about to lose more. So what does he do? He shouts, 'Freeze! I'm infallible!' Then everyone moved. Half the problems of the Church today come from that mistake."

The policeman tapped him on the shoulder. "You can't say that."

"Eh?" My friend looked around for the first time.

"You can't say that about the Holy Father. You don't understand the nature of his mission."

My friend stared for a moment, then bowed low and waved the young man in. Within minutes the policeman was in the midst of their argument. Of course, he was on her side. Their attitudes were identical. He stayed the afternoon, phoned his sergeant and stayed for dinner. They were all good friends before the evening was over. What's more, they stayed good friends. I think she was as relieved to have a little support as her husband was to have some stiffer opposition. The officer was five years younger than they were and was suitably innocent and enthusiastic. He gave a whole new impetus to their marriage. They often saw one another during the week, but their fixed rendezvous were for church on Sunday morning, followed by lunch and a good argument out somewhere, after which they would sit around and chat at the brownstone. Spending so much time with a company vice-president (that's what my friend did) nourished the policeman's ambition and he began to do well in his department. On the religious front, however, he was gradually overwhelmed. My friend's remarkable intelligence and intellectual purity weren't of much use in the corporate world, so he was pretty wound up by Sunday. Their arguments stretched on for two years, until, in fact, late on a miserable Sunday afternoon in November. They were sitting cozily around the fire emptying a bottle of Pétrus, which brought up the subject of communion wine. My friend began to bait the other two.

"I wouldn't go as far as Luther, but your priests' unjustified superiority in refusing you a sip of the blood, well, I've always found that a perfect example of how a large organization serves itself."

"I admit it's something I don't understand," the policeman said. "The Apostles got the wine. Why don't we?"

All three of them fell silent. They waited. The policeman said nothing more. He showed no disagreement. Then they all became aware that he had been won over lock, stock and barrel to the High Church argument. Even the young man himself had not realized how profoundly he had lost his way; not until that very moment. Their alliances had shifted. A small smile crept onto the husband's face, but as the silence persisted his smile waned. The policeman stumbled to his feet and left without a word.

Forty-eight hours later my friend's wife deserted him for the policeman. She moved into his little apartment way over on the West Side near 1st Avenue. I suppose she had heard all of her husband's arguments. I suppose she was bored. On reflection it did seem to me that a slack expression had grown in her eyes over that period of two years. The marriage must have been worn out in more ways than she admitted, but religion was her excuse. The policeman was fresh in every way.

As you can imagine, my friend was distraught. So much so that he resigned his job, sold his house and left town. He drifted about Europe for a few months, looking without seeing. This had been going on for a good six months when we met up in Paris and had dinner together at Chez Georges. I found him depressed; lost, you might say. The next day he was wandering aimlessly around in the 6th – well, not entirely aimless. He was looking for the Chinese restaurant in which Ho Chi Minh had washed dishes. That task satisfied, he went over to the 5th to look at the Musée de Cluny, then cut down past Saint-Julien-le-Pauvre, across the Seine, past the facade of Notre Dame, thought of going to get a sorbet at Berthillon, but instead turned back and went into the cathedral, where he paced up and down the aisles in an increasingly manic way until there, behind one of the pillars on the north side, he had some sort of religious experience. This had nothing to do with our meal the night before. Pure coincidence. I say "some sort" of religious experience because he was already a believer. What this vision did was to show up his High Church obsessions as transparent and super-ficial. Instead, he saw the great mother of Catholicism with all her contradictions and hypocrisy as a large warm sea in which one and all could bathe. The waves came rolling down the aisles of the cathedral and swept him up. Only years later did he find out that Claudel had had his own illumination behind the next pillar. He mentioned this particular fact to no one except me. I suppose he was quite pleased to share some beachfront property with Claudel. On the other hand, it cheapened his own experience to discover that it was a bit of an imitation. Or a repeat. And he wasn't Claudel, nor was he going to be. This wasn't a conversion that would fill theatres around the world. It also raised some interesting questions about the concrete geographical manifestations of divine intervention and therefore the probability of saintly powers. After all, God himself was unlikely to be hanging around between two pillars waiting for likely prospects. Surely he had broader issues to deal with. So perhaps it was a franchise – some particular spirit had sway there or, dare it be said, some particular saint.

This sort of thought became food for doubt much later. At the time he floated around the cathedral in a trance until the English-language confessional welled up on a crest before him like a Mulberry harbour. He threw himself on his knees at its side, grasping the wood tightly with each hand, and poured out to the priest half hidden by the grille precisely what had happened. He asked this obscured face for help. The two men – the priest was an American – spent the rest of the day together walking the streets of Paris and talking it out. One month later my friend was received into the Catholic Church. Then he went back to school and began preparing for the priesthood. This he did in Virginia; anywhere but New York.

He had not exchanged a word with his ex-wife since his original pleading with her to come home had failed; that was one month after she had moved out. It was not a coincidence that his formal conversion had taken exactly the same length of time. He still loved her. I'm sure of that. Perhaps that was the key to his sudden love for the Catholic Church, but there you have a cynical outsider's guess; in fact, this is nothing more than another surreptitious attempt by the narrator to stick his nose in. My friend hid his broken marriage and divorce proceedings from the Church. I make no comment.

It was six years before he was a priest and well-enough established to get himself accepted at Notre Dame. One of his duties was to work the English-language confessional. The cathedral, however, is large and that booth was on the south side – the other side from his own holy pillar, a good eighty yards away. The confessional beside the pillar of his conversion was in the hands of a Père Lafolie, seventy-five years old, who had himself stretched padded silk over the inside walls of his booth to make it cozier, perhaps a little warmer in the winter. After four months of being wheedled, chatted up and eventually wined and dined, the old man agreed to switch confessionals. He relented in the end to the argument that there was more light and therefore less damp on the south side. From that point on my friend spent as much time in his new cubbyhole as possible. His obsessiveness may appear to you to lack the proper elements of devotion, but the explanation for his action was that he secretly believed his first illumination had been only half an experience. There was more to come. He was certain of it. Now that his official booth anchored him within a few feet of *the spot*, he grasped every opportunity to hang around the pillar exuding a nervous expectation which cannot have been much use to the travelling sinners who made up most of his clientele. And travellers do sin; more than at home. And they are more open about their sins in foreign confessionals.

In the spring of the seventh year after the vision, his ex-wife and her husband came to Paris for an Interpol conference. They stayed at the Lutetia – the Gestapo hotel in the 6th which was then converted into a convalescent home for death camp survivors. Finally it reverted to its original hotel mission, which Hemingway had described in the 1920s as the evocation of pure middle-class boredom. While her husband compared criminal methods with his global colleagues, she wandered about the city. He had done very well in the police. She had put on a little weight – they both had, it was the Irish in them – but her hair was still blond and she hadn't changed, except I suspect there may have been a slack look of boredom in her eyes; the look I had seen once before. I am guessing, as I wasn't there to witness any of what followed.

On her third day she made it as far as Notre Dame and ended up at the English-language confessional. Had she come on purpose, by accident, drawn subconsciously by some need? Was this the second miracle my friend had been waiting for: God bringing him face to face with his most profound human weakness? With the failure of his marriage? With his failure as a husband? Whatever the reason, at the sight of the booth and the priest's black shoes sticking out, with a tourist in orange kneeling to one side, she was overwhelmed by a need to confess, and the moment the spot was free she fell to her knees and released all of her guilt. It consisted mainly of her being tired of her second husband, with whom she lived in sin in the eyes of the Church. She was indeed a foreign sinner, and being far from home had gelled her frustrations and made her feel free to express them. The worst part, she confessed, was his High Church stance. His arguments were so convincing that she felt herself falling away from Catholicism without meaning to. But how was she to resist? His simplistic view of right and wrong, drawn from the enforcement of law, combined with his "fervour of the converted" to make him unbeatable.

Her ex-husband listened to all of this from behind his grille without saying a word. He had recognized her immediately. He could feel himself trembling within and without; trembling with uncertainty. Was this merely the devil come to tempt him, or was this in fact the second half of his vision? The trembling which he felt, the loss of distinction between air and solids, the wood around him, the cathedral of stone outside his confessional, all melting into a mist, were so much like the elements of his first experience behind the pillar that he could not believe this was the devil kneeling beside him. When she had finished he made an attempt to control himself and began to advise her in as neutral a voice as he could muster.

He also had the fervour of the converted, and so he was able to give her the answers she lacked; but in the process his enthusiasm snuck out, aided no doubt by the emotions raging through him. A flash of electricity seemed to crack through the grille. Or the veil was rent. Either way, he began to mumble then fell silent. Neither of them moved; not for a good minute. After which she got up and walked around and lifted the curtain. He was unable even to twist his head up. That lifting of the curtain, it was as if she had stripped off his cassock. Oh, he knew it was still there, though he could sense her looking down past his face in the shadows and his expanse of black cloth to the few inches of bare calf that showed above his short, cheap socks. Seconds later they were in each other's arms. The cathedral was fairly empty and some pillars protected them, in particular the pillar of his vision, against which he pressed her. The cassock came between them like a frightening reminder of sin; though they were, curiously enough and in the Church's eyes, still husband and wife. Then she managed to yank it up above his waist.

The next thing they did was run off in search of a hotel, which they found in the Quartier Latin on rue Saint Jacques. It was a small students' place and they spent the afternoon in bed. She paid, but she wouldn't tell him where she was staying and disappeared from his life as suddenly as she had reappeared. When my friend went back to his confessional the next day, he felt the whole cathedral was empty; not of faith but of expectation. The pillar no longer held anything for him. All had been delivered.

After that he suffered a few weeks of confused guilt and even considered confessing all that had happened to some unknown priest. Sins of the body are not rare among priests, although he himself had been unrelentingly celibate until this one experience. As to his emotions, whatever he confessed he knew that they would not be understood. He himself perhaps understood them, but they could not be explained. In the end he said nothing and made no attempt to clarify his own feelings even to himself. Instead, he let the terrible confusion within simmer away and went on with his normal life. Now each time he sat within his confessional, he noticed the damp. Worse, he smelled the sweat of the old priest who had sat there for twenty-three years. The old man belonged to the anti-bathing school once so popular in France. And each time my friend looked at the grille, he sensed his ex-wife on the other side. He ripped out the silk, but that changed nothing. Each time he passed his miraculous pillar, he imagined her leaning back against it with her skirt raised. Then one day, as he walked through the streets on his way to the cathedral, he realized that he could no longer see the beauty of all he passed. Instead, he had the same vacant, disappointed, bitter eyes that he had so often noticed in Parisians. The next morning he began trying to transfer himself back to New York.

It took a few months. He was sent to a church in Spanish Harlem on the northeast side of Manhattan. Once there, he sent her a postcard of Notre Dame with nothing written on it except the address of his new church. Two weeks later she came to confess. Nothing in particular was said between them. She sought guidance – arguments, in fact, to be used against those of her High Church policeman. And my friend did give her fresh ammunition to fight back. This priestly conversation was followed by an awkward pause, after which they went off to a hotel. Again she paid. From then on she came once a week. The confessional and the comforts of a simple hotel bed gave her the intellectual and emotional fibre to continue her marriage. In fact, by regressing into a theological ménage à trois with some extra sex, they all went back to living happily ever after, or at any rate up to the time of my writing this.

Now, there is a story filled with nice people and a happy ending. What good has that done? Do you feel better? If so, good. But is it necessarily my job to bring about this feeling? I'll tell you this, I've discussed the whole thing with my friend Howie, who periodically flies down to New York. He is in the mattress business in Toronto. Howie is a remarkable fellow. I'll tell you about him some other time. For the moment you need know only that he got out of Hungary in '56 and has since done very well. Very, very well. When I told him about my two friends and their policeman, Howie seemed scarcely surprised. Nothing I say seems to surprise him, and yet over the years he has heard almost every story I write before it is written. Howie has a good nose for the unbelievable truth, which I am forced to discard because my business is belief. Truth is an agreeable but marginal sidekick.

When I expressed surprise at his lack of surprise, Howie just said, "I respect your talk. You're mentally educated." He often tells me that, as if it explains everything. "Speaking about your lady friend," he added, "it was all by way of comparison. She wanted to put her shoe on the other foot."

I mention Howie simply because his feelings towards me are a good expression of what yours might be. Of course, you think I'm going for the quick laugh in order to win you over. That isn't so. The context of his comment was quite complicated. Howie likes to involve me in his negotiations. He believes that my mental education and my profession – storyteller – make me the perfect psychiatrist; and since his big concern is always to understand his competitors, he believes my advice could be useful. A few weeks ago he was in town trying to buy out a specialized box-spring company. We had lunch together at Manny Wolf's steak house just before the key session and he whispered to me, "I want you to come to this meeting to help me feel them up." He misinterpreted my startled expression and added, "I need you, Tom, I trust you simplistically." The reader might take a lesson from Howie. In truth, I don't really see why you should be surprised by the kind of people I've chosen to describe. Something has drawn me to individuals unacquainted with happy endings. Mrs. Revere summed it all up quite nicely: "If you should be better and you aren't, well, then you're worse."

Whatever my faults, at least I haven't used this personal intervention or my stories to make any of the standard narrator claims. I have made no orgasmic boasts on my own behalf – neither seven a day nor three in a row. I have not stated the opposite sex's worship of the narrator's persona or physique, in detail or in general. I have not even offered evidence of my undisputed intelligence or unusual powers, concrete and metaphysical.

It's just possible that narrators and authors who assign remarkable sexual talents to themselves are, how shall I put this, somehow related to sex maniacs who engage in actual rape and murder. What separates them? The maniac carries out his frustrated and warped fantasies on one or two unfortunate individuals. The writer does it on the page, where he can be certain both to succeed (adding to his sins that of liar) and to reach a larger public; the only saving grace being that the public will survive. Is it worth adding that narrators who describe themselves as having large and/or particularly active sexual organs and who stand for noble causes have moved dangerously close to the Napoleonic syndrome. That is, people who mask their sexual problems with delusions of grandeur.

Queen Victoria is a fertility symbol in Bangkok. The oversized statue of this oversized woman is constantly decorated with garlands left by ladies who are having conception problems. I mention this because not far away from her monument-cum-idol there is another shrine; this one dedicated to male potency, or rather impotency. At the centre of a small garden there is a two-yard-high standing wooden penis with wooden balls. Around this erection lie piles of smaller wooden penises. Smaller, but not small. Depending upon the supplicant's financial means and degree of desperation, these erect carvings range from a foot to about four feet long. If you pass that way at night you are almost certain to notice a forlorn male lurking behind a bush contemplating the large offering he has made.

In some inexplicable way this shrine reminds me of late-twentieth-century fiction, centred as so much of it is on the author himself and the outsized dimensions of his own personality, force, sins and virility, rather than on the personality of the characters he is supposed to be creating.

I am not suggesting anything about the private lives of first-person-narrative, interventionist writers. I know nothing about their lives. How could I – a mere fictional

narrator, devoid even of the real flesh and blood necessary to walk – know anything about the real lives of real
writers? It's just that each time I see a writer raise his ego
on the flagpole of potency at the centre of his fiction, I am
reminded of the Bangkok shrine.

11
CONVERSATIONS
WITH DICTATORS IV

IT WAS A PROVINCIAL BULLRING built of wood and brick. I suppose we had driven about an hour and a half from Madrid. A young English journalist I'd met a few days before was at the wheel. He was a stringer for several papers. Not many thought Spain was worth a full-time correspondent. Anyway, Peter had been taking me about and he liked to have a good time. So he liked Madrid. It was an eating, drinking, even dancing town once you got away from the bureaucrats and politicians.

He had suggested that we go to the rally just for the fun of it – as if to a museum of curiosities. Franco was long dead and the annual celebration of his landing from North Africa and therefore the formal beginning of the Civil War couldn't help but be a curiosity. His survivors were old remnants who could scarcely win a seat in the Cortes.

So I was a little taken aback at how far away we had to park. It was a big crowd – they'd come from all over – but it wasn't just the size that struck me. The mixture was odd. There were the energetic young men rushing about or working on the stalls outside. Young men with purpose. I suppose there are always young men with purpose ready to serve ideological causes, particularly if a uniform is included. Photos, postcards, books about Franco were on sale along with Hitler paraphernalia. There were lots of lapel pins – swastikas, Falangist yoke and arrows, fasces in various qualities: plastic, silver, iron. A few images of Mussolini were mixed in. It was a July evening. The eighteenth, to be precise. The heat was easing. The grass outside was surprisingly clear of litter and everyone appeared happy. There were a lot of middle-aged women in perfect neat dresses and patent-leather shoes. The hair tended towards blue rinse, permed firmly in place. They might have been off to some middle-class ladies' club. Their husbands wore blue shirts, the party uniform. Given the ages of the men, a lot of the shirts were filled to the straining point, with flesh pushing through between the buttons. I suppose it wasn't their fault that clothes are usually cut to average sizes. And these being fascist shirts, it followed that they would be cut with young athletes in mind. In any case, there is always something particularly unpleasant about a uniform pulling on a big stomach. The most remarkable element was the girls. I've never seen so many beautiful girls in a single place, except perhaps in Northern Italian cities during the *passeggiata*. Spanish women, when they are beautiful, have something extra – a sort of self-sufficiency which heightens their looks.

"The fascists get the best girls," Peter whispered. He had a wry sense of humour.

The girls seemed to be with the older men. Perhaps they liked the uniforms.

"What are they doing here?" I asked.

"They're into purity. The purity of the cause. Old men are like grandfathers. Maybe they get a little extra sexual flutter out of the flags and the chanting."

It was a quiet, polite crowd. We showed our press cards and were directed down through an archway onto the sand-covered oval in the centre of the bullring. We walked around looking up. There was only a handful of other journalists, looking dejected. This was not a fashionable story. The fifteen thousand seats were filling up. Every second or third person seemed to have a flag. I'd seen no one carrying these into the ring, so they must have been laid out in advance. They were being waved mostly by the middle-aged men. The overall effect was impressive, but if you focused on a single male he looked ill at ease, large body swaying in a slightly undignified way, his gaze cloudy as if uncertain of what to focus on, worrying about how things were going at his garage or shop or insurance agency. However, the background to the flags was not these awkward stares but the sea of blue shirts. Periodic chants were taken up and spread through the crowd. "*Caudillo! Caudillo!*" When these ended, a patriotic song burst out from the PA system. The crowd took it up and drowned out the loudspeakers. Slowly but effortlessly the quiet individuals who walked in were converting themselves into a boisterous mass. When the official speeches began Peter and I went to stand below the podium on the shady side. The warm-up speakers weren't very good and all energy seeped out of the crowd.

By the time Blas Piñar appeared they were pretty quiet. Almost depressed. This was, after all, a celebration among losers. It takes an effort to keep your spirits up. Piñar was a minor figure from the Franco era. But he was also one of the few who had a talent with crowds. So the grand ministers with their effusive manners and big fortunes had faded away into retirement and Piñar had swollen into a parody of Franco, the Christian gentleman.

His talent was immediately apparent. With a dismissive gesture and a few quiet words he grasped hold of the crowd. It was a matter of seconds. In the manner of an orchestra conductor, he then pulled them together using a few abrupt sentences which established absolute calm, then a few more words released a cheer – or rather a marshal cry. He worked them up and up towards a seemingly unattainable peak as he shouted louder with each word – a carefully measured increase – and their response followed at matched decibels. It was a remarkable bit of work. I leaned over to say as much to Peter only to find him looking pale and staring down.

"Are you all right?"

"Bastards," he said quietly.

When Piñar got them to the peak he abruptly threw out a slogan, which I missed, and they shouted it back and thrust their arms out at that intriguing, slightly erect angle that constitutes a *Sieg Heil*. I could hear Peter breathing heavily.

"Bastards. Bastards."

He was sweating. People often surprise themselves in the way they react when faced by experiences for the first time. I remember fainting while watching a knee operation in China. It wasn't the blood. It was the yellow fat which seemed to leer up at me when they cut the skin open. I simply keeled over. I suppose Peter was out of control because he hadn't expected to feel anything. Piñar made people feel things, whether they wanted to or not. To be overwhelmed with loathing, abruptly, unexpectedly, could be pretty disturbing, I suppose. Particularly for an experienced journalist. Peter would have seen Nazi rallies on television, in movies. We have all seen clips of Leni Riefenstahl's *Triumph of the Will* – the invention of the modern hero, the hero's plane arriving through Wagnerian clouds, the Caesarean platforms for speaking down to the crowds, the lighting from below. In other words, with the right presentation you can turn a dumpy middle-aged man with no distinguishing physical characteristics into a heroic figure. But that is all treated as the past – a safe memory of evil. It was as if Peter's intellectual structure of moral indignation couldn't deal with reality. It was crumbling.

I remember sitting in a theatre in London during a performance of George Steiner's *The Portage to San Cristobal of A.H.* In the middle of the Brazilian jungle an aged Adolf Hitler is found in hiding by a platoon of Israeli soldiers. They try to get him out to be tried in Jerusalem, but the security services of the world's various superpowers intercept the platoon's messages and send their own soldiers to grab hold of Hitler. Everyone wants to own the devil. They think they want him in order to gain the credit that will come from judging him. What could be a greater assertion of a superpower's superiority than the power to judge the devil? Perhaps more important, this would be an opportunity to settle the meaning of history. The Israeli soldiers therefore had to deal with Hitler before the forces of the competing superpowers found them. They set up a court in the jungle, each of them assuming a role – judge, jury, prosecutor, defence attorney. But Hitler, played by Alec McCowen, insists on defending himself and in a spellbinding monologue justifies everything he had done. And it was a convincing text. After all, Steiner wrote it. And McCowen's performance was an amazing evocation of Hitler's emotional and intellectual strengths. When he finished, the audience leapt to its feet crying bravo. Good middle-class, probably left-of-centre Londoners. Then the applause petered out as they realized what they had done and everyone sat down sheepishly. I suppose Steiner had proved his point.

"Calm down," I whispered to Peter. He showed no sign of having heard. I nudged him insistently. "Calm down. This isn't the place to throw a pro-democracy fit."

Piñar dropped into a whisper and the crowd strained forward to listen. In the silence I felt that all fifteen thousand of them could hear Peter muttering. Then the tone began to rise again, slowly, ever so slowly. Piñar was in perfect control. He was playing them as one would a bull – the passes, the occasional twisting cape, the hypnotic relationship between matador and animal. I began to feel very exposed standing out on the sand in full view with an Englishman who was sinking into an unpredictable fit of loathing. Bulls don't leave the ring alive, in spite of their rightful loathing for the matador. By the time Piñar was finished there'd be lots of men looking for someone to kick.

"Come on, Peter. Let's get out of here."

He still didn't seem to be hearing me, so I grabbed hold of his arm and pulled him firmly through the scattered journalists, staring at us with the hungry curiosity of someone looking for a story. Peter was shaking, and each time Piñar jerked the crowd one way or another, his breathing got worse. Outside, some of the young men were packing up the images of Franco and Hitler. In little isolated groups on the deserted grass they seemed to have lost their energy. In fact they were a wan, even scrawny, group, none of whom adequately filled their blue shirts, which hung off their shoulders in a manner so pristine, so uncreased, that the material must have been polyester. And yet they didn't look hot and they hardly raised their eyes as we passed.

12
TRUE LOVE

I WAS SITTING IN SILENCE on the long late-summer grass by the edge of some still water that disappeared to either side in a maze of streams, canals and marsh. A lawyer friend was standing on my right, flicking at the surface in the hope of brown trout. I'd given up. As in the setup to a classic joke, another friend, a doctor, was working his rod on my left. The bugs were biting us more than the trout were biting our flies. My origins make my skin a bit tougher, and when in such places I coat myself with something invented during the Second World War by a man experimenting on naval paint thinner in Nova Scotia. Its effect on mosquitoes is unforgiving. The longer-term effects on the human liver are probably the same, but you're dead anyway in the long run. In the short run I could lounge happily, their hordes kept at a distance.

In these damp places of the Canadian Shield there is a soft haze late in the day as the summer winds down. My friends seemed out of sync with the quality of light, working their rods too hard, the doctor in particular.

"You know, Michael, I envy you."

He glanced down at me uncertainly.

"Sick people stagger up to your door, pause and stare at your brass plaque –"

"Plate."

"What?"

"Plaques are for dead people. Christ." He'd lost his rhythm.

"Concentrate, Michael. So they stare at your brass plate –"

"Aluminum."

"Whatever."

"Cheaper to replace when you add a partner."

"Right. So they stare at your cheap aluminum plate, forgetting how expensive you are, and they see, as in a dream, no, as in a fantasy: MICHAEL FOWLER: PRIEST, GURU, SAVIOUR. You will make them well. They will rise up."

"Fuck off."

"No, Michael, I envy you. Writers spend their lives searching for the heart of man. You see him naked, transparent, totally emotionally dependent, up to eight times a day, ready to confess anything, ready to tell you things they've been hiding from their wives, their husbands, for years."

The lawyer broke his cast with disgust. It struck me that his eyes were filled with perpetual disappointment, the lines on his face deep, though he was scarcely forty.

He looked past me to the doctor. "All you see are bodies and fear. And fear is cheap. It's the most common human emotion. Seeing it teaches you nothing. The heart of man is in his property. I see people naked to their heart and further, and in ways you two couldn't begin to imagine."

The doctor, with the pedantic calm of his profession, reeled in the line and began packing up his rod. "Normally I'd agree. I don't see much. Mostly fear, as you say, and sublimated dissatisfaction. I never see the positive emotions." He fell silent, apparently forgetting about us as he arranged his flies. "Well, I suppose when there's a pregnancy people are pretty positive. But they don't come to me about that." He had a prosperous doctor's air about him; scrupulously clean, he had put on weight in the first flush of life's comfort and, with the fashion of the time, had now beaten the fat back off, leaving him with a wrinkled look; a balloon once blown up doesn't quite regain its sleek line when the air is let out. He seemed to be fussing unnecessarily over his flies and then looked up, revealing a confused expression. "It's quite unethical to tell you, but the proof of what you say is that I've got a problem I can't handle. The complete elements of this problem, and therefore, I suppose, of the solution, are here this weekend. You two could help me ..."

We are all members of a hunting and fishing club in upper New York State. At the centre of its two-thousand-odd acres laced with streams and ponds there is an elegant big house built of wood in 1820. We crowd in there at weekends and dine on duck and pheasant, bass and trout. It has the added advantage of a good wine cellar.

"Michael," I broke in, "if you're going to be unethical, make it quick and sharp. The rest is hypocrisy."

"Well, I'll tell you this. I'm really stuck. It's Peter and Anne-Marie."

The lawyer laughed. "I'm their lawyer and I've never seen a better balanced pair."

"Property doesn't account for everything."

My own overdeveloped sense of doubt made me fall silent, though Peter and Anne-Marie McCarthy appeared to be a perfect couple. After fifteen years of marriage, they were as much in love as they had been on their wedding day. All three of us could testify to that, as we had been at the marriage. I use the word "love," an old-fashioned, imprecise term, to imply I don't quite know what. What other word is there? They are devoted to each other. This two-way devotion has been extended to include their daughter, no further. They are nice enough to their friends, but we always feel we are in the way, like a fourth corner trying to intrude upon an equilateral triangle. The only disruption in their smooth flow came when they realized that Anne-Marie could not have a child. This they quickly resolved by adopting a baby, Sancha, who turned twelve last month. She is a sweet girl, quickly turning into a teenager. I'm very fond of her. Whenever we are all together, she and I go into a corner and talk about litera-ture. It is quite amazing what she reads without her school or her parents being involved. You might say that this represents a bit of complication in their perfect triangle.

All the same, such satisfaction within a marriage, such absence of rumours about other interests, is pretty rare in New York, particularly in that sort of group – people who work without needing to work very hard. They fill the day in order to satisfy a latent Protestant work ethic. I say this although the McCarthys are practising Catholics; again, rare in such a group. The Irish are to be found here and there where there is comfortable money, but only here and there.

Anne-Marie is not Irish. She's French, or rather her grandparents were. Apart from the name and the religion, she also inherited a French figure carried to the extreme. Her body has the shape of a neat little box, as if her rib cage touched her hips and thus eliminated the waist. The impression is of great energy, much of it sexual. Apart from devoting her energy to Peter and to Sancha, she devotes it to herself. Never have I seen her without detailed makeup. Never without hair forced or pulled into something specific. Never without a little uniform, which the French call style, and which, she being waistless and energetic, suits her body.

Peter, on the other hand, has a potato face – lots of flesh, no bones. It is, in fairness, not a big, flowery potato, but a finer variety; closer to a new potato. I suppose with time he will grow into the commoner breed used for french fries in the winter.

"What about them?" I said eventually.

Fowler had again fallen into indecision. "Look, I can't tell you. But keep your eyes open. If things get out of hand, I mean … do something."

The lawyer gave a half-laugh. Awkward.

I hesitated, but couldn't help myself. "That's ridiculous. If you want our help you must tell us."

"I have your help. Both friendship and curiosity will make you keep an eye on them. I can't tell you more." He stood there, clearly confused, caught in a professional trap, and then, as if describing people with terminal cancer, "They might work it out by themselves."

We walked the two miles back to the clubhouse in a sullen mood; the doctor nervous, I suppose, because he wasn't sure he'd done the right thing; and we caught between concern, unsatisfied curiosity and admiration for his self-control.

There are only three large tables in the dining room. It's a friendly sort of club and we usually eat in groups. I came down from my room early enough to make certain I would get a seat with the McCarthys. In fact I was able to grab the chair beside Anne-Marie. Peter was across the table from her. With the summer sun hanging on, the only other light in the room came from large fussy candelabra that flickered like a warning of imminent darkness. We ate pheasant with squash and Peter bought champagne for our end of the table. He was as blissfully happy as ever and full of Sancha's success at school; particularly her success in history, French and science, because he knows I consider them to be at the heart of a good education, especially for those who hope ever to write. You have to write about something and you can't write about literature, so there's no real point in studying it. What you need to do is read it, and for that matter read everything else.

Anne-Marie took little part in the conversation, which I thought unusual, but she seemed happy enough. A little excited perhaps. Nothing special. In fact there was no sign of the explosion expected by the doctor, who sat at another table, keeping his distance no doubt. Late in the evening something made me turn and I found his clinical stare coming my way from across the room. I smiled at him. He smiled back without enthusiasm.

We were up the next morning at five to walk out to the duck shoots. At first I noticed little, but it grew upon me as the haze cleared from my intellectual faculties, then from my motor functions, that Peter was terribly agitated. He seemed not to have slept all night; yet he was laughing and enthusiastic as we made our way across fields that had recently been turned. I stumbled along, silent, periodically glancing at him. One thing struck me: it was he who had chosen to share a blind with me. I'd have preferred to leave any revelations for later.

My silence obviously displeased him and his agitation grew while we waited in the brush hut seated back from the two openings. He made several attempts to get the conversation on the road without managing to provoke more than a one-word response. Then to my horror I realized that the mosquitoes were in full dance and I had forgotten to bring my killer repellent.

"I've some news, you know," he threw out.

"Shows."

"It does, does it?" The tone was ambiguous. "Well, it's big news."

"Uh huh."

My lack of interest made him pause a minute or so, then he blurted, "I'm going to be a father!"

My eyes must have betrayed astonishment, because he gave a grunt of satisfaction. "Big surprise, wouldn't you say?"

"Big surprise," I agreed warily.

"Anne-Marie's been going to doctors. They can do a lot more now than when we first married." He looked out of the blind, his gun moving about in his hands. "She gave me the good news last night."

"That's great, Peter. Just great."

We were saved from any further words by a first flight of teal. I fired ineffectually, which further annoyed me as I'm a good shot. Peter fired wildly, but brought down two birds. I was amazed. He is not a good shot.

"Well done."

He made no reply but leaned back on the rough bench inside the blind, his enthusiasm suddenly exhausted. We waited in silence for the next flight; it was twenty minutes. I made an effort this time and brought down one. Peter again shot wildly but with accuracy. He reloaded in a frenzy and made as if to fire again, though the birds were past, then in frustration sank back onto the bench without breaking his gun. His finger was still on a trigger.

"Kill her," I heard him mumble.

"Break your gun." He obeyed like a child. After a time I added, "You said something?"

"Nothing." He sat transfixed by his gun before looking up at me. "I said I should kill her."

"Anne-Marie?"

"It's not my child. I worked it out last night. I was away for almost a month in the Far East in June. You remember? Why did she wait so long to tell me? It's obvious."

"I don't think so. She loves you. That should be proof enough. The dates are never so simple that you can be sure."

He seemed not to have heard. "After all these years," he said more to himself, "after all that time with the doctors and then not even mine." The anger seemed about to turn to tears.

I had not seen the ducks come, but Peter sprang to his feet, threw himself forward and again brought down two. I have never seen such shooting. He scarcely aimed, and the birds were almost overhead. Again he reloaded.

I looked over at him. "Break your gun." He obeyed, then sank into a funk. "Peter, I don't understand what you're talking about."

He looked up. The expression was wistful. "Are you saying that what I've told you doesn't make sense?"

"Doesn't wash."

"So then no one will believe it. They'll all think it's my child."

"Especially if you keep your mouth shut."

He looked at me again, even more wistful. "She acts like it's mine. I can't stand it. I guess people wouldn't understand how much I love her. She was on the pill when we got married. Did you know that?"

"How would I?"

"That was pretty adventurous for a conservative Catholic." As if this weren't obvious enough he added, "Things weren't the same then."

"I was there. Remember?"

He gave me a wan smile. "We wanted to have a good time for a while, so she kept on taking the pill. We decided on three years. Then she stopped. After a year we started to wonder what was wrong. Anne-Marie doesn't really like doctors. She's shy about personal things, so I went off to see Michael Fowler. Since I was there and Anne-Marie was embarrassed, he said he'd start with me. He made me jack off so he could check for sperm. I didn't tell Anne-Marie. It was sort of degrading. I didn't think she'd like to know. A few weeks later Mike told me I had no sperm. Sterile, you see. He did a few more tests, but … the more I thought about it … it drove me crazy. I couldn't bring myself to tell Anne-Marie. She wanted children desperately. I was sure I'd lose her and I couldn't face that. I didn't know what to do. Then one night at dinner, I was a bit drunk, and I told her that I'd hidden something from her. About my past. That I'd got a girl pregnant at university and she'd had an abortion. I hadn't planned it, the story I mean, it just came out. I was so terrified of losing her."

"Of losing face," I thought to myself, but that was unkind. Out loud I asked, "What did she say?"

"Nothing much at first. The next day I found her crying, and she kept saying, 'I wanted a child so much.'

"'Go see Mike,' I said. 'Maybe he can suggest something.' Don't ask me why I said it. I was half crazy. I had to phone Mike that afternoon and beg him to keep his mouth shut about me and tell her she was sterile."

"Surely he didn't agree to that?"

"We're pretty old friends. We went to school together."

"I know."

"Anyway, Anne-Marie didn't go beyond Mike. After a while I suggested that we adopt a baby. Then word got around that she couldn't conceive, you know, the way it does."

"But what happened when she went to all those doctors?"

"I just made that up. I mean, that's the logical story, isn't it?"

"It certainly is."

"You know what she said to me last night?" The

question was accompanied by an incredulous expression. "She said it was a miracle. She said she couldn't believe it herself. She said she's been offering masses at St. Patrick's every day since she found out."

I watched some ducks come over, tantalizingly low, but neither of us moved.

"Maybe it is a miracle."

"Don't be a fucking idiot. I should kill her. But if I do that, I have to tell her first. I have to tell her that I know she cheated on me."

"Then she'd know you were sterile."

He nodded. "You think I didn't tell her because I was ashamed. You think I'm afraid it would make me less of a man. Well, you're wrong. It's because I love her so much. I couldn't bear to lose her."

"Then why kill her?"

There was contempt on his face. He almost whispered at me, "You just don't understand, do you? I mean, you've never been married, have you? You've never had a child."

"You're talking garbage, Peter. Total shit. Total self-indulgent garbage."

After that we didn't have much to say to each other. We concentrated on the shooting and did quite well. Walking back he asked me to keep my mouth shut. I said I'd think about it. I said it would depend on what he did. If he were reasonable, I'd be reasonable.

That afternoon I was sitting near the house under a great pine which cast total shade. I was thinking and didn't hear Anne-Marie come up. She sat on the patchy grass beside my chair. She sat with great energy and immediately said, "Peter is asleep. He drank too much at lunch." She looked inquiringly. "What did he tell you about my being pregnant?" Her hair was cut short and brushed back so that her face stood out larger than life.

At first nothing came to mind, then the silence seemed a bit long under her gaze. "I congratulated him."

"But not me?"

"He asked me not to mention it yet."

Her eyes never left my face. "I wonder why."

"You tell me."

"I guess it means he doesn't believe in miracles."

"Do you?"

She went strangely passive. "Why not? What's he going to do?"

"He says he's going to kill you. I'd say he means it in a very practical way."

"Who cares." It was thrown out with lassitude. "Do you think he should?"

"Should? No, of course not. But there are circumstances under which people kill people, and within the realm of emotional norms they're considered pretty acceptable circumstances, even if the killer is later executed. The laws of reason don't eliminate the laws of emotion. It's an uneasy tandem."

She watched me with a cool eye as I talked, and after a brief silence between us she said, "You're pretty pompous." There was another short silence. "Why shouldn't I kill him first?" I couldn't read her expression, except that it was tortured.

"Why should you?"

"Because a friend forced me to see a doctor last year and I found out I wasn't sterile. Because it was almost too late. Because I loved Peter and trusted him and he has almost destroyed me. Do you understand that word? Destroyed – taken from me my primary function. Once I found out, I got myself pregnant as fast as I could, before it was too late. Do you know how difficult that is when you don't want everyone to find out and still want a decent father? I couldn't have some anonymous donor. Do you think I wanted to sneak around luring appropriate men into bed?"

"Who is it?"

"Don't bother."

"Why didn't you just leave Peter?"

"What about Sancha? She wouldn't understand and I couldn't explain." These words came out as bad acting.

"Come off it."

She snorted with a kind of laugh before doubt could temper her assurance. "Anyone could figure it out. He stole my love for fifteen years with his cheap little pride. Now I'll steal his. He loves me, he says. Well, let's see how long before this love turns into a cancer."

"I think you're a fool. You want Sancha to grow up in a poisoned atmosphere?"

"Sancha is his child. If this poison begins to affect my child, I'll leave. There's lots of time for that."

"I think you should send Sancha away to school."

She glanced at me with a veneer of indifference. "What do you think he will do?"

I ignored the question and got to my feet. "You should send Sancha away to school."

I went inside to find Michael Fowler. I found him on his bed, reading the thriller of the day. He had recommended it to me with enthusiasm, as if to say I might hope to do as well if I applied myself. He sat up with sudden interest.

"Has something happened?"

I don't know why, perhaps it was the tone of his voice. I lost any desire to win his support. "Peter told me his concerns," was all I said.

Mike nodded impatiently. "Did he tell you everything?"

"Everything."

"What do you think?"

"I've just seen Anne-Marie."

He paused and fixed his eyes on me. It was the examination of a doctor searching for signs of a disease. "What did she say?" When I hesitated, Fowler lost patience. "Well, what did she say? Does she really believe it's a miracle?"

"Hard to know."

"Incredible! An incredible situation. Do you think he would really kill her?"

"Certainly," I snapped. "Certainly he would. Will he? That we'll see, I suppose."

"What a cold thing to say. Are you such a bastard? Observing it all from a distance."

"Am I? And why did you lie to her in the first place? Why did you support his ridiculous pride? Was that warm and considerate?"

He brushed my remarks away as if they were naive or, worse, unprofessional. "Oh, he's an old friend, you know. We went to school together."

"I know."

13
CONVERSATIONS
WITH DICTATORS V

A PRIVATE TALK by Gianfranco Fini? What a bizarre idea. And in London? Who could be naive enough to offer him credibility?

I took a quick look at the invitation. I'd be in France around that date. London was a hop away. February. A horrible time of year in England. The ethics of accepting? I considered them for a few seconds. My presence would be irrelevant, being neither English nor Italian. And at these special Chatham House gatherings seats go quickly.

But Fini? The first fascist, neo-fascist, ex-fascist, whatever, perhaps even he doesn't know, to gain power in Europe since the Second World War? The custodian of Mussolini's political inheritance? And at the Royal Institute of International Affairs? I mean, really, who thinks of these things?

Most Chatham House talks are just announced and whoever comes comes. There's plenty of room and a rather retired audience, to put it politely. The Royal Institute is familiarly called Chatham House because that's where it is – in a townhouse which once belonged to Pitt the Elder, Earl of Chatham.

I'd say Chatham's ghost is still there, the great man who fulfilled every tribune's dream by dying on his feet, in Parliament, even if it was the House of Lords, in the midst of a speech defending an ethical issue – justice for the American colonies. To be exact, he was stricken, collapsed and was carried out to die, a month later. All the same, it had been a matter of existential ethics.

Sometimes the hall inserted into the basement just isn't big enough. When prime ministers come. Or a political figure with star qualities. This must have been Fini's case. After all, stardom is its own content. And Fini was a youngish, good-looking, disco-dancing, indeed fashion-able, fascist, with the intriguing twist of denying he was one, sort of. The triumph of form over content.

Anyway, in these cases an invitation goes out to members. First come, first served. The confirmation that I had a seat arrived a few weeks later. They had actually moved the meeting to the Queen Elizabeth II Conference Centre, opposite Westminster Abbey. Could the demand be that big? I'd have thought this was more of a specialty event.

The day – when it came – was indeed a February London day. The ground the colour of the walls the colour of the sky, all three pulled together by the drizzle. My taxi driver drew up behind a crowd. He pointed through them to the other side of the square.

The people were standing four or five deep with their backs to me, up against a metal crowd-control fence, with police facing them. I became conscious of my dark suit. They were methodically chanting. A bit too methodical, I thought. But they had come. They were playing their role as citizens. Perhaps if I hadn't been a foreigner I'd have made the same choice.

A policeman told me to skirt around to the far end of the barricade. He seemed to understand instinctively what I wanted. "Show them your card, sir." He smiled, a friend's smile.

From the other side of the barricade I could see that the conference hall, like so many concrete structures designed for the gatherings of managers, resembled a bunker. Thanks to air conditioning there was no need for architecture. Any old square or circle or rectangle would do. The shapes of a child's game.

I was directed upstairs. The wide, red-carpeted staircase gave on to a lobby, also carpeted in red, always the right colour for making people feel important. The lobby was grand, although without any distinguishing characteristics. As incapable of giving offence as it was of inspiring doubt. I wandered across to the plate-glass wall of windows. There was a panoramic, soundproofed view over the bleak square outside. The demonstrators offered no colour but did provide animation. They moved their arms and heads, placards swayed gently in the rain. Their gestures had an almost nostalgic air. The street lights made their bulky coats – over heavy sweaters I suppose – seem even bulkier, as if growing out of the sidewalk. It might have been a scene in some troubled Middle European capital, I don't know, Bratislava, with Soviet-inspired concrete and a much put-upon but hopeful crowd. There were no ghosts in this building. No Pitt. Boredom doesn't provide the spirits necessary for a ghost. The interesting thing about Pitt wasn't that he represented purity or the loyal husband or the good churchgoer. There was lots of corruption about him and scrambling for power. But he was driven by ideas. You might even say ideas of the public good, ideas of *the other*.

There was a light touch at my elbow. A young research assistant from Chatham House indicated that I should cross over to the theatre. I took the last empty aisle seat, halfway back. The room was a continuation of the lobby, minus windows, plus standard folding chairs with red plush seats. A standard head table set up for three. A draped cloth so that legs could fidget unseen. Water. I looked about. There were perhaps three hundred seats. I might have been anywhere in the world.

It wasn't a typical Chatham House crowd. Most of them had an air of being there on business. Most were the age of senior civil servants, but not top level, and senior managers, but not the presidential sort. A room full of assistant permanent undersecretaries, ambassadors, political advisors, vice-presidents, directors. Men, of course. A gathering of the corporations, or rather delegates of the corporations, public and private.

At exactly five thirty, a door to the side of the head table opened and Fini came in with two other men. On time, like a good train. It's curious how head tables file in, the way suspects do for a police lineup. The translator, then Fini, then the chairman. I missed his name. Sir Somebody Something, ex-ambassador to Italy, currently vice-president of a City bank. He sat himself with exquisite neatness and managed to look like both.

His first words were of protest, mind you in the softest of manners. This meeting, to be precise the holding of this meeting, had been questioned, indeed opposed, by some members. There had been controversy, he suggested.

Fini stared out at the audience. There was no penetrating glance. No magnetic projection. The gaze of a successful accountant. Present but bored. Conservatively fashionable glasses. A classic Italian double-breasted dark suit. Standard international shirt and tie. Neat haircut. The appearance of a perfect technocrat.

The Royal Institute's role, the chairman persisted, was to serve the cause of debate. And that was exactly why ...

There was something intriguing about Fini's indifferent stare. He was thinking what? Nothing? Or perhaps how bizarre it was to find himself here. Or perhaps that this was the cost of building respectability at home – an afternoon of ritual self-humiliation in a dreary room with dreary men. Or perhaps how much they resembled their

Italian equivalents. Or that here, in this room, was an illustration of the true meaning of corporatism, exactly as Mussolini had explained it: everyone would act in the immediate self-interest of their group; that is, if you let them do it. And having a bit of power, as he now did, he was in their self-interest, as Benito had once been and would have remained, had he not made that terrible mistake of lining up with a German raving lunatic. If he had stuck to practical matters, the real meaning of corporatism, he'd have been the friend of the fathers of the people in this room and others like them, well, to the end, like Franco. Of course, for all I know he was really thinking about dinner. But he looked too bored. No. Not bored. Dispassionate.

The chair had moved on to introductions. Fini was from Bologna, a communist city. His father had been a civil servant, his mother a teacher. As a young man, he had "discovered that any opposition to communism led to being called a fascist. He had the steel, he says, to respond by becoming a real fascist."

This was pronounced in a neutral tone. He finished with the standard sterile but elegant flourish, inviting the speaker to speak.

A member jumped up somewhere behind me. The chair tried at once to interrupt him, explaining again that everything had been taken into consideration. But the protestor had a good public-hall voice. "I am the son of a former director of Chatham House and I find the welcoming of a fascist demeaning …" The rather fleshy face of the current director – an American who had made his career in England and recently been knighted for services – was just visible as he sat discreetly low in the front row.

It was a solid emotional outburst, full of ethics. I could sense the crowd hating it. Their job was to be there. To listen. To ask specific questions. To report back. There was no need to personalize things. This was about professionalism and the wisdom of professional conformity. About structures and running things properly.

A peculiar sound, a sort of grumble, began to build in the audience. It was fascinating; those whose very profession turns on discretion metamorphosing themselves into a crowd.

The sound of bored anger came rolling out, here and there, around the room, as if to say, "Let's get on with it. Process is what matters. We're professionals. Cheap ethics are for students." A curious formula which always raises the question of whom expensive ethics are for.

There is a particular way in which men in ties shout. The body rarely moves. It is still being managed, even as the larynx slips out of control. There is something touchingly animalistic about a torso seated – an artificial position, after all, limited to Western culture and reasonably recent – with its arms on the lap and a head which swivels to shout. It's a little bit the way seals bark. I don't necessarily mean that as an insult. It would be too easy.

Too cheap. After all, the finest bred and trained dog will remain seated and swivel its head to bark in precisely the same manner. The very finest. It is a form of expression proper to many of us in the animal kingdom.

The ex-director's son persisted. "... a fascist in an Armani suit ..." That was an unexpectedly snappy line. He called for immediate adjournment, then paused. There was no sign of agreement from the chair, from the hall, from myself for that matter. Just one of those difficult silences. He hesitated, still on his feet, then stalked out. That's what you have to do. You stalk out. Stiff, awkward, striding, pitched at a forward angle, narrow focus, unsure of your facial expression. Your class – the people you went to school with, the people with whom you share an accent, a tailor, or at least a style of tailor, a type of shirt, an education – sits in rows watching you as you go, as if you were a bug, dismissing you as marginal and, worst of all, emotional. Then you're gone, and the chair takes control of the silence in order to refinish his introduction, gradually, in a comforting way, filling the void you have left behind.

I was still thinking about the protestor's exit when I noticed that Fini was on his feet. No, it wasn't an Armani suit. Something better cut, more anonymous yet less mass-market. Perhaps from Cenci in Rome. Something carefully designed to blend in. The salesmen at Cenci would be happy to have a new category of clientele, now that so many of the old Christian-democrat and socialist leaders were out of power, if not in jail. This was the perfect image for a corporatist. Far more effective than the heroic costumes of the 1930s.

All the same, I wasn't prepared for the voice. He began, well, to drone. You could hear it in his tone even before the translator intervened.

"It is difficult for me to explain exactly what Alleanza Nazionale is …" He started to read out an intricate analysis of political power with almost no reference to content. "Over the last two years there has been a real democratic revolution in Italy." There was no indication of revolution in his tone. "… only two forces remain … a clarifying process … the Right and the Left … the ideological period is over …" I sat there, separating the words out. He says no middle remains. In that case, only ideology remains. There would be a question period. Perhaps I'd ask him about that. His tone was calibrated not to resemble an ideologue. He didn't even sound like the Gianfranco Fini I'd read about, boasting that a new generation of politicians had arrived, men who danced the latest dances in public and stripped off their shirts on beaches. Of course, that was precisely what Mussolini had done. He had been a great dancer and bare-torso jogger. He had invented the modern leader as jogging populist – fun-loving athletic Hero. Hitler had been a much more old-fashioned plodder when it came to personal details. Now, that would be an interesting historic point to ask him about. Or there was the business of there being no middle.

In any case, the whole shape of twentieth-century ideology has been based on the either/or principle. The centre was meant to be no more than a refuse dump of ill-considered soft notions jumbled up with short-term interests and filled with Mensheviks, Girondins, Kerenskyites, liberals, weak, wet, wankers, well-intentioned political garbage. The Nazis, fascists, Bolsheviks, neo-conservatives, all believed – believe – that history has no centre because moderation is a betrayal of truth.

Not that he was putting it that way. This was an intimate chat. I glanced at Sir Somebody Something. He nodded periodically, with an understanding smile – the unconscious gestures of a man who likes to be in agreement. Or at any rate whose career has been about being seen to be in agreement. A lover of calm, of unity among those in the know. I don't suppose he was even considering the central argument being put forward.

In defence of the chairman, Fini's words were not immediately recognizable as an argument in favour of two extremes, because these extremes had been converted into an expression of normalcy. Moderation, on the other hand, was extremist and dangerous, because it wasn't clear or efficient, or indeed professional.

So the extremes had become democratic, while the middle undermined democracy. It was very clever. He was sewing together into one the original fascist corporatism with contemporary managerialism and the rising forces of neo-conservatism.

"What is the guarantee that we belong to the democratic right? Everyone knows that the Alleanza Nazionale cannot be seen to be neo-fascist." Seen to be? Seen to be! It was all strategy, appearances. Now, that would make a good question. I looked about. The audience didn't seem to have noticed. "We were not neo-fascists yesterday. We are not today. The proof: we have been in power for nine months without endangering Italy's alliances." But Mussolini was in power for years without alliances changing. Surely someone would ask him about that; if not, well, I'd never get the floor more than once. I'd have to choose my question.

A few moments later he sat down. The audience applauded. A solid sound for a fixed period of time.

"Lord Henry," the chair said, pointing to a figure in the audience whose arm was on the way up. He asked about the EEC treaties. Would Fini honour them? A long, obscure answer followed.

"Sir Marcus."

The question was about markets and the answer seemed to be that the modern face of corporatism was relatively unchanged. "Free markets" meant putting everything into the hands of interest groups.

I put my hand up.

"Mr. Everett-Boxer."

Mr. Everett-Boxer asked in a gentle way about racism. Fini replied that the old racist laws were "a mistake that led to a horror." The chair nodded. People nodded.

But a mistake is only a tactical error. I put my arm up more insistently. The chair's gaze seemed to be searching the room. His eyes danced around me once, then back and around the other way, on a complex slalom course, until they found a nervous, mid-level, Foreign Office type.

"Mr. Scott."

The fellow stood up, as if relieved that he had not been forgotten, and asked carefully about Mr. Fini's policy on the Slovenian border. Almost apologetically. There was an old Mussolinian claim to a good slice of Slovenian land; what had once been Yugoslavian land. It had been a justification for war. The question felt like something written by an undersecretary and then handed down to a desk officer to be memorized and the asking guaranteed by a telephone call from the writer to the chair, a former colleague perhaps. The answer escaped me, except that in his technocratic verbiage Fini was justifying the claim.

So this was the new fascism: relaxed, boring, reassuring.

The chair's eyes dipped and swayed as he chose another questioner he could name. Then another. All careful questions. Some seemed prearranged, others were from safe, responsible types. You might say there was a shape to the whole performance. I kept my arm up, but I suppose there was too much tension in it, too much aggressivity. Then, perhaps in an effort to give the impression we weren't being managed, the chair chose someone he couldn't name.

One of the characteristics of the technocratic or

courtier-like mind is the absence of judgement. It just isn't necessary. Judgement is replaced by relationships and by structures. And when they do take a risk it is suddenly like buying a lottery ticket. After all, their skills relate to the management of the known. You could see how he made the mistake. The man he chose was dressed right. Had an appropriate haircut. There was nothing odd about his manner. Not agitated. Not aggressive. As calm as anyone in the room. But judgement is all about unknown relationships. The uncontrolled. Good judgement is dependent on some sort of central belief system. Almost any belief in any system will do. It grounds you. Feeds your intuition. Helps you judge the meaning and consequences of events.

"Mr. Fini, you have never publicly condemned Mussolini." Discomfort blew across the room. A great gust. Just like that. The chairman momentarily lost his calm expression. There was a hint of panic in his eyes. Then, almost like one of those windup toys which hit a wall, turn over, then right themselves, you could see the mechanisms of experience reasserting themselves as he began to focus on the questioner, who sat down, saying, "London would perhaps be a particularly appropriate place for such a condemnation."

It lasted no more than a few seconds. The interlocking fabric of all the careful chairing and the droning, the almost staged questions and answers, seemed to have dissolved, like nylon when a match is put to it.

Without hesitation, as if to a child, Fini shot back, "I think history has condemned him. I don't think I need to." The absence of the founder's name was almost too deliberate, drawing attention by its absence. And the double use of "think," to soften the reply. And yet it was the answer which had captured everyone's attention. The dismissive contemptuous tone, as if the question were beneath the dignity of a professional.

I let loose a louder-than-conversational "Facile!" and stuck my arm up again. My neighbours leaned slightly away on their folding chairs. Nothing you could measure. A psychic leaning. A de-solidarization.

But the unnamed questioner was back on his feet. "That's not an answer, Signor Fini. We deserve something other than evasive rhetoric!"

I noticed the handful of non-conformers separating themselves out, leaning forward, ready to jump in. Suddenly the room was alive with a hint of reality. But the chair now saw his chance. With a smooth, reassuring, even, drawn-out murmur he suggested that the question had been dealt with and, as he was speaking, pointed in another direction so that without any dangerous pause he was able to say, "Sir John."

Sir John leapt into the void with an obscure economic question. The riot was over. As fast as the disquiet had blown in, it blew out, carrying the energy of the non-conformers with it, leaving only passive pessimism.

Then an executive from the Chase Manhattan Bank

was on his feet. "You say your prime minister should be able to complete his three or four key economic policy reforms by April, in time for an election. Which is more important? To complete them all or to vote? In particular, what about pension reform?"

A banker meets a neo-fascist and wonders about his investments. I gave up raising my arm and tried to withdraw from the atmosphere by leaning back, as if in search of the distanced independence proper to a writer. In the process I caught a glimpse of the fellow who had asked the condemnation question. He was leaning forward, his arms resting on his knees, his hands clasped together. In that position it would have been natural for him to be looking down at his hands. Instead, his head was forced back and up so that he could stare at the chairman. Not at Fini. There was a loathing in his eyes. A sort of pessimistic loathing. Well, London was his town. He had to live with these people.

In truth, an odd discomfort had come over me. I don't know. Discomfort or agitation. Or perhaps familiarity. Like an old film or a book or something. Something. But of course! This was the atmosphere of 1938. Of course. A desperate, quiet desire to be agreeable. The appeasement atmosphere. The nudge, nudge, wink, wink, all insiders know that this-is-the-way-the-world-works atmosphere. We all have to deal with nasty types. We all have to get along with them. Eventually they'll see reason. In any case, they can't touch us unless, through ill-considered movements, we disturb the calm waters required for an interwoven continuity. A sort of early globalization.

By the time I refocused, the chair was thanking Fini, generous yet careful, then fast onto his feet, leading the way out through the side door. The room rose in general, unperturbed chatting. I was still in my seat, considering what had happened, when the young research assistant who had earlier got me to my seat came by, shepherding the director out.

I greeted the recent knight of American origins. He nodded down at me with the care of the outsider who has made his way on the inside and no longer knows how to talk to other outsiders. I got up and reminded him why he knew me. A soft, noncommittal smile came to his face as he kept moving towards the exit.

"Well," I said, to stop him, "that was a bizarre event."

He stared quizzically at me rather than respond. At the word "bizarre" his eyebrows had jumped ever so slightly. Such a non-intellectual, non-utilitarian word. Then he mumbled, "Oh, you know, we were caught in an awkward ..."

I broke in. "Bizarre that a man who takes over an officially neo-fascist party, members and all, then says it isn't fascist, can't bring himself to condemn Mussolini."

"Oh, you know," the director began again, "it was such a difficult position for ... People like that, well ... I wouldn't make too much of ... you know, just one of those things ..."

"Actually, Director," the research assistant jumped in, "perhaps you didn't hear him at lunch. Signor Fini said he would be politically dead if he condemned Mussolini."

The director chuckled, as if to say, "Of course. That's what he really is. A careful type. Careful of his position. Everyone with a position has to be careful." He turned to chat with another member.

14
A VICTIM
OF ROMANCE

THERE WAS NO REASON why Eleanor should not have been married. After all, she had been, to quite a famous portfolio manager who had been born with money and made more before dying. He had left Eleanor their apartment on East 78th, all the objects she had put into it thanks to his signature, and what her accountant once described to me as "a fascinating portfolio" of shares, bonds, parking garages (three), and a condominium at Vail, rented to others, because unlike her husband Eleanor did not ski and did not feel that tight trousers suited her thighs. On the outer edges there was a small bulge she preferred to disguise. Cellulite wasn't a word she knew.

That aside, I could find no clear reason for her failure to find a husband. The first had died of natural causes, though at an age well below the national average. A cancer of the colon had somehow been allowed to get out of hand – too many clients, too many bonds – and carried him off at thirty-eight. He had been, as Eleanor correctly stated, a generational victim; that is, disenchanted with fibre and "preferring the processed pabulum of postwar prosperity." Her phrase.

She was not, as you can see, stupid. Quite the contrary. And well-read. She was not too old (never truly relevant anyway). Nor lacking in looks. She was of the blond type, with good bones kept well in view by dieting and exercise. There was a surprisingly delicate air about her, which had more to do with attitude than with physical reality, and no lines, because she had always kept out of the sun – perhaps she travelled so much that the idea "holiday/sun" had not occurred to her. Nor indeed the idea "holiday." I suppose she had never accepted the commonly held dictum that life is a pile of sandwiches and death the empty fridge; that each sandwich has a filling – the good part, the periods of relaxation – sometimes cream cheese, sometimes caviar, but in any case surrounded by slices of labour, the long-life white of the assembly line or the seven-grain intensity of Madison Avenue, stale or fresh.

Eleanor didn't eat bread. It was bad for her hips. She ate her caviar with a spoon.

When we were together, which we were from time to time (she was the sort of woman people felt they couldn't invite without carefully pairing off, and I was an acceptable half-pair), it sometimes struck me that she was short on luck.

I mention this because four and a half years is a long time to be on the lookout – she had been a widow for five – when you have so much to offer. She sometimes wondered out loud to me about her various prospects and one thing was clear. Eleanor knew what she wanted.

Two years ago, for example, we were beside each other at a long table in honour of a fellow who had once made quite a noise as secretary of state and had cashed in on that as a consultant to aimless chief executive officers. When they were in despair over their market share they could call up the great pundit and he would recount his latest conversation with Boris or Helmut or Margaret. It made them feel better. Eleanor seemed overexcited, but not by the company. She wasn't a snob or a social climber. She was primarily impatient at finding herself trapped in yet another social event. I probed, and after some fencing she confided,

"I've reached the stage in life" (hardly the way to describe forty, but then she was very American in her worship of youth) "when I'd like a man who wants to do something. Something real. Not business or politics. Find a cure for cancer, that would be real. Don't laugh. Why not? That will be done. Or paint. Really paint. Or take the Met in hand."

I agreed that the opera had sunk pretty low, then teased her, "You mean, live vicariously? Why not do something yourself?"

She pinned a bit of chicken to her plate, raised her fork, stared at the meat, pinkish-white, and released it back onto the plate. "I don't want to! Perhaps I should and I suppose I could. But I don't want to. I want to help someone else do it."

It was a point of view I could understand without accepting. She had spent four decades under the protection of a double-edged myth – the role of women and the role of money.

As if to scotch my thoughts she fixed her eyes on mine in admonition. "You don't understand, do you?"

With a shrug I admitted that I didn't.

She had the remarkable talent of seeming to blink only when she wished. She blinked now and whispered, "I don't believe that money is essential to life or that with it all can be bought. But look at New York. It is becoming a Third World city. The rich five floors up and descending only to enter their cars. The middle-class sinking down into a state not unlike that of the poor, because they are obliged to live and travel together, suffering from the same filth and crime." Regret came over her face. "I don't want to be part of that. I want a man who can do something about it. Either that or a man who can do things in spite of it."

Eleanor belonged to the compassionate tradition of rich America. "Money is a protection, and those who are protected should extend their arms to enfold others. Not fewer private elevators, but more people in them."

She had been hopeful that evening. The object of her hope, I found out from friends in common, was a man obsessed with converting the pornographic heaven around 42nd Street into a haven of ideas and culture; the latter being, I suppose, the residual of the former. I don't know what went wrong, but he never did include her in his plans. Nor did anyone else.

That delicacy of Eleanor's, there was something disconnected about it. Not from people, but from the reality people lived in. And it wasn't because of her money. Other people had that and held on to their hard edge. In the immense flow of the world where some people swam along and others struggled and some drowned, Eleanor sat on the edge without getting her toes wet. Of course it wasn't really so. You can't sit on the edge. We are all carried along on our short trip towards the end, but Eleanor's trick was to appear to be ashore and dry and perfectly stationary. She wanted to manage her life, to choose options carefully, to preplan their execution, to execute without unforeseen consequences. As all of this was impossible, she passed her time sitting on the edge, reaching out periodically over the waves with the best of intent but to no effect. Nor, of course, could anyone reach up to help without her getting wet. Eleanor would have a monogrammed hand towel within reach.

Last month she asked me to her apartment for a small dinner and I found her in a bitter mood. She had continued to dress beautifully, to organize interesting gatherings, to travel and to be on the lookout; but despair had seeped into her eyes. That evening she had assembled a politician, a writer, a film director and their women.

I overheard her conversation with the politician. It was centred on his sailing off Cape Cod. At one point I butted in to ask him about nuclear arms. He was preparing a senatorial report. Eleanor cut me off. I stayed on for a while after dinner and she began by bawling me out.

"You know better. You should never ask a serious question prematurely at dinner parties. It can be fatal. You must start low key and feel the mood."

"We were eating dessert."

She ignored this and subjected me to a bout of moaning, which could be summed up as "Never have there been so many rich. Never has it been so unfashionable."

That was the first time I had heard her cast doubt upon her own myth. If the cramming of her private elevator were not even perceived to be a good thing, not even admitted to be a sign of proper social advancement among those in circumstances similar to her own, well, the myth was hardly worth holding on to.

This change of fashion clearly depressed her, though I had no idea at the time to what extent. How was she to find a husband in those conditions? She felt trapped not by her habits, but by the trappings that made her habits necessary.

The telephone call I received yesterday was not of the sort I expected from Eleanor. It involved no careful social planning as a spearhead to something worthwhile. She asked simply if I were free, and if so would I spend the afternoon with her. When I say "simply" I do not convey the excitement in her voice. I cancelled a minor appointment and was at 78th Street before three.

Everything in her apartment was, as it always had been, carefully placed and perfectly clean. The impression was of a set, without any suggestion of rooms lived in. I allowed myself to be placed on a medium-hard chair, one of a pair Eleanor had picked up in Paris some years before. At the time she had told me they were signed "Jacob." She sat, and without a word, not even to offer coffee, passed across the gulf between us a neat blue folder. As she reached forward, it struck me again that she was a truly handsome woman; an old-fashioned description, but the right one. Had she been relaxed, she would also have been physically desirable. This unkind thought was drowned out as usual by the evidence of her great and good intentions. They drew upon my sympathies and I gave her a warm look before opening the folder. In it was a schedule, printed in pencil:

JUNE 15TH:

Appointment					
1	3:30 p.m.	IRT Local		76 St. Station
2	4:00 p.m.	"	"	66 St. Station
3	4:30 p.m.	"	"	59 St. Station
4	5:00 p.m.	"	"	51 St. Station
5	5:30 p.m.	"	"	42 St. Station
6	6:00 p.m.	"	"	33 St. Station

Beneath the schedule was a page of want ads from the *New York Review of Books*, dated June 1. Three ads were circled and numbered with green ink. The ad numbered 1 read, "Woman 40, young appearance; seeks husband intelligent, ambitious, with purpose. Desire: devote life to him. PO Box G 31 Z."

I flipped over the sheet to discover a page from the *Village Voice*. Again it was of ads, again three were circled and numbered in green, this time from 4 to 6. I glanced at 5. "Young widow ready to give up independence in return for original husband who will take command. PO Box 1612."

I looked up, but Eleanor gave me no time for questions.

"I've decided to settle the matter. I asked myself, how can I do a survey of the whole market? Easy. Two newspapers. I don't think I'd be interested in anyone who reads the *News*. Or the *Post*. Three ads in each paper. Each ad tailored to attract a different group of men, but each group, you see, meeting part of my needs. I received seventy-three replies; forty to the *Village Voice*. I selected two replies from each ad in each paper, wrote them, spoke to them on the phone and eliminated half. That leaves a total of six. What a pity I can't have them rolled up into one." With a pretty little smile she confirmed that she was enjoying the whole business.

"All right, Eleanor, fine." I paused to look her over, but she seemed perfectly normal, or rather, as I had always known her. "All right, but what about the subway? I don't see how that fits in."

"Simple. I don't know these people, do I? What's more,

I'm going to eliminate five of them. I thought, how can I meet them in a public place where I can avoid a sticky situation, where I can get away easily without being harassed. If I meet them in hotel bars they might follow me." It hadn't occurred to her that none of the six might be suitable. And what if the one she wanted didn't want Eleanor?

"Six in three hours?"

"I've made up my mind to do it, so best get it over with. I have all the information, all I want is the physical confirmation. You see, I sent them a photo but asked them not to send one to me. Women don't really care about men's looks. Not in the long run. Their voices are more important. There is so much more of their feelings and their character hidden in their voices. The telephone was perfect for that. Twenty minutes on a station platform should be enough for the rest." The disbelief must have been growing on my face, because she paused with a concerned look and in a reassuring tone added, "There are even benches to sit down, if one wants to."

"And I ..."

"You, Dong, you come with me, if you don't mind, just to be sure nothing goes wrong. Anonymously, you understand. Just travel in the same car and wait a few yards away on the platform, so that I can call you if need be."

I have a little reputation for going to rough places and dealing with rough people. That was probably why Eleanor chose me. Why not? She looked at her watch. I looked at mine. It was 3:10 P.M.

"Time to go," she said and stood up.

We walked over to Lexington and down to 76th, where Eleanor insisted on paying my fare. At 3:25 the downtown platform was empty except for two young women. There was a quiet, shabby feel about the place; the air warm and damp, holding a history of dirt in suspension so that the smell although strong had a homey edge. Eleanor placed me against the wall halfway along and strolled a further twenty yards to sit on a bench. She sat well. Calmly. In fact with greater ease than was normal for her. She gazed straight over at the facing platform and not to either side.

Nothing happened for two minutes. Then a train came in going our way. Graffiti resistant paint had been introduced in May, but already the secret artists had found a blend that would hold and the cars were again covered in soiled swirls. The train stopped. Two women got on. A fat man and a woman got off from separate cars. His trousers hung down limp over his rear end. He looked around, then headed for the exit.

Another minute passed before a train came in on the other side, heading uptown. A man got off the first car at the front end. He was dressed in a standard Brooks Brothers way and carried a briefcase, perhaps a little on the large size. The briefcase, I mean. He was forty-five or fifty, fairly thin and just under six feet. The face was without special distinction and although a bit dark, probably that of an Anglo-Saxon. A bank vice-president, I would have guessed. He looked anxiously up and down his platform, and when he saw no one waiting his shoulders seemed to sink with regret or perhaps relief. There was something sympathetic about him. He waited for a moment, holding his briefcase before him with both hands on the handle, then his eyes came up onto our platform, where they travelled from his end, down, over me and on to Eleanor, who looked calmly ahead. They stopped at Eleanor and fixed themselves there as the man walked up his platform until he was opposite her. Eleanor still stared straight ahead, so they were now staring at each other. After a moment, Eleanor smiled and nodded. She might have known him for years.

He nodded back and in an agitated half-run went to the exit, climbed the stairs and, I suppose, crossed the avenue, because he reappeared on our side having had to pay another fare. He walked down the platform at a much slower pace. Passed me. As he approached Eleanor, she got to her feet and introduced herself.

I couldn't hear the conversation, but I saw him invite her to sit. She seemed not to register this. A train came in and went out. Eleanor was doing most of the talking while he listened in awkward silence. It was the way I had seen her treat out-of-town guests who came with an introduction but turned out to be not quite on an adequate social or financial or intellectual level. Ten minutes later another train came in. With polite smoothness she stretched out her arm, took his hand and shook it. The length of the arm held him back while she eased onto the train just as its doors closed. She did it so quickly that he could not possibly have followed. I had scarcely enough time myself. As we pulled out I saw the man watching me from the platform. Perhaps he had noticed my letting the first train go by in order to hang around on the platform.

I pushed through the doors connecting my car to the next, ran forward and through another set to where Eleanor stood with her hand on a metal pole for balance as if it were a Doric column.

"Boring," was all she said.

"What was his purpose?"

"Some sort of business deal." She looked at her watch. I noticed for the first time that it was a diamond-and-enamel object in art deco style. "We're almost late. Don't stand near me." The train began to slow. "Go to the end of the car, then walk down the platform away from me."

I did as I was told, my eyes fixed on the linoleum floor. It was grey marbled with white.

There was a handful of people waiting at the 66th Street stop. Once the train had gone and the half-dozen passengers to get off with us had reached the exit, I saw a plump man pacing along the platform near the centre. He wore a worsted suit and carried a bunch of roses.

Eleanor walked up to him without hesitation and he took her hand with grace, then gave her the flowers. He talked as if he were laughing, which immediately communicated itself to Eleanor, because I heard her laugh. They sat down to talk, with great animation. I regretted not having read her other advertisements, nor having seen the replies. And there I was, just standing around on the platform without even a paper.

Two trains went by. As the third pulled in, Eleanor rose unexpectedly to her feet. The man recovered in time to give her a last smile, but she was on the train and gone.

I stayed in my car and concentrated on its walls. They were grey-green. The doors were brown. We reached the 59th Street station almost exactly at 4:30. A small crowd of potential Bloomingdale shoppers got off, another crowd with and without plastic bags got on. The train left and the station cleared. There was a man sitting on a bench at the far end. The moment the platform was empty he jumped to his feet and strode up to Eleanor. She hadn't really seen him come and gave a little start. He was healthy and athletic with an open-neck shirt and a light sports coat. He took Eleanor by the arm before leading her back to where he had been seated and had left his briefcase. I was a good distance away, but the size of the briefcase caught my eye.

I moved slowly down the platform towards them, past a newsstand, where I bought the *Post*. He was seated with his back to me, but I could see that Eleanor was engrossed in whatever he had to say. There was something in the shape of the head, though not the hair. The way he held himself. No. It wasn't that. The briefcase. It was large and of imitation pale leather. Two trains came and went. I was ready for the third. Eleanor, as expected, got to her feet, but he had her by the arm. She reached up with her free hand to stroke his cheek, which caused him to lose his grasp and she was away.

As we pulled out I got a good look at him and he at me. Then I understood! I rushed forward through the cars until I reached Eleanor.

"That man, he was at your first meeting."

She gave me one of her looks of bright social surprise. "What are you talking about?"

"It was the same man!"

"Don't be silly. The first man was in business. This one has a health village. I suppose if they resemble each other at all, it's because they're both a bit to my taste. This last one was quite nice."

"Eleanor, I'm telling you, you're wrong. He was the same man."

"Go away. You'll spoil it."

She moved down to the end of the car and turned her back on me. Her mood had changed. She was no longer amused, but consumed – comparing, I imagine, what she had seen so far. Her right arm was stretched up to grasp an overhead hook shaped like the handle of a light machine-gun and made of steel.

The 51st Street station was crowded with people waiting to get on. We were out of place among the first commuters rushing home, though Eleanor showed no sign of recognizing this. She stood on the platform as if in her own hallway waiting to greet a guest. The crowd did not clear away. People poured down the stairs for the next train, so Eleanor walked slowly along the platform, exhibiting herself, or so I wrongly thought, because she suddenly stopped before a young man who carried a white cane and wore a solid narrow band of steel curved over his eyes in place of glasses. He was elegantly dressed in a Milanese way, a voile shirt with three buttons open, linen trousers, wafer-like loafers, all in two tones of mauve and grey.

But why did he need a wife if someone dressed him so well? And who read him the ads in the papers? He could not see me, so I began to move closer. Then such pure voyeurism made me shy and I walked away from them to sit down and read. The paper reported in detail an interesting case of multiple rape in New Jersey. A train came in and left. Then a second. I stood up to be ready for the third only to find there was no sign of Eleanor. Nor of the blind man. He could have walked past me to the exit, but where was she, unless already on her way to the next station?

I felt like an idiot. All she had asked of me was that I keep my eyes open and I had not. Instead, I had to fidget on the edge of the platform until the train came in and then fidget in the crowded car.

The platform at Grand Central Station was jammed with secretaries and businessmen. It was like a precarious island, with trains coming in on either side and heavy square blue columns running down the edge of both platforms to obscure the view. Even the centre was broken up by a series of benches facing alternately one track, then the other. I pushed my way through the people towards the downtown end of the platform. There was no sign of her. How could I have been so stupid? It was hot in the station with such crowds of people jostling. Or was it my nerves? I worked my way back through the crowd towards the other end. They were on the last bench with Eleanor facing me. I say facing, but she was being kissed by a man who held her in a full embrace. His hair was thick and black and brushed straight back with a shine. His jacket also was black. I saw a gold chain curving around the nape of his neck.

Eleanor did not seem to be fighting him. I came closer to get her attention, only to discover that her eyes were closed, in satisfaction. Then I saw the briefcase at his feet. I moved out a bit to get a look at his face. The expression was egotistical, a decided look, quite different, but it was the same man. Perhaps my stare was too hard, perhaps I made some sound in my astonishment, because he loosened his hold and looked up to see me. I tried to turn away, but it was too late. He swore something at me – I could not hear the word, but its meaning was clear – and jumped to his feet, pulling Eleanor with him. He shoved a way for them through the crowd until he was at the far end of the platform beneath the exit stairs with Eleanor in the corner, blocking all access with his body.

He was remonstrating with her, I could see that, and

she was reassuring him each time he gestured behind himself in my direction. I came forward to put a stop to it all, but Eleanor shot me a look. I stood back a few yards, refusing to go any farther, even when he looked around and saw me still there and shouted at her again. The scene was confused by the stream of commuters and the trains rushing in and out of the station.

Eleanor managed to calm him until once again he had his arms around her and was talking in a passionate way, to which she responded. I was amazed to see someone so controlled melt on a public platform into a victim of romance. But who was this man? How had he picked out three of her ads? He was like an actor switching from type to type.

Eleanor playfully pushed him back a small distance to give herself some space to talk. I saw her soothe his arms and make some sort of promise, which at first he refused then reluctantly accepted. Somehow she effortlessly got herself free without taking her eyes off him and moved out from under the stairs towards a train coming into the station. He followed, putting out his arms, but she moved slowly, keeping just clear, and managed to get in as the door closed. I was in the next compartment.

I pushed through the connecting doors, forcing my way past the jammed passengers.

"Leave me alone!" were her only words.

"The man must be a nut. It's the same man. You realize that?"

"I didn't ask you to interfere. I asked you to watch from a distance. Now just leave me alone. I told you, you're going to ruin everything."

"Ruin what?" There was no answer. "Eleanor. Listen to me. Ruin what?"

She turned her back, and when we reached 33rd Street she shoved her way through the crowd to put a distance between us. Across the sea of heads I could just see her, waiting at the uptown end. I didn't know what to do. I was so mad I felt like leaving. That was what she wanted. But no, I wouldn't.

Nothing happened for ten minutes. A number of trains came and went, but nothing happened. Most of the time I couldn't see Eleanor. For some reason, that didn't concern me.

At a quarter to six a train came in and there was a commotion at the downtown end. Someone pushed his way forcefully out of the car, so forcefully that there were shouts. I was tall enough to make out his progress along the platform in our direction. The first thing I saw clearly was his disordered hair. Then his face. There was a shadow of a beard and his eyes were wild. Wild, but intelligent. He wore a dirty white nylon shirt. As he pushed by, he caught sight of me, and only then did I consciously register what I had been unconsciously expecting; that he was indeed the same man. He had no briefcase. I suppose he no longer needed it, this being the last appointment. He leered at me in fury and pushed on. He was a few yards past before I pulled myself together and tried to follow, though he shoved his way ahead much faster.

I couldn't see Eleanor through the crowd, but the moment he found her, there was a scream. The crowd on the platform fell absolutely silent and I heard a slap and another scream. The crowd drew back, making it even harder for me to get through. I could see nothing, only hear broken phrases.

"Do you think you can treat me that way? Do you think you can send that man after me?" The voice was strained and uneven with passion.

I couldn't hear Eleanor's replies. They were mumbled or whispered.

"Why should I believe you? What trust do I owe you? You whore!"

"Let me through!" I shouted at the people blocking my way. "For Christ's sake, let me through!"

I heard another slap and could see the movement of struggle beyond the few layers of the crowd that still blocked my way. The first sounds of a train coming in caused them all to draw back from the platform edge and I lunged that way to get by. The screech of the train braking drowned out the man's shouts. I was just in time to see him throw Eleanor onto the tracks. I saw her for only a second, then the train arrived. There was no cry. Only silence.

The crowd drew back farther as from an escaped wild animal. He saw me and screamed with rage as he charged.

I kicked as hard as I could at his groin and as he doubled over struck him on the temple with my clenched fist. He crumpled to the platform.

There was another moment's silence before the crowd pushed forward to insult his inert body. I saw a woman spit on it.

15
THE
CRIPPLE

I WENT TO STAY at the Arizona Biltmore in March this year. Why? That was what my New York friends asked. They were suffering their way through the winter rains or flying to New Yorker–sodden islands in the Caribbean and thought that a proper and normal pattern of life.

Frankly, I didn't want to see any of them or be seen after the initial inquiry into Eleanor's death. It was not easy to explain how she came to be on that platform, how I came to be there, how one man had come to play four different roles, including murderer. The *Post* latched on to the heiress, masquerade-murderer, writer angle. A redefinition of the classic triangle. I think they wanted revenge because Eleanor hadn't placed any of her advertisements with them. They made it a story about the degenerate rich. You could hardly blame them. It was a good story. Day after day it dominated page six. I suppose it could have been wonderful for book sales if I'd accepted the endless interview offers, which I didn't. Eleanor was due some dignity in her death.

So I went off to Arizona. The weather is perfect in March and the hotel remains an exquisite memory of Frank Lloyd Wright. A friend of mine lives in Phoenix and she promised to get me a room looking out over the geometric maze of gardens and bungalows. Teresa was waiting at the airport and drove us through the mess that the city has become until she had delivered me into the womb of the Biltmore, from which I didn't intend to move. My friend is an architect. She promised me there was nothing else worth opening my eyes for in the city, so I suggested she come back at eight for dinner.

I unpacked with the languor of an important event and stopped from time to time to examine the details of the room. I'll admit that those last glimpses of Eleanor would continually push back into my mind without warning. And so I focused hard on the details around me. Even the towels had been designed by Wright.

When that was done I stood in an open window, staring out at the laden orange trees. From among them a pretty woman appeared pushing a man in a wheelchair. She pushed with the distance of a butterfly manacled to a rolling rock. My room was one floor up, and as they came closer I saw that he wasn't old; in his early forties perhaps, with a detached expression.

It was only later in the afternoon, as I sat out of the sun in my cabana beside the mosaic pool, that his face reassembled in my mind and I could attach a name – Phillip Hartman. I hadn't seen him for a good five years, just after his accident. I had known his wife since child-hood. He was an engineer from a famous Massachusetts family and Margaret, his wife, was a buyer for a depart-ment store. They had dropped out of sight once he was crippled.

I rationed myself to a glass of orange juice, then succumbed to a Campari and orange juice before strolling back to the hotel. As I came through the orange trees, Hartman rolled into sight. I walked over their way and called out so that I wouldn't have to run after them. Hartman twisted his shoulders – he was apparently still paralyzed from the waist down – and stared at me as I approached.

"Hello, Phillip."

He recognized me, but he didn't say anything. Just stared at me. He'd been a good-looking man, in a Germanic way, and in spite of sitting in his wheelchair for four years still had a healthy face with what would probably be called wonderful bone structure. His hair was still blond and thick. There was no doubt, however, that his stomach bulged out from under his jacket.

I called out my name. "I haven't seen you in a good four years, Phillip."

He managed a small smile, forced. Rather than talk to me, he introduced his nurse, rudely, I thought. "This is Carol," and nothing more, as if to make her push him on.

She came out eagerly from behind the chair to shake my hand. "How nice to meet an old friend of Phillip's.

How long are you here? You must have lunch with us."
She had the grace of a hired hand. Touching and lonely.

"I'd love to." I turned back to Phillip. "How is
Margaret?"

He stared at me accusingly. "How would I know?"
This left me bewildered, which must have shown, because
he went on, "We're divorced. You can find her in New
York."

I began an apology, but he cut me off with sharp
instructions to his nurse, "We're late enough, Carol."

He hardly said goodbye. I was shocked though not
upset. But I was surprised at Margaret. She'd always had
a passion for him, far more than he for her. She could
never understand what he'd seen in her. I suppose somewhere in his heart neither could he. But for Margaret to
drop him because he had become a burden, well, it was
the sort of thing I hoped I wouldn't do myself.

I had dinner that night with Teresa in the great dining
room beneath its gold-leaf ceiling. The food was all right;
the taste of Middle America with a bit of hollandaise sauce,
in recognition of the clients' money. The tables around us
were peopled by a collection of golfers, corporate tennis
players and the odd television star, who left an impression
of dyed hair and overfilled clothes. Teresa and I stretched
out the meal. We really weren't sure whether to go to bed
together or not, so we didn't talk about it. Instead, we
talked of other people, other things.

I described my strange encounter with Hartman.

She hadn't known him in New York, yet she grew increasingly interested as I described what had happened in the garden.

"So that's who he is."

"What do you mean? How long has he been staying here?"

"He doesn't. He must live somewhere in Phoenix. But every time I come to the hotel, there he is, being pushed around the garden by his nurse. I've never seen them eat here. No. Once, I saw them have tea on a Sunday afternoon. Then she drives him off in an old Chevy. I think they come here to spend their day in decent surroundings without having to spend any money."

"But that doesn't make sense."

After Phoenix, I went to San Antonio to give a talk, then crept back to New York, where everyone wore the expression of a shabby raincoat lining. The Eleanor business seemed to have quieted down.

The day after I arrived, I met with the editor of a fashion magazine who wanted me to write a story for a spring issue – something they could tie advertisements to. After half an hour of banter the editor could see I wouldn't do what they wanted. There are depths to which … Anyway, I knew he wanted me and would give in sooner or later. There was a knock at the door and in walked Margaret Hartman. She didn't apologize for interrupting. In fact, she was so intent on giving the editor instructions that I became invisible.

It was only when she turned to leave that Margaret noticed me. I don't know why I did it, nervous reaction probably, but after a few words of greeting and glacial friendliness on her part, I mentioned that I'd run into Phillip in Phoenix. There was a sudden break in her expression. She stared at me. From within the hardness there was an abrupt glimmer, as if I'd wounded her.

But it was only a glimmer and she turned away, then left with no word of warmth. I asked the editor what she did at the magazine.

"Do?" he replied. "She doesn't do. She runs the place."

"Margaret?"

"Toughest bitch I've ever met. Smart."

"Has she got a husband?"

"Listen, it's enough to know her professionally. Anyway, she never leaves the place."

As I went out, the editor's secretary picked up her phone and said a few words. By the time I got to the elevator, Margaret was walking by. She was a little more friendly and drew me into her office, sat me down in the large, cold room in an equally large armchair, then curiously enough retreated behind her desk and sat bolt upright. Around the walls were photos of Margaret with various Kennedy women and other popcorn of the New York fashion world past and present. I noticed poor Eleanor in one group shot. And Sunny Spenser in another.

"How was Phillip?" The question was asked in a professional way.

"Don't ask me." I was a bit edgy. "He wouldn't talk. I guess I brought back memories of the old days before you left him. He had a nurse pushing him around."

Margaret blushed a deep red. "Nurse! What nurse? That was his wife."

She could see I was taken aback.

"I grant you," Margaret added, "she is a nurse." The distance and coldness had suddenly disappeared. She sat now with her weight resting on her desk. Her self-confidence had melted into humility of a sort I had never seen in her, not even before she married.

"When that accident happened, we had very little money saved. Phillip's company took no responsibility. The insurance covered the medical side, but he couldn't work, would never work again, and all I had was a crummy job with a crummy salary. We went through a very hard year while I worked day and night to get a better job and more money. We had to move into a two-room apartment on the Upper West Side. I won't say I found it easy. Everything disappeared from life except my job and looking after Phillip.

"Margaret, I didn't –"

She stopped me with a gesture. "Well, you didn't try to find out, did you?"

I began to get up to leave, but she went on talking, as if she had never told the story and needed to get it out.

"By the end of the year I was making enough to get a part-time nurse. That took some of the pressure off me.

Phillip was terribly morose. God, it was unbearable to see him. He couldn't believe his life was over. He couldn't believe he'd have to sit like a zombie in a wheelchair until he died. I suppose he could have found a way to do some work, but the willpower wasn't there. Every time I left him alone, I was afraid I'd come back to find he'd killed himself." She looked at me. Her eyes were shining. "Why should you remember how much I loved him?"

"I remember."

"He couldn't stand to hear about my work. My slaving reminded him that he did nothing. Anyway, getting the nurse gave me more time to work. More time to get more money. That was all I concentrated on, because we were still living on the borderline of poverty. It took me another two years before I was making enough to get us back to our old standard and back onto the East Side in a half-decent place. Through all of that I hardly saw Phillip. I couldn't. The only way I could help him was to work myself sick. He hardly noticed. His life consisted of his little problems and the series of nurses he gave a hard time to. He ate them up. None of them lasted more than two months. It was about two years ago that Carol appeared. You met her in Phoenix.

"She came as a full-time nurse. We had an extra bedroom, so she actually lived with us. Somebody had to be there in the evenings. I never knew what time I'd get home, and Phillip still hadn't come to terms with his state. I was certain he would kill himself if I left him alone. It became a fixation for me. I showed my love by making sure someone was with him every minute.

"I had to find some way to show it. We could hardly talk to each other; I mean, have a real conversation. Before, we had always told each other every detail of our day. Now he had no details of his own and he didn't want to hear about my successes. All he would allow me was to relay gossip about people. Working in this world," she gestured at the photos on the walls, "gossip is a staple of the day. I'd arrive home from the office either in time for dinner with Phillip and Carol or too late and too tired to eat. Then Phillip would have made up a little fiction about me having gone to a dinner party. He'd encourage me to describe who had been there. What they'd said. I could see he was laughing in his bitter way at the play we put on for Carol, who sat silent, almost afraid to ask what Furstenberg was really like. In those days I thought it was a silly diversion. Now I understand better. Phillip didn't want to feel guilty. He didn't want to be reminded that I was his sole support, that I was working late into the evenings to make his life possible.

"So we never mentioned money. We never mentioned work. I would arrive back in my wonderful clothes – which I got wholesale, if not for nothing, thanks to my job. I would appear and, as Carol opened the door, transform myself from a driven career woman into a frivolous, fashionable socialite, full of amusing stories from my inconsequential job – hobby, really – or from dinners or parties or plays, which I rarely saw, never had the time or money, but I read the reviews.

"The only mention of money would be when Phillip threw in from time to time that I or my friends understood nothing of money, that I was lucky to have such an easy life. I know it sounds crazy, but I suppose Carol thought we were very rich. How else could we pay for her without Phillip working and with me amusing myself in a minor job?

"Whatever she believed, I didn't care. She knew how to handle Phillip. She was the first nurse to last more than two months. In fact, she lasted more than a year. She became part of our family, as if she were the mother. I was the spoiled daughter and Phillip the stern father. I suppose it might have been different if Phillip and I hadn't stopped sleeping together. But that was another of his obsessions. Before the accident, he'd been so active, wonderful really. He took me in hand and made me happy. Suddenly he couldn't move. I had to do everything. We tried it a few times, but he hated it. It reminded him of how good he'd been. I felt so inadequate. So we stopped for a while, to give him a chance to forget the past, but we never started again. I was almost afraid to take the initiative and he never gave me an opening. His spirit was such a delicate bird. And I was always tired.

"After Carol had been with us for a year, I could see that Phillip was coming out of his permanent depression. For the first time in three years he had plans, ideas, an interest in the outside world.

"Then one night I came home and he was gone. He and Carol. They'd run away together. There was a note from her, not from Phillip, saying they loved each other. It was written like a letter from a mother, scolding her daughter – now you must pay for your frivolous life.

"I couldn't believe it. I didn't know what to do. I was so shocked that I acted as if it were the next act of our little play, not reality. They couldn't have been serious. They'd taken nothing, just a few clothes.

"A week later I heard from our lawyer. Phillip wanted a divorce. Would I cooperate? I did. I don't know why. I didn't know what else to do. My life had been made up of doing what Phillip wanted ever since we'd been married. What else could I do?

"Four months later it was done. The only thing that went through my mind during those months was that she must love him more than I did. I mean, I had first discovered him beautiful and active. She found him crippled. All those days together, she must have found a way to make him want to make love. I knew what it was – she carried no memory of how he had been before.

"Anyway, I went on ... you know, I went on ... I became obsessed by my work. The irony was that I was made publisher of my magazine two weeks after the divorce. Then one morning the receptionist rang through to tell me there was a woman waiting in reception who wouldn't give her name. I went out to find Carol.

"She walked into this office, looked around bitterly

and said, 'I knew it.' What, I couldn't imagine. She didn't leave me time to guess. 'Phillip has either gone crazy or you got his money in the divorce. I knew he was a fool. But not that much of a fool.'

"'What money?' I said.

"'His money!' she shouted at me. 'He says he hasn't got a penny. He says he never had a penny.'

"'He never did.'

"'You're lying. You tricked me. You wanted to get rid of him, you bitch. Do you think I'd have taken him if he had no money? How can we live? He says I'll have to work. The way you did.'"

She remembered Carol looking around bitterly at the photos on the walls. "All those people I had told her about. I was overwhelmed. She thought she was getting a crippled millionaire. She didn't love Phillip at all. The most disturbing thing was her eyes. They were literally filled with contempt and hatred. 'Poor Phillip,' I said without thinking.

"She saw her opening and made an effort to control herself. Instead of raging on, she described the tiny apartment they were renting. She had begun working part-time. That meant Phillip was alone. He'd fallen into a terrible depression. She was worried about him. By the time she'd finished, I'd agreed to give them a small allowance, providing she looked after Phillip full-time. It isn't much, not enough to live in New York. So they moved to Phoenix. She's from there. They're living in a room in her parents' house somewhere in the suburbs."

"My poor Margaret," was all I could say. I wanted to embrace her, but she was locked behind her desk.

She willed the iron protection back over her eyes. "It's too late for all of that now. I'm on another road. I prefer not to remember."

16
CHATTING WITH
A DICTATOR'S ASSASSIN

IN JANUARY THE GOVERNMENT announced that the preceding year's inflation rate had been fifty percent. My friends said this was an official number, by which they meant mythological. I could see no change in Belgrade. It remained rundown. Indistinct in a clammy, yellowish coal smoke of the sort that over the winter months had once enveloped every European city.

The best restaurant was still in the basement of the Writers' Union, a nineteenth-century stone palace across the road from the Officers' Club, which had the power and the money, but not the chef. That is to say, not the papal legate's ex-cook, Ivo, who had controlled the kitchen of the Writers' Union for years.

In spite of St. Francis and the Christian tradition of physical purity, the pope's senior officials around the world have always had a taste for good food. Perhaps sauces make up for sexual abstinence. Perhaps the best way to identify which cardinals keep their vows of celibacy is to eat at their tables.

As for Ivo's restaurant, everyone ate there. Officers, diplomats, the secret service and the writers. And not simply for the food, but to overhear, to spread rumours, to see. All of that was unchanged. Even a searching glance at the crowd of diners would not have told you that the Marshal had been dead seven years. My friends claimed that there was an invisible vacuum, in the restaurant and in the country, which only the military could fill – or rather, inevitably would end up filling. The inflation was unbearable. It couldn't go on. Foreigners could stuff themselves at Ivo's for the price of a fast-food snack in the West, but for the locals it was another matter. I was working my way through a second bowl of *kesten-pire sa šlagom* – chestnut purée with cream and chocolate – while my friends shouted about the crisis and smoked. They were relatively typical Yugoslavs – the product of Serbs sleeping with Croats sleeping with Bosnians sleeping with Montenegrins sleeping with Slovenians sleeping with Russians sleeping with Germans. As writers, they knew that in an era of obsessional racial purity their haematic reality was irrelevant. Events would identify them as pure something and deal with them accordingly. For the moment they were Serbs.

Quietly under the noise Dara leaned over and said, "You ought to meet Archduke Ferdinand's assassin." Her tone implied that this would clarify everything.

I put my spoon back in my bowl and looked carefully at her before replying, "Princip died in an Austrian prison in 1918."

She laughed, which was far enough out of character with the lugubrious talk around the table to draw the others' attention. "Not Princip. Vaso Čubrilović. There were seven assassins. It was a terrorist group. Čubrilović is the last one left."

I suppose I was looking bemused by this unexpected historical detail, because Aleksandar, the only historian among us, broke in from the other end of the table. "Three of them started out for Sarajevo by train in late May with a suitcase full of pistols and bombs. This gave them one month to prepare for the Archduke's visit. In Sarajevo their local control, Ilić, helped them recruit three more men – a Turk in his late twenties and two students. Čubrilović was one of them. He was seventeen, I believe. The plan was that each would have a bomb and/or pistol. And cyanide, of course, so they could commit suicide rather than be tortured and risk implicating the others. When the royal party arrived on June 28, the six assassins mixed into the crowd lined up on the quay. Each was fifty metres apart. The Turk was first, Čubrilović second, on the corner of the Cumurja Bridge. Čabrinović was third. He threw a bomb. It bounced off the back of the folded-down top of the Archduke's car, one of those high, long, sleek limousines." He paused, visibly searching. "I don't remember the make, although …" Dara threw a piece of bread at him. "All right. Details matter, you know." Aleksandar looked mildly wounded. "Anyway, the bomb rolled under the vehicle behind and exploded. There were twenty wounded. Arms blown off. Disfigured faces. The victims were mostly courtiers and aides-de-camp. People who care about their looks."

"But what did Čubrilović do?" I interrupted.

"Oh, he was very young. Not a professional terrorist. Neither was the Turk. They both lost their nerve when the Archduke rolled by. And when the bomb went off they all panicked and ran, except for Princip, who tried to get into a position to fire. The Archduke was a sitting duck. To be exact, he climbed down from his car and wandered around comforting his wounded courtiers who were spread out on the ground. Very grand seigneur. Very courageous. Not a thought for his own safety. But Princip couldn't get a shot off."

"What do you mean?"

"He was too short. He couldn't see over the crowd. Princip was a miserable little creep."

"Aleksandar!" they all shouted at him.

"Oh, the national hero! Give me a break. He was a weak, unintelligent, unhappy runt of a failure. He was killing the Archduke to prove himself. The classic inferiority complex syndrome." Aleksandar seemed chastened by his own declaration. "Anyway, it was pure chance that he got a second opportunity in the afternoon. A second chance and a clear shot at close range. Fate! I believe he turned his head away before pulling the trigger. Two shots to the heart, I mean to the hearts of the royal couple. At first it wasn't clear what had happened. The Archduke's uniform was so tight, the material thick, her corset, all those layers of clothing. There was no visible blood, yet they seemed to have lost consciousness. The crowd had to be cleared, the limousine backed up to the quay, then they drove in a panic along the river to the bridge, back along the quay on the other side, up the hill to the local royal residence, carried them through the corridors, up the grand staircase to their suite, laid them out on their beds side by side. The protocol around those Habsburgs was really something. The very idea that someone might handle them in a personal way. And there they were, in a provincial capital, far from Vienna, surrounded by provincial officials and servants, all of whom knew they had failed, that their own careers were now ruined, as much the smart young people who had accompanied the Archduke from Vienna as the local lot. Eventually someone unbuttoned his uniform and the blood poured out."

"So Čubrilović got away?"

"No. They were all caught and tried. Ilić was hung. Princip got twenty years. Čubrilović got sixteen, I think."

It is always amazing what history doesn't retain. The other assassins for a start. And their trials – the legal examination of a civilization. The arrangement of Europe, which had been produced on the battlefield of Waterloo a century before, was swept away. And the Austro-Hungarian Empire disintegrated as if it had never existed.

In place of my reflections I simply asked, "You mean these local patriots assassinated the great Satan and the response of the evil empire was to give them a fair trial? They weren't tortured? Raped? Their tongues weren't pulled out?"

This was greeted by what I took to be a mournful silence. At last Aleksandar said, "Well, they were under age."

"Doesn't sound like much of a dictatorship."

There was another silence. "You should meet Čubrilović," Dara repeated.

IT TOOK TWO DAYS to arrange. I used the forty-eight hours to find out more about him. His prison sentence had been commuted after the war. He'd gone back to university and eventually become a history professor, then a communist. During the Second World War he had served in the Marshal's guerrilla army and had gone on to become a cabinet minister. With the gradual elimination of Tito's rivals he had become the leading ideologue of the Yugoslav movement.

I was told to go to the Academy of Sciences and Arts where, as an historian, he had an office. Dara had agreed to translate, although it turned out that he spoke some English and French.

The academy was one of those grand provincial clubs of learning which had sprung up all over the West in the late nineteenth century. There was no one walking up or down the marble steps outside, no one in the great hall, no one in the reception rooms. A deep silence. Then doors opened and closed with that hollow sound produced by empty halls with overly waxed floors. Dara appeared with a sort of club steward, I suppose from somewhere in behind. He led us up to the second floor and left us in a very small room. A desk. A chair behind it, two chairs in front. Nothing on the desk. Nothing on the walls. Everything was either dark polished wood or cream paint.

Ten minutes later the steward reopened the door and the assassin came through. He was slightly taller standing than I was seated. Čubrilović looked at neither of us, but made a rapid concentrated movement towards his chair. He wore a heavy, perfectly pressed, grey-brown double-breasted suit. A ministerial suit. Thick glasses. A Neville Chamberlain moustache, which suggested that he had fixed his self-image in the 1930s, in early middle-age. Men tend to do that, just at the moment when their public disguise crystallizes. His skin was the parchment of a ninety-year-old. There was very little flesh.

The moment he was seated he took out a large black fountain pen and placed it in the centre of the desk, pointing from right to left. It lay there as a weapon that could be picked up at any moment to draw a line along the middle of the surface between us, like a tennis-court net or a metaphysical trench. But for the moment it simply lay there, somehow looming ever larger. More than a barrier. A wall. A wall of rubble. The rubble of potential written words. There was no paper. He placed his hands, fingers interlocked, just behind the pen. Then he flashed a stare at me and shot out, "Alors, monsieur?" It was a clear, sharp sound.

I was so taken aback that I heard myself saying what I was thinking. "Can you pay too much for a nation?"

Before Dara could begin translating, he dismissed my phrase.

"Oh, the old question!" He picked up the pen and threw it down a few inches closer to me. Still parallel between us. "You mean was it worth killing the Archduke given the slaughter of the world war it provoked?"

"More or less," I replied sheepishly.

"I'm an historian. There is no 'if' in history. Only what happened. What didn't happen."

It was very odd. His body remained immobile in the way of a store dummy. But his head snapped about and he moved his arms as if he had fingers beginning at the elbows.

"You surely don't mean that war is always inevitable?"

He smiled as if to say that now I was asking proper questions. "That's not the point. It's a matter of real-ities. I was born in a narrow little Serbian world. The broad, inclusive Yugoslav mentality we have now didn't exist. The assassination was a practical reflection of our situation. Besides, the Habsburgs were semi-feudal ..."

He trailed off abruptly, as if bored by the classical inter-pretation of history. How many times? Those words? Those explanations? Then with a fresh surge of energy he grabbed his pen back and almost shouted at me, "Now, with television and computers, nations have little import- ance. Software will lead the way."

"You mean you're an optimist?"

"Why not? History always corrects its mistakes. You want to talk about violence. I tell you, countries which still go to war are undeveloped. I believe in progress. I see it everywhere. Yesterday I met with a group of Japanese computer experts. It is perfectly feasible to link Yugoslavs together by an information network which can penetrate to the local level."

He went on about the romance of technology for some time. I was tempted to remind him of the romance of tech- nology preceding the First World War. What I wanted to ask him was how he had felt waiting in the crowd on the quay for the Archduke's car to pass. The people around him must have been there to gawk or to cheer and he was there to die, because his own death was the probable, in fact the planned, result of him firing a shot. He must have had the cyanide in one of his pockets along with the pistol or the bomb. Or was the cyanide somehow pinned to his clothing? There was the standard spot for the anarchists of the late nineteenth, early twentieth centuries. Pinned under your lapel. Close to your mouth. Less time between deciding to die and dying. A few centimetres to move the hand from the lapel to the lips. But from a pocket, well, that could be fifty or sixty centimetres. Almost a full physical gesture from way down there. So much distance over which to hesitate. On the other hand, how would a vial of cyanide be pinned under a lapel? Would it be hard to unpin? Would it require a conscious mechanical act? And how had he felt as the car passed with the royal couple waving; that is, as he failed to pull out his pistol? After all, that was his moment. The perfect existential moment. He had come to act, determined to act, certain that he would act. And then he had stood, frozen. Hands trying to move. Not moving. If he was sitting there in front of me it was because of a personal failure. Then there was his statement at the trial – "When I saw the Archduke I could not bring myself to kill him." I suppose his lawyer or his parents had forced him to take the respectful approach. Or had he simply been reduced by then to the paralyzed state of a frightened teenager?

Čubrilović made a last comment on modern communications, pocketed his pen, heaved himself to his feet and put out a hand to say goodbye. One of those handshakes of people who have done it all their lives for a profession. The strength of the grip, in the end, far exceeds the strength of the body. I left Dara in the street and went back to the Hotel Yugoslavia, a Stalinist block trembling on the side of the autoroute, which it faced. With perfect modernist logic, freed of all romanticism, the building backed onto the Danube, as if it were a ditch, to be ignored. I walked along the bank in the grey-yellow light perhaps half a mile to a small bar floating on pontoons out on the water. It was meant to be an amusing, summery place. I sat inside on a metal chair. There were no other customers. The waitress was dressed up. There were frills on her gown. She wore thick red lipstick in the style of the 1920s and had a black moustache. I ordered *žito sa šlagom* – crushed wheat, walnuts and dried raisins with cream – and thought about the old man.

Princip had talked at his trial of "sweet and bloody revenge," although the local military commander was probably the real, unintentional, killer. Despite prolonged rumours of an assassination attempt in the works he had decided to save a miserable little sum on his annual budget by not ordering in extra police protection. And the Archduke was a liberal reformer, out to help the minorities. He was distrusted by the courtiers in Vienna. Of course, even if the Empire wasn't particularly oppressive in normal times, it was pompous, insulting and vicious when threatened, like all empires. And it was there. Then there was all that Bosnian blood, so special, waiting to express itself. How could the world be other than better off for such purity?

The failed assassin-become-minister had also become bored with blood over the years. That seemed to be at the core of his optimism. He was now exalted by software. Perhaps he sensed that some new mythology was necessary to distract people in a time of political emptiness. Certainly he'd had the time to consider the ramifications of blood worship. As things turned out it was a good three more years before they started to kill each other in earnest.

"I BELIEVE YOU KNEW my father."

He had walked forward in a deliberate way so as to force my eyes up from where I sat. His face was familiar, but only the familiarity of someone passed periodically in the street.

"Not to my knowledge." I said these words politely and made a sign for him to join me on the sofa if he wished. The seat was low-slung, deep, scarcely inflated by tired feathers, easy to sink into, difficult to escape. Had we been elsewhere than a club, there'd have been no offer.

Only in London would I bother belonging to that kind of organization. In New York, clubs are fatuous, in Paris irrelevant and in other cities merely a confirmation of provinciality. However, most of what I do in London happens not far from the West End and it rarely involves more than two meetings a day. Apart from that I see friends, perhaps do some research at Chatham House or the British Library, go to the auction houses, the galleries and the bookstores. So a club becomes a way station. Useful.

This may sound an unadventurous approach to London; but it's that sort of city – a place to make money and to strive after comfort. Not comfort as the rich see it in New York, with their beseiged-fortress attitudes; nor in Paris, where it is a thing to be enjoyed as a secret right. No, London, for those who can afford it, is a place of relaxed comfort, a city of invisible walls behind which you can hide without noticeable effort.

That I didn't know this fellow member now sitting beside me was not surprising. I don't seek new friends when I come to St. James's. I seek only peace. And had I been in the seeking mood, he would not have figured on my list.

He was one of those Englishmen who have grasped successfully at the least imaginative of what their class and their means offer them. I could have drawn up a list of where he bought or had made every item he wore, probably even his underwear, without seeing it. I could have done the same for his opinions and would still have discovered nothing of interest. He was probably a banker.

He lowered himself onto the sofa in a proprietary way until his dark blue blended into the olive-green slipcover. I closed my book to gaze at him. There was an awkward superiority in his manner. I suppose he wondered how a North American had got by the membership committee; how he himself had not been more vigilant.

"My name is Harry Williams."

I nodded in reply, but "Harry Williams" meant nothing to me and he saw this.

"It was only recently that I learned of my father's connection with you. It was through his diaries. His solicitor was also his close friend and he, the solicitor, took it upon himself to keep the notebooks. I was finishing school at the time and I suppose he thought it best to wait and see. The fellow died in January of this year – the solicitor. His junior partner came upon the notebooks while running through the files and sent them to me, unopened, or so he said."

Having got this far, Williams paused, unable to disguise the uncertainty that crept over his face. I guessed that he had rehearsed only his first words and was now ahead of his thoughts. I offered him a drink. He refused silently.

"My father was an American," he let fall, "like you."

Nothing could have surprised me more. I'd have guessed that Williams's father had been what Williams himself appeared to be – a perfect model rising out of the depths of the English upper middle class, southwest variety, all soft edges and careful tones. As for my being Canadian, I sensed he wasn't the sort of person for whom this detail would matter.

"Not my mother," he added with haste. And then with curious ease, "It took me some time to work out that you were the man. Only subsequently did I learn that you also belonged here. It was an unexpected coincidence." He had veered off track and now threw himself back on. "But it is not so difficult to find out about people and their back-grounds once you set your mind to it." This was said with an attempt at significance which fell clumsily from his mouth, and when he saw again my patient incomprehen-sion, he added almost sheepishly, "Funny that you should have made such a mark on him and yet you remember nothing."

He was beginning to bore me, even within the confines of politeness dictated by where we sat. But before I could protest, he had got to his feet.

"If you stop at the porter's desk on the way out, you'll find I've left a few pages for you."

He made an awkward, broken gesture to indicate farewell and turned to go. I went back to my book. I have never ceased to be amazed by the extent to which people think their lives are relevant to yours when you have become famous enough for your life to be known to them. On my way out later the porter reminded me that an envelope had been left with my name on it.

I got back to my hotel in the early morning after a long dinner and wandered around the room turning on the small lights, which threw uneven haloes across the darkness of the panelled walls. It was a hotel that special-ized in comfort. Even the darkness had a warm feel to it. I undressed, collapsed in bed and only as a last thought pulled the envelope towards me from the side table. It held four photocopies of pages written on by hand. They appeared to have come from a small bound notebook, as two pages showed on each photocopy. The handwriting was large and clear. The line was heavy, the punctuation assured. I flipped through without reading. Each day began on a new page, and as some days had few words devoted to them there was a lot of blank space. The visual impression was a bit stolid, an overbearing insistence on simplicity and yet also of elegance.

At the top of the first page someone else had printed with a black felt pen on the photocopy itself, "1969." I suppose Harry Williams had done it for my benefit.

4 NOVEMBER

Left London 10 A.M. Arrived Paris noon. Straight to flat. As always, a sense of relief and freedom. Phoned B. Lunch alone at Le Duc. Napoleon exhibition Grand Palais. What a phony, with his clan favouritism dressed up as reform. Met B for dinner. Brasserie of the Closerie des Lilas. As usual, made me wait. Really, what a hollow body. Apart from the extra-ordinary appearance, the sleekness, the insolent assurance, there is nothing. Insolence about what? With what justifica-tion? There isn't an idea, a taste, not even a real emotion beneath the skin. I'm sure of that. How can the anticipation and the momentary pleasure be worth the rest? I cannot see it when I consider all rationally. I write this with B lying beside me, so comfortable beneath my sheets; and so beautiful if contact is limited. I should like to reach out to take the hair in my hands and shake it, but I know I won't.

5 NOVEMBER

Left Paris 11 A.M. Arrived London at same hour. Straight to
office. Immediately the boredom comes over me. The shock
of these returns is worse than the elation of escape. Lunch at
my desk to catch up, then to London Library for a break.

I did not mention yesterday that a young man sitting
across from us at dinner seemed to take a particular interest.
Each time I looked up, I found him staring. No doubt we
make a strange pair. For a start there is the difference of
age. Then there are B's looks. I suppose also my ridiculous
behaviour.

Today, as I came into St. James's Square, I saw getting out
of a taxi ...

The page dropped from my hands. Where had the
memory been hidden? Of course! Of course! Williams.
Charles Williams. I was consumed by embarrassment
though alone and lying in half-darkened silence.

By November 1969, I had been in Paris six months,
having come to France with the excuse of studying, but
in reality to write, though I hardly knew it myself at the
time. Naive romanticism in part had drawn me there;
in part the realization that without money, as I was, it
would be impossible to go on doing nothing in North
America. Paris is not a romantic place. It is a temple to
egotism. That is what draws writers and painters – a
place where no one feels self-conscious about their own
poverty while they are finding out if they have any talent.

And if it turns out that they haven't, well, they go home to become stockbrokers or brassiere salesmen and their Paris period is remembered in a soft haze as a romantic interlude of youth.

I was then in the full throes of egotism and poverty. I lived in a small hotel on Avenue de l'Observatoire, just across from the Closerie des Lilas. The room cost eleven francs a day, cheaper than the Cité Universitaire in which I'd begun. One window, a small bed. It was on the sixth floor, a shared toilet on the landing, a locked bathroom on the fourth. You paid for each use of the tub. The other rooms were filled with students and political refugees. Paris always has an overload of both. Across the hall from me there was a Romanian painter – a self-declared refugee – and his wife, once beautiful, still with an aura of past beauty floating about her. To make extra money – he sold little – she acted as night clerk and told fortunes from behind the desk.

What money I saved on the room was kept for eating. It is hard to explain, now that food and wine are like religions. There was then a more practical side to restaurants. For example, there was always a great contrast between the expensive bourgeois restaurant of the Closerie des Lilas and its cheap simple brasserie. These two arms were separated by the bar, the heart of the place. I suppose I went there often because so many other writers had done the same; the ghosts of Proust, of Hemingway, of Gide, of Lenin were still there. And because it still had the feel

of that great Paris invention, the American bar. The cock-
tails were as complicated as they had always been. No
one ordered gin martinis, because they were the most
common object on the list.

I ate in the brasserie, a long, thin, enclosed pavilion
built out over the sidewalk of Boulevard Montparnasse.
From there I could hear the piano player in the bar work
his way through a litany of tunes without noticing myself
which was which. In the summer I had invariably ordered
fish; once winter arrived I had switched to steak tartare
or oysters. They were cheap enough then, and a dozen
oysters provided more than enough protein. There were
two rows of tables with a bench running down each wall
and a row of chairs facing each of them. It was a small
room with a low awning as ceiling. I went there whenever
I was alone and made a point of eating slowly while
fiddling with pen and paper.

The month had been damp from the first day, which
was expected of November in Paris. The rain had
somehow got through to my ego, so that I half-wondered
what I was doing on my sixth floor; the realities of living
on nothing are clearer in cold, wet weather than in the
dry heat.

The fourth of November was particularly clear because
of what happened. I had tired of my room by late afternoon and gone down to run through the rain to the
Closerie, where I rubbed my hair dry with my scarf and
ordered a beer, a Belgian beer, which I nursed until eight,

then got to my feet long enough to move from the bar to the brasserie and order another beer with lamb and white beans. These I ate slowly while working on some poem, long since hidden away.

Shortly before nine my eyes were drawn to a man entering the room. He was sixty, I suppose, and of average height. He was American, but not American in the sense we mean today. He was American with the elegance of a Scott Fitzgerald character. His clothes had a fine detail of line and colour, and yet there was also an ease, an informality, about him. Elegance and informality are no longer ideas that we put together. That marriage has been lost in an age of extremes and compartmentalization. Never has there been such an age of uniforms as this one. Never has the dictatorship of massive insecurity come down so violently in favour of single, colourless solutions. "This is informal!" they say. "Wear this or die!" and an army of blue jeans goes by.

He could, I suppose, have been English; something out of Coward or Waugh. But no, what made him American was the masculine confidence with which he carried himself. The ease of his movements. He slipped onto a bench across from me and put his grey felt hat on the ledge behind him. He had not carried an umbrella, so the hat was speckled with rain. The felt was soft and pliant, the brim just a bit wider than expected, but not too wide, the ribbon a shade lighter and at first surprising. It was a very fine hat.

As was the face. It was not an unusual face; there were no features I could fasten on to that made him a handsome man. Everything was in order and in proportion. It was a clean face, not just clean-shaven, but covered by a smooth, firm skin; though none of that was what made it remarkable. My attention was held rather by the elegance of the face itself. What showed in the clothes carried on into the way the man moved his mouth when he said a few words to a waiter; an effortless clear way of talking; the lips neither held tight nor puckered nor opened too wide nor expressing any emotional insecurities nor betraying any ignorance of the self. The same was true of the way he moved his eyes. They pierced no one and yet did not hesitate to look. The gaze was one of acceptance. It was the elegance of spirit that held my attention; something that I had never truly seen before – the man's profound urbanity. But for these two words – elegance and urbanity – to take on their proper meaning, you must try to see them without the normal superficial appendages of class and of style.

In place of class and style he radiated intelligence and understanding. I felt instantly that behind this face there was a man who had grasped the meaning of all around him and made use of this knowledge to live his life without drama.

I could see his feet under the table. The shoes were light and formed to his shape; laced, but of calf. He ordered a whisky sour and without looking at the list told them to open a specific bottle of wine. I knew it wasn't one of the brasserie's limited choice, so it must have been from the restaurant list. He apparently knew the place well. It was curious I had never seen him before.

There was a slight slouch about the way he sat, and when his drink came he took a small gulp with pleasure, then gazed up and down the room. I went back to my poem.

The next time I looked up it was well after nine. The man was fiddling with his empty cocktail glass. I noticed a slight change in his manner. The easy calm had an exasperated edge. I noticed also at least seven colours in the thin stripes of his shirt, but they blended so perfectly one into the other that it was impossible to describe them separately. The collar rolled in to button behind the tie.

As I watched, he swung to his feet with a brusque move. The suddenness was surprising in him. I followed his stare. He had risen to greet a young man who strode down the aisle towards us. The aisle was too narrow for a stride, half-blocked as it was by people's chairs, but he strode in any case. It was an overly conscious way of walking; an approach to life, if you like, which I guessed he would attempt to impose on any surrounding.

The young man was thin and he held his body, wore his clothes, in the same way that he walked. It was all a preconceived notion; a rigid idea of style, which is the opposite of the real thing. He wore a blazer and grey flannels with a pale-blue shirt and a narrow tie. The whole outfit was no doubt the conception of some shop on the Champs Élysées; at best, of Saint Laurent. A little uniform.

The two men shook hands at a maximum distance from each other for the briefest of seconds, their palms touching just long enough for the newcomer to manoeuvre himself around onto the banquette, leaving the outer chair for the older man, whose face I could now no longer see. But I sensed a light reproach from the movement of his head. He was interrupted by the Frenchman, who moved his lips and their entire supporting apparatus of flesh and muscle well out in front of his teeth before beginning to talk in an articulated manner. It was a justification for his lateness, which the American indicated was unnecessary by a nod of his head.

"Que veux-tu manger?"

"Les huîtres et un filet," the young man insisted, as if it might be refused him.

The American called the waiter over without seeming to make any sound and ordered two dozen oysters, half Belons, half Portuguese (they had not yet caught their mysterious black death in the sea and so could still be bought in Paris), number 3; that is, not too large. He then asked the young man his news. Bernard – that seemed to be his name – unleashed myriad minor preoccupations, each accompanied by difficulties. He worked in a shop where he was victimized by his employer. The hot water system had broken down in his apartment. He had been insulted by a policeman – "Un sale flic! J'aurais dû l'insulter à mon tour" – and a dry cleaner had shrunk his other good trousers.

The American listened to all of this patiently, with good humour; even interjected little suggestions and, when it was over, asked if he had yet seen the Napoleon exhibit. The man seemed not to understand the question, so the American went ahead to describe what he himself had seen and felt. He was listened to in silence. No, not listened to. Bernard was silent, and when the description was finished he made no comment. They said nothing more to each other until the oysters arrived. The American drank his from the shell; his friend put a spoonful of vinegar sauce on each and used a fork.

Eating oysters is such an involved business that there was no call for conversation, but when they had finished the silence persisted. The American pointed at a poster on the wall and asked if Bernard had seen the exhibition it advertised. The answer was no. He encouraged his friend to go, the way a father might encourage a son to educate himself. Braque, he said, might appear to be a boring painter, a painter lacking in colour and spirit, but he was nevertheless a genius. There was genius in the fineness of his execution. He was never the one to produce the most evocative painting of a given style, but he would be the one to take that style to its logical conclusion. Technically he would take cubism, for example, as far as cubism could be taken.

Bernard waited with impatience for him to finish, and yet when he did finish had nothing to say himself. They sat mute until the American found another subject; this time it was music. He had heard of a new pianist who played often in Paris but had not yet come to London. Polini. His friend stared straight ahead.

Never have I had such a sense of purchased time; certainly not among my meagre experiences of life that preceded that night. There was a pain. There must have been a pain, because I felt it. By rights it should have oozed from the purchased young man. He was the exploited. He was the Marxian victim. He was there because he had no choice. And yet I sensed no emotion from him. Perhaps experience had taught him how to wall it in. Perhaps it had been killed by whatever marginal life he had led. Or perhaps he was simply too transparent to know any emotion other than petulance, justified or unjustified. In any case, the pain I sensed came from the American. The nature of it I could not guess. I could see that he wished to draw his friend into the warm fold of his own knowledge and calm and, I suppose, to give some dignity to their relations by taking them beyond the bought dinner and the night that would follow.

The pain, which I suffered on his behalf, because we are all creatures of the herd, made me lose interest in my poem and stare up at them whenever their eyes were not turned in my direction. I say their eyes, because the window above the bench threw enough of a reflection for the American to see clearly behind himself. Of course, more than human empathy held my attention. Curiosity went along with it and I'd be foolish to pretend otherwise.

A number of times they caught my eyes fixed in their direction and I was forced to look down. The nature of their conversation – or lack of conversation – caused them to eat quickly and by eleven they were gone. It was another half-hour before I myself left, passing beneath the shadow of Marshal Ney's statue, placed where he had stood before his firing squad and died. I crossed over to my hotel. The Romanian night clerk was behind the counter brushing her hair, which was long and thick with a burnished chestnut colour. She opened her generous lips to give me a warm smile and I wondered what would happen if I tried to kiss her.

I was up early the next morning to take the train to London. The trip had been planned for some time. I wanted to consult documents at Chatham House, where I had a student membership, to buy some books, to see a friend who had gone to live in England at the same time I had gone to France. From Charing Cross I took a taxi to St. James's Square, and there, as I stooped to get out, my eyes twisted up to focus on a man strolling by. My stare would not break, yet I didn't know him.

He was English, probably a businessman of the conservative school; he had that shambling way of walking, as if to efface himself. He carried a heavy black umbrella with a rubber tip on the wooden end. His feet were protected by heavy black shoes, well shined. He wore a suit of thick grey wool, pinched in at the waist in a stiff way, and the broad, bold stripes of his shirt were witness of Harvie and Hudson, the shop preferred by successful businessmen who wanted a striking colour that could not be misinterpreted. He had the look of a man who walked a great deal and did it not for his health and only peripherally for any pleasure that might be found in the surroundings.

I stared so long that the taxi driver was obliged to do the same, until the passerby found his own eyes pulled in our direction. When he saw me he broke his stride. A look of disorder came over him. It was only a second before he recovered and strode on along the north side of the square towards the London Library, a large, private institution. I paid the driver and took my bags into Chatham House, where I explained to the porter that I was expected. Only then did it come to me.

The American of the night before! I had seen him first as a fine, rare beast in particular circumstances. Here, in London, he had transformed himself into a most ordinary of beings – a perfectly predictable Englishman – solid and unimaginative. But no, it wasn't possible. The clothes could be changed, perhaps even the way of walking, but not the manner, not the ease, not the spirit. How could a man banish one soul and summon up another? No, it was a case of vague resemblance. But why had he panicked when he saw me?

I turned my back on the porter and ran out onto the square only to see the man disappear into the London Library. He looked behind him as he went in and I thought it a furtive glance. He saw me, seventy yards away, staring at him. A second later he was through the door.

Long after he had disappeared, I stood staring after him, then walked along the sidewalk until I stood outside the library. Why? Even now I can hardly say. At the time I thought about it not at all. My actions were just that and nothing more.

I have always been drawn by the unexpected, which this clearly was, so I stood before the door trying to digest what I had seen. There were no ulterior motives to my curiosity, only astonishment at the ingenuity of the man. I don't know why, but after five minutes, instead of going back to my business I went into the garden in the centre of the square and sat on a bench where I had a clear view of the library's glass door. Other members went in and out. The air was damp and cold; a penetrating cold once you stopped moving.

I suppose it was then that the writer's mind first intervened, because I began to imagine the scenarios surrounding the little I knew. An hour later a taxi drew up. My man came quickly out through the library door and slipped in. I rose to keep him in sight but could not see his face – he was turned the other way as the taxi went past. Could I really be so certain it was the same person? His actions seemed suspicious, but were they? Or was it because I sought meaning in them? Why shouldn't he leave by taxi? Why should he look at me?

I got to my feet and was carried by slow steps towards the library, hesitated a moment outside, then strode forward to pull the door open. Behind it was a porter. I approached him with a confused air. "Excuse me, but I've just missed my friend. He drove off in a taxi as I arrived. I was late."

"Mr. Williams, you mean, sir?"

"Yes. Could you help me? I don't have his office number with me. I ought to phone him to apologize. Would you have it?"

"I couldn't give you any telephone numbers, sir, but," he had started running through a list of members, "here." He turned the book around for me:

> Charles J. Williams
> Chairman
> Bentley Holdings
> 16 Upper Brook Street
> London, W 1

I made a note of it, thanked him and walked back to Chatham House. Again, why I did all of this I cannot say. I simply did it. Once back at Chatham House I gathered up the documents which had justified my trip to England and went to work on the first floor in a small high-ceilinged room that looked out over the square. This had been Chatham's private study in the years that he owned the house. After less than an hour my concentration dissolved.

As if by automatic pilot, fingers brought the scrap carrying Williams's address out of my pocket to be stared at, then legs sent me in search of the London phone book. His company was there. I noted the number then turned to look under "Williams." There were pages of them. I worked my way through without finding him. Either he had an unlisted number or he lived in the suburbs. Which would be most likely? *Who's Who* might have given the answer, but there was no mention of him. I went back to my work, found myself still unable to concentrate, and so gave up for the day, collected my bag downstairs and took the Underground to my friend's flat on Craven Road, north of the park.

That night I thought a great deal about Williams. It was the sort of story a writer might search after all his life. I could almost have written it without knowing more, but my fascination for the reality still unknown was greater than the fiction I knew could be invented.

In the morning I walked over to the Underground on my way back to Chatham House, but once beneath the earth I found myself staring at the maps posted on the platform and realized that the distance from the Green Park tube station to Williams's office was not too much farther than the distance from the same station to St. James's Square, where I was meant to be going. Either way, it would be a pleasant walk. Feeble reasoning? I avoided the question while waiting on the platform and avoided it again on the crowded train. When we arrived at Green Park I pushed my way off, took the escalator up to the surface and began walking along Berkeley Street. Fifteen minutes later I was at 16 Upper Brook Street. It was an eighteenth-century brick house converted into offices. By the door was a single engraved name – Bentley Holdings – which implied that they used all four floors. I walked up the three steps of the porch, pushed open the door and found myself in the reception area. A middle-aged woman gave me a tentative but matronly smile.

"Excuse me," I said, now unsure of what to do, "I'm interested in your company's portfolio. Could I have any information on it?"

"You're not on our lists, then?"

"No, I'm not. But I'd like to be."

"Well, perhaps you could leave me your card?"

I certainly looked hapless for a few seconds, but recovered. "Let me write it down for you." I pulled out my pen and she pushed her notepad forward. I printed my name and the address of my hotel in Paris.

When she saw this she made a little sound, a restrained "ah." Her natural matronly qualities were surfacing. "So you live in Paris. Lucky you."

I smiled obligingly. "That's why I wanted to come here while visiting London. I hoped you might have some documentation."

"I could give you our annual report, if that would be of interest."

"Oh yes. That would be of great interest."

She got to her feet and moved – there was some weight upon her – out of the room. I looked around. It was all very plain. The walls were cream. A fireplace sat as it must have sat in the original hallway. The waiting room furniture was solid English stuff. There were no pictures; only a half-dozen framed stock offer forms. A second later she was back with a large but thin envelope. I thanked her and made my way out. It was just after 10 A.M. I wasn't more than ten yards away when a Rover pulled up outside with Mr. Williams driving. He glanced at me before going in; it was a solid disinterested look. Surely this was the same man. It wasn't my imagination. Why had we been drawn together? What was expected of me? I walked on to the corner and there turned back to contemplate the illegally parked Rover, then jotted down the licence-plate number. A young man in shirt sleeves came out and drove the car away. I suppose he was the office boy charged with parking it.

I walked back to St. James's Square and Chatham's study, where I pulled the brochure out of its envelope. Annual reports have always been a mystery to me, even when glossy and photograph-laden, as was this one. The various investments made by the company were laid out. Bentley Holdings seemed to be some sort of fund in which people could buy shares. The fund then profited or floundered on the quality of the particular investments made by the management. A list of officers was printed at the back, along with their home addresses. I suppose that was a legal obligation. Mr. Williams lived in Kingston upon Thames – good solid stockbroker territory.

Not that it was a place I'd been. It was only a name that surfaced now and again in novels. Of one thing I was certain: the other half of Mr. Williams's paradox would be found there. In Paris I had caught a glimpse of a private life; or rather, one face of a private life. The other face was in Kingston, not at Bentley Holdings. I thought about that for a while, then phoned the railway stations until I found the right train and its times. Only then did the ridiculousness of it all overcome me and I put the sheets aside.

This loss of interest lasted until the afternoon of the next day. After lunch, I found myself on a train. It was a short trip, and from the station to his house was a half-hour walk. It was on a curving road with properties of one or two acres. The house was Victorian Tudor, large, with a conservatory on the right side. I stood at the gate and stared in. The garden which surrounded the house struck me as beautiful. My experience was so limited that I couldn't have justified this judgement, apart from noting that the garden was filled with a profusion of different greens, melting one into the other so that the flowers were a mere bonus. Fruit trees were somehow tortured into growing flat against the brick walls. The leaves were down, but colour still managed to surge from the borders. The conservatory appeared to be walled with stained glass thanks to the blur of flowers within. There was a peaceful atmosphere about the place and no sign of life.

I walked on down the road a hundred yards, where I found a bench. On this I sat and pulled from my pocket a copy of Céline's *Mort à crédit*. The weather was cool but dry. It was a nice place to read. Periodically I got to my feet and wandered back to stare at the house. No one had appeared; in fact, few people drove either way on the road. It was close to five when a small car came past, driven by a woman in her fifties. Beside her was a teenage girl. The woman was not so much good-looking as pleasant. She had fair hair backcombed into a fixed state. There was something in the way the daughter held her head that drew my eye. A moment later I heard the car brake. So it was they I had come for.

With short steps I moved towards the house. The car had been parked near the front door while the two women unloaded some parcels. By the time I reached the edge of the garden, the mother had walked back out to the road to close the gate. She wore sensible clothing.

"Excuse me," I said. My tone was feeble. "Could I ask your help?"

She paused in the midst of pulling the barrier across to examine me. It was a direct and engulfing examination; very much a mother looking at a child. She said nothing, but acquiescence was implicit.

There was no choice except to continue. "I came out on the train to look at the town. I've been walking around for two hours and now I'm not sure how to get back to the station."

"And did you think it was pretty?"

"I'm sorry?"

"Was it worth the walk?"

"I think it's great. We don't have gardens like these. They're amazing."

She smiled with pleasure. "The climate makes it easy. Where are you from?"

"Well, I'm studying in Paris, but before that I was at college in New York, but I'm from Toronto." She hadn't asked for a pedigree. My nerves were showing.

She seemed to put this down to North American clumsiness. "It's not far from here to the train station. Just straight ahead, more or less." She hesitated. "Would you like to come in for a moment? I'm about to make some tea."

"I'd really like that. Thank you very much." I came forward through the gate and she closed it behind her.

"My husband was born American." She walked beside me down the path. "He is the gardener. I think the first thing he loved about England was the gardens."

I pointed at the fruit trees. "I've never seen anything like that before."

"They're espaliered." She gave a little laugh. "You're the one who lives in France. My husband trained those fruit trees. I'd never have the patience."

I gave her my name and she said hers was Sarah Williams. Now that I was no longer trembling with nervousness, I could look at her properly. She had a slightly fixed-in-place look, like her hair, but apart from that was a pretty woman, a wonderful soft colour in her face, gentle full breasts, long tapering legs. The motherly expression had gone from her face to be replaced by a kind of open enthusiasm; a form of innocent passion. She was far more alive than her husband, the chairman of Bentley Holdings, at least from my few glimpses of him in London.

She led me inside the front door, across a hall and through a long drawing room to a second, small square sitting room. There was about it all a supremely comfortable air. Oh, I could see even in my ignorance that there were lots of nice pictures, some good furniture, good rugs; but it all had a furry look about it, a soft, overcooked look into which you could sink. And none of it had a specific character. There was no one thing I could notice. It was all of a kind. Family stuff. Or the sort of belongings that become family stuff. In the larger drawing room an effort had been made to create a formal air, but even this had been compromised with concessions to comfort.

She called through a door, "Audrey, put a third cup on the tray, please," and then to me, "In the winter we have tea with the plants."

She led the way into the conservatory. It was much larger seen from within than from without – an almost square glass room, with five oleanders along one side, each trunk the thickness of a small tree but with branches clipped back and covered in peach-coloured flowers. Two clementine trees on the other side seemed to have both flowers and fruit. The rest was a mixture of plants, some in flower, some not. In the centre were four armchairs around a low table, all in clear birch. She later told me they were early nineteenth-century Russian. The chair cushions were coloured in an elaborate eighteenth-century design. I recognized this from my Paris museum visits. There was a curious atmosphere about this room. Each plant had a specific, chosen air about it. Each thing stood out and yet each was part of the whole. It was an elegant place. More elegant than the house.

Sarah Williams sat down and gestured for me to do the same.

"This is my husband's room." She looked around at the plants and said with genuine admiration, "He has a marvellous talent."

I hastened to agree. A few minutes later the daughter came in with the tea.

"You won't mind having Indian?" the mother asked.

I didn't mind one way or the other. I was so busy asking myself what I was doing there, I hardly heard the question. The daughter had just finished school and was filled with the idea of going to college in the States. After all, her father was American, at least that was what I read into it. She herself was slim and fresh and in other circumstances

I'd have wanted her phone number, so to speak. There was, in addition, nothing American about her. She was filled with breathless enthusiasm, short sentences, usually unfinished, and an apparent ignorance of cynicism. She wanted my opinion on her going to the States, because her father was against it.

That was easy. I made a little speech in favour of transatlantic educations, which her mother dismissed with subtlety and charm. By then I'd had three cups of tea and they were ready for me to leave. Mrs. Williams had only to add that she'd have driven me had she not been waiting for her husband, who would be back any minute, to get me on my feet.

Walking back through the house I noticed a collection of photographs on a table and glanced over at them.

"There, you see, that is my husband in his younger days." There was a ring of devotion in her voice; real devotion, filled with tenderness and caring; a reverberation of love still very much alive.

I paused to look closely. One showed him in uniform; another as a student, in white. There, in those silver frames, was the elegant man whose ghost had been visible in Paris.

"I can see," I murmured, "that he is American."

"Oh," she corrected, nicely but firmly, "he was American."

I suppose I was a couple of hundred yards down the road in the direction of the station when I noticed his olive-green Rover go by. It caught my eye and I turned to see it slow, then come to a halt without pulling off the road, then slowly back up until it wasn't more than fifty yards behind me. The driver's door flew open and Mr. Williams swung sideways on his seat with great speed, a leg coming out, a foot striking the pavement. But instead of bounding out, he leaned his head sideways to stare at me. At first I thought it was an inquisitive glance, but then I realized it was bald fear. I had never seen it before, but like the heat of flame before a child this burning glance brought with it the certainty of understanding. The fear penetrated into my body and ricocheted around. Suddenly I realized. It was me that he feared. What a fool. Afraid of an idle student with literary pretensions. I suppose he thought I might tell people. Tell whom? I knew no one.

But the gaze held until I wrenched myself away to avoid it and walked, half-ran, towards the station.

Sitting on the train, remorse overtook me. What had I been doing? What a stupid idea it was to pry like that into a man's life. His wife would tell him about my visit. What would he think? The image of that solid businessman petrified by the sight of me, that image came back again and again. I was bad company for my friend all evening and I slept badly. At six I was already awake, lying restlessly on the sofa where a bed had been made up.

There was only one thing to do. I must reassure him. I must explain that my motives were mere nosiness and then I must disappear from his life. If I went immediately I would get to Kingston before he left and it would be easy to ask for five minutes with him. Perhaps he would be frightened when he first saw me at his door, but I would plan my words, my apology, and soon put him at ease.

I was in Kingston just after eight and at Williams's door just after eight thirty. There was no sign of life. Only the Rover was parked outside. I went through the gate with ease and determination. Thinking about it now, it amazes me, but it was the assurance of youth. I paused only a moment at the door before ringing the bell, a good solid ring. I waited a minute before ringing again. There was still no answer.

Then it came to me: perhaps he was working in his garden, at the side or the back. I walked around the house to the right. No one. The conservatory came into sight. That was it. I walked up to it and discovered a glass door I hadn't noticed the day before. What with the contrast of light and the outline of plants it was difficult to see inside. I tapped on the glass. It made a hollow sound, but there was no reply. I pushed the handle down and the door swung open. I put my head in. The table was there with the four chairs around it. The remains of the family's breakfast were on the surface. So I had been right. I stepped in and called out, "Anyone there? Hello. Mr. Williams?"

It was the strangest thing. Hearing my own voice like that, suddenly ringing out alone in a strange house, well, it brought me back to reality. What in God's name was I doing? I mean, I was standing inside the house of someone I didn't know, having walked in just like that. And what for? Completely crazy. I had no right to be in that house; no more than a thief had. I could hear my heart beginning to beat. It was the stupid sort of thing you do if you think things out alone.

I listened carefully, with stealth, dreading that he might find me there. No. There wasn't a sound. Thank God. I crept towards the door, eased it open, stumbled out, eased the door closed and walked quickly across the garden. It was all I could do not to run. But no, I mustn't run. Later in the day, back in the security of Pitt's study, I remembered forgetting to close the gate onto the road and, once on the road, beginning to run. I couldn't stop myself. The pounding of my heart had forced me. I didn't run far. A few hundred yards. Only until a semblance of calm had returned and I could think. And what did I think? That I was an idiot. Certifiable.

The curious thing is I hadn't thought of Williams for years; not since then, and suddenly, reading those few words in his diary, it had all come rushing back. I looked around my hotel room filled with the opulent shadows of Victorian decoration. The pages of the diary were lying on the opulent linen bed cover on my lap. I picked them up. It was the second page, November 5. Halfway down the entry began again.

Today as I came into St. James's Square, I saw the same
young man getting out of a taxi. At first I thought it mere
resemblance. The world is full of young men whose hair
is a bit too long, who wear ill-fitting clothes and have the
enthusiasm of youth. But I looked hard and it was the same
boy. He wore the same clothes except that he had put a tie
onto his checked shirt. I stared at him like a fool – in all these
years it is the first time that Paris and London have touched.
He stared at me. I broke away and walked on to the library.

My place near the window upstairs was free and I was
happily reading there when I glanced out and noticed the boy
standing on the pavement below. What did he mean by that?
I went back to my book, but the pleasure had been ruined. I
found myself continually looking out the window. There was
nothing to see except a perfectly ordinary person. After a time
he went into the gardens. But he sat on a bench just outside
the library where he had a good view of the door. Again, I
began by thinking it a coincidence. But, no. His eyes were
fixed on the door. He was waiting for me. I suppose I should
have gone down and faced him. Far better to get it over with.
Had it been in Paris, I'd have done that. But not here.

I waited another half-hour. He hadn't moved. I went downstairs to ask the porter for a taxi. When it came, I dashed
out and gave him my destination from within. And when we
passed the man in the garden I looked away. Why did I look
away? He knows my face. Life is so filled with delusions of
visibility and invisibility.

6 NOVEMBER

Is this a bad dream? Is this the ugly moment I have been awaiting for so many years? I arrived at my office this morning to find the boy of yesterday leaving it. I had already put him out of my mind. Forgotten him. How did he find out about me? He was as surprised as I yesterday on the square. Or was that my imagination? Did I see clearly? Perhaps he had meant to leave a few minutes later to waylay me and that failure explained his appearing off-balance.

Marjory is a good receptionist; no more of a fool than most in that job. I suppose I should thank her. She got his name and address. He lives in Paris in a seedy little hotel across from the Closerie. At first I thought the address was a sort of veiled threat, just to remind me that he knew. But I rang up the hotel and he does indeed live there. Has for the last few months, on the top floor, Room 19. Marjory says he spoke like an American. What does that mean? Nothing perhaps.

I tried to pull myself together, but how? The whole business is badly timed. I've so many decisions to make for the company and I need all my wits about me. The rest of the committee want to sell the Argyle shares. I don't know. Blakey is provoking them. I tried to think it out today. They say Argyle is in more trouble than we think and that our ten-percent holding isn't enough to have any influence. I don't know. I like Mackelrey. He's a good, tough president. He ought to be able to pull them around without the shares collapsing. And if we try to sell, I fear they will collapse before we get out. I talked to Mackelrey but resolved nothing in my own mind. I could think of little other than that American.

7 NOVEMBER

I was almost at the house tonight when, suddenly, there he was again, walking away from our gate. I knew it immediately. I don't know what came over me. At first a great anger. I stopped the car and backed it up. Better to confront him. Either pay him off or frighten him. Hit him, if necessary. But I stopped the car before I reached him. Still, I opened the door with decision and began to get out. Then I caught his gaze. It was a blank, meaningless stare. There was nothing in it. No apparent malevolence. No gloating. Just a meaningless stare. It wasn't what I'd expected and I was overcome. Overcome. What does that mean? I sit here in peace, surrounded by my plants and the word goes down easily. Fear surged out from somewhere and disintegrated all my willpower. I sat half in, half out of the car, unable to move. Then he walked away.

He is trying to frighten me. Before he asks for money, he wants to destroy my confidence. Sarah told me that she had invited him into the house; that she had given him tea. Here. In the conservatory. I came close to shouting at her. I might have hit her. What was she doing? But I was very calm, very interested. He says he is a student. He claimed he was lost. He played on her weakness for Americans. I suppose she saw some of what I once was in what he is. Surely not. What does it matter? I listened to her, knowing with every move she made, every word, that I love her. That I still love her hard.

Does he think he can frighten me by coming into my house?
I am trembling with anger. I made up a story about robberies
and told her not to let him in if he ever turns up again.
Audrey seemed hardly to believe this. I can't blame her. She
is a smart girl with a good nose and she knows me the way
only a child can know her parents – better and worse than
anyone else. It is also because she is so taken by everything
American. I can smell his presence in my house. And yet, I
am not frightened. I can always pay. For the moment I must
wait. He will reappear.

8 NOVEMBER

I thought myself so calm. How many lies do I tell myself? This
morning after breakfast, Sarah and Audrey went out. They've
driven to London to shop and wanted to be there early. I
dawdled in the bath, thinking about this Argyle business,
then heard a noise downstairs. I went down wrapped in a
towel. There was no one at the front door. Just to be sure I
walked to the back. There was a sound in the conservatory.
I went to see, thinking Sarah had forgotten something and
come back. At the last moment I saw his head. Thank God
it was before I came too close. I don't think he saw me. I
stood at the corner of the drawing room where I could watch
without his realizing, unless he came into the room. He was
walking around the conservatory, inspecting it. He smelled
the oleander. Didn't know they are without scent. He leaned
over the table and examined the remains of our breakfast.
He picked up a spoon and I thought he was going to steal

it. That would have been good. At least I'd have known he
was a common thief. But no, he held it close to his eyes to
see Sarah's family crest, then put the spoon down, carefully,
in exactly the same place. He had an unshaven look about
him and wore the same tie, an old, thin paisley. I could see
it was spotted. Quite suddenly, he stood up straight and
looked nervously around. Had I made a sound? The look of
a frightened animal came over him and I realized just how
dangerous he would be if cornered. He crept away. Perhaps
he is crazy. But that would be worse. That would make him
uncontrollable.

I must not let him get away again. I must not let this
drag on. I thought about him all morning at the office until
Kennedy came in to tell me that the Argyle shares were off
two pounds. So I was wrong and have lost half the investment. I told him to sell fast. Now it will only get worse. How
I wish I had not brought any outsiders onto the investment
committee. Now everyone will know the mistake was mine
and was caused because I dithered. Blakey in particular
is dangerous. I am sure he would do me in if he got the
chance. I am sure he is fast spreading the news of my
senility.

Still, that boy is in my mind. He left his footprints on the
floor of the conservatory. I don't think he noticed even that
the ground was wet. But no, why assume the best? He could
have left them on purpose, so that I would know he had been
there.

The man was an hysteric. He had understood nothing. No, really. I could see that his son would be upset in reading the diary, quite apart from the homosexuality. The only solution was to see him and to explain myself. I slept badly and went to my club about ten the next morning. I didn't expect to find Williams – it was too early – but I thought he might have left a message for me. Nothing. I questioned the porter about Williams's movements. There was apparently no pattern to them. He came in from time to time. The porter looked him up in the membership book. His office was in the City, so it would be quite a haul to come in for lunch. He was a vice-president in one of the big clearing banks. I thought of telephoning him there. Then of sending him a note by messenger. But what was I to say? That I wanted to see him? He knew that. Why else would he have given me the diary. A fragment of the diary. I suppose he wanted me to crawl. Well, I would crawl, within reason. Why shouldn't I crawl? I had been stupid in the way only an immature egoist can manage.

I had a book to read – *Il barone rampante* – and little to do, so I sat there for the morning, went upstairs for lunch, went out for one meeting with my surprisingly happy publisher and dropped back in later. No sign of him. Well, there it was. I had an agreeable evening with friends before me and still one more day in London.

While it is marvellous to do nothing, it is a difficult thing to enjoy when you are waiting for something to happen. By late the next morning I was fidgeting and reconsidered telephoning the man, then put aside the idea. Why should I give him that pleasure? It was enough to know that I should have to crawl when I did see him.

Mid-afternoon I was sitting in an armchair near the bow window, theoretically because the light was better there. In fact, my mind was empty. Suspended. I saw Williams come in but at first could not focus on him. He paused in the doorway, a silhouette without original form. He surveyed the room, saw me and walked forward with deliberation.

"There you are." He said it without any particular emotion. It was as if we had an appointment. He stood above me and made no move to sit down.

I felt obliged to stand.

"Look," I said quietly, "I remember your father only too clearly. Looking back on it, I can hardly believe I acted in that way. But I did. And I can only apologize to you for having done something I still have difficulty understanding."

"Your apology does not interest me." His eyes had not left mine and yet it was not a hostile stare; more an unblinking observation from which emotion was absent.

"I can understand your attitude now that I've read your father's diary. You see, the terrible thing is that he misunderstood my meaning. He assumed that I had some vicious –"

"You don't suppose that I gave you those pages in

order to hear you justify yourself. What you say your intentions were has no bearing on the case. None at all."

"Nevertheless ..." I heard my voice rising and could feel it radiating out across the room. There was only one other member there, at a good distance, but I stopped and began again in a near-whisper. Williams stepped back as I began, so I could not be certain that he heard me. "Nevertheless, the reason I wanted to see you again was to explain –"

"That certainly was not mine." He was a banker, and he spoke as if refusing a loan. Before I could say a word he took another step back, "Good day," and was gone.

I tried to sit down, but within a minute was back on my feet, walking up and down in front of the window. The bastard! The prig! What a mean little mind. In disgust I left the room and turned to leave the club. The porter leaned out of his lodge as I passed.

"Excuse me, sir. Mr. Williams left this envelope for you."

It was brown and large enough to take full sheets without folding. My fingers ripped it open and pulled out the pages. I turned around so violently that without pause I was propelled back into the drawing room. There I chose an isolated chair and brought the pages close to my eyes. The first was dated November 10. Where was the 9th? What game was he playing? What was he hiding from me? I shuffled through the pages to see if they were out of order. But no.

10 NOVEMBER

Investment committee meeting this morning. As I expected,
Blakey made a sortie. He is so direct that he defeats himself.
Of course I was wrong about Argyle. I have the right to be
wrong from time to time. I did a small in-and-out operation
on Blader yesterday and made back a third of our loss. That
sort of fast business is not meant to be my territory, but
shows that I can move when I want to. It was enough to blunt
Blakey's attack. Still no word from the American. Perhaps
it was a false alarm. It has all come and gone without major
waves. Sarah noticed my state but put it down to business.

11 NOVEMBER

Worked in the garden most of the day. My thoughts were
filled by B. Is it my thoughts or my nerves? When I am safely
here, I forget about the disgust I feel in Paris. Surely within
B's personality there is more than I find. How can I feel so
much at a distance and so little on the spot? But then, is it
surprising that B should aggressively close off the heart and
the softer pleasures of life? Why should I find it surprising
in someone who has had so few opportunities; someone so
dissatisfied with the nature of the desires that rush out of the
body without the mind being able to control them? The truth
is, we have not known each other long enough. L was much
the same when we first met. Look how bright L's life has
become. When you allow yourself to grow, you do grow. Grew
until I was no longer necessary. Well and good, though at the
time it was hard to bear.

When I begin to think of B a true desire overcomes me. I know it is real desire. I can think of nothing else and Sarah evaporates from my consciousness. She noticed I was unsettled at dinner. Never have my feelings been less in tune with the realities of my life. I could blot everything out by getting on a plane tomorrow morning, but how could I go to Paris? The American must know where B lives, works. That must be how he got on to me. Overheard B gossiping, boasting or complaining. He is probably part of the same group, but only an element within it; the sort I have always managed to avoid. The cheap blackmailers. I must wait. How long? How long before I know that all has calmed?

12 NOVEMBER

Blakey wants us to get involved in electronics. His candidate is NewWays, a small company on the rise that is desperate for cash input. If we move fast we can have effective control and still leave the management in place. It seems a good idea, apart from its source being Blakey. If only I felt my mind were clear, my judgement cool. It would be an important risk.

13 NOVEMBER

Home in bed. With what? With nothing. And yet I cannot move. My temperature is up.

18 NOVEMBER

I will go to Paris. I'll see the American. I'll pay him and be done with it. Sarah asked if I was well enough to travel. Two hours after I decided, my temperature had dropped and I felt both well and clear-headed.

The NewWays deal is almost in place. Blakey sent the figures out here. They look good and the market is still rising for electronics. I gave my go-ahead and will catch the 6 P.M. plane.

19 NOVEMBER
On arrival from London I went to my flat and rang B who claimed to be busy. I insisted and of course the fact of the resistance/insistence means that a larger present will be expected. We ate in a new place on Blvd. St. Germain called Pactole. Everything steamed in seaweed and very fresh. Apparently it's the latest thing. The new cooking. I questioned closely about the American, but B protested complete ignorance. I probed every crevice. Perhaps I was wrong, though B's ignorance of the matter does not eliminate the blind-gossip theory. The relief, the simple relief to be back here, made the night wonderful, not just in anticipation and retrospect, but in reality.

This morning I sent a post-office courier to the American's hotel with a note asking him to meet me at the Closerie Bar at four. That is a good, empty hour. I typed the note myself and didn't sign it, but it was clear enough.

I arrived at 4:15. He was waiting at the end of the bar in the darkest corner, sitting with his back to the wall. He didn't have a drink in front of him. Such an insignificant figure. Someone who, seen like that, seated in a bar by a passer, would go unnoticed. A marginal sort. There is no sparkle of character or intelligence. Just a muddy look. A plodding look. I am the proof of that – he had fallen onto a sucker and he won't let go. I stopped halfway through the room at the bar and ordered a bottle of champagne with two glasses. I waited there with my back to the table until the champagne was ready, then I asked the waiter to put it on the table in front of the American. When this was done, I walked over to join him.

He attempted to rise to greet me. Attempted to shake my hand in a French way. He managed neither. I sat down across from him and filled the two glasses. I was friendly.

"This is to celebrate our agreement." I passed him a glass and by holding my own glass up made him do the same. We both drank.

He did not seem to have changed his clothes. Again he wore his tie. I asked him what he wanted. He began to reply but lost the thread, so I took over. I explained that I wasn't interested in a long-term relationship. That I wanted to be left alone. That his actions in going to my house were unaccept-able. That whether we came to an agreement or not, if he ever again used such harassment I would have him dealt with. He asked me if I was threatening him. I assured him that I was. If things were to come to that, I suppose I could find someone to deal with him. That is not such a mystery. L would know someone and I will not allow this boy to destroy me. In any case, I gave him no time to reply with counter-threats. I offered him twenty-five thousand dollars. One payment. Story over. He was astounded. I have always found it best to do difficult deals fast and, by coming in high, to avoid bidding.

He made me repeat myself. Greed lit his eyes. How often I have seen that look in business or with young people like B. They, everyone when the right sum is placed before them, lose control of their reason. That sum appears to be the solution to so many problems. The nervous system separates itself from the body. The eyes glow in a way disassociated from the face. I could see that I had won. Then abruptly he turned away and told me to telephone him tonight. He tried to stand up, but I blocked his way. He said he also wanted the affair terminated. It was a harsh, cold little statement. Curiously enough, he then asked whether my offer was serious. I assured him that it was. He said something half under his breath; a self-justifying sort of statement. But then he finished off by accepting my offer. Funny how the most evil of people feel obliged to express regret at the moment they complete their acts. Again he told me to telephone him tonight in order to organize the details. I insisted – Did he mean he agreed to my terms? I might withdraw my offer in the meantime, I said. I might pass directly to action. He jumped up, brusquely repeated that he had agreed and pushed by me out of the bar. Good. Good. Thank God.

I must not panic. Perhaps I have not miscalculated. I must play this out. I telephoned at 11 P.M., according to my plan. It took him some time to come and he was out of breath. I suppose the only phone is in the lobby. I suggested we meet in the morning to organize payment. This time I was cold to him. He replied that I should telephone him in the morning to fix the time. I began to say I would prefer to fix the meeting now but we were cut off before my sentence was finished. I dialled again only to be told that he had gone out. He has more greed than intelligence. He wants more. Well, I will find out how much and settle the business fast. Tomorrow morning I will telephone, exactly as he has asked. I have no choice. The time of choice is finished.

Some sort of noise must have escaped from me, a moan, a sigh, I don't know, but it caused me to look up at the other members in the room. They were making a point of not noticing me. I suppose it didn't really matter one way or the other. Williams had not understood me at all. It was as if another character were playing my role; as if Williams could not see me. Quite probably I wasn't a very impressive sight, but that is not the same thing. I understood better now that he saw only himself. He was lost in his anxiety. I have already mentioned my ego as a young writer. His had remained at that stage, caught in the never-never land of his divided life.

Nowhere did he consider that my silence in Paris had been nothing more than that. I asked only that the matter be forgotten. Until his note arrived suggesting a meeting I had even given up going to the Closerie for fear of meeting him. I admit this one thing – I could not get him out of my mind. Why, I cannot say, except that his image floated back into my imagination whenever I relaxed my guard, or into my dreams. And I could no longer write, could scarcely concentrate enough to read. I suppose the sudden revelation of my power over another man had done it – what I could have done to that man had I been another sort of person.

His note had been the last thing I expected. I came in from a desultory walk in the Luxembourg and lunch at a cheap little restaurant on Monsieur-le-Prince with a French girl who might have become more than a friend had either of us made the effort; but for our own reasons neither of us had. The Romanian woman at the desk gave me the envelope. It was the first pneumatique I had ever received. There wasn't that sort of urgency in my life. I don't suppose many came to that hotel, except as convocations from people owed money. I owed nothing. I took the envelope back outside, walked down to the Observatory Fountain and sat on a bench with a view of the bronze horses. Perhaps I had been expecting it.

Perhaps that was why I couldn't get him out of my mind. It wasn't finished between us. Even without knowing what I now know of his feelings, I had already seen his fear. That is a great bond, a chain. We were linked, and his little note was an invitation to break the link. I felt at ease for the first time in over two weeks.

I went across to the Closerie precisely at four. The place was almost empty. I chose a discreet table and waited. And yet when he appeared my calm was shattered. I swear that he was like a ghost – an elegant ghost of a prewar world long disappeared. Not a hint of his London character remained. All that had been heavy was once again light. All that had been solid assurance was again finesse and understanding. His clothes were only a detail of this. It was as if he had lost years and pounds, as if hair had disappeared from his earlobes, his skin taken on another quality, his eyes become enquiring, unafraid of contact. And with this return of his other persona, my own confidence disappeared. In London I had felt embarrassment for him, his humiliation and my own dismay. I had felt his protector. How can I explain the sense of superiority that had come over me? But all of that dissolved the moment he appeared in the Closerie.

At first I was unsure he had seen me. He stood at the bar talking with the bartender, a good-natured plump man. Then the champagne was brought to the table, Williams following behind it. The closer he came, the more he appeared to be a ghost. No, not a ghost. Not transparent. More the opposite. Somehow more clearly defined than a real person, almost as if there were a spotlight upon him.

He forced me to drink his toast, just as he described it, and while I concentrated on my glass, he sipped his, put it down and gazed easily at me. Then he asked me what I wanted. Well, it wasn't the question I'd expected. I had been prepared to apologize and to assure him of my goodwill. Now the idea seemed presumptuous. He had no need of my goodwill. I felt as though I needed his.

I began to explain what had happened, but in a halting way, that is true, and so he interrupted me. I found it much easier to listen. I could only agree with his condemning of my actions, though I said nothing myself. He was making my speech for me. I fully intended to leave him alone. When he threatened me I summoned up a half-hearted protest – my motives had not been understood – but to my amazement he simply confirmed that threat. He had no idea how far out of my depth I was.

But all of that was nothing. It was the offer that swept all else away! My shame, my intention to apologize, my indignation at his misunderstanding of what I was doing. Those words – twenty-five thousand – shone through them like an ultraviolet ray. I was at that time surviving on three thousand a year. In those days an executive was making fifteen thousand, a bureaucrat ten. And that was in the United States. In England the figures were a third less; in France, still lower.

I didn't have to think it out. I knew what his offer would do for me. The freedom, the time. And it would amount to the same thing as my apology. He could afford it and I intended in any case to leave him alone. So I said yes. Without thinking. Without hesitating. I accepted. Once done, regret swept over me. Not really regret; but I began to consider the other side and so tried to play for time. He threatened me again and somehow I no longer saw clear. Everything swam in a haze. I shoved my way past him and outside. I ran towards the Observatory, where there was a small café. I spent the next hours there drinking and trying to clear my head. I knew that I should not have accepted, but was I in fact feeling any real regret? Though I tried to convince myself otherwise, the answer was no. It was that absence of the expected emotion which upset me. When before in my life had I been asked to make a real choice? And now that it was upon me I found I had none of the moral reflexes necessary to make the right decision. Money contains no moral quality. That was what I told myself. No goodness. No evil. If you can get it and you know what to do with it, your life can be easier. Not better, but easier.

I remember all the arguments I put to myself, and I remember repeating them and not going back to the hotel until late in the evening. I suppose I secretly hoped he would already have called, assumed that my absence meant lack of interest and dropped the matter, but I had no sooner climbed to my room than the intercom buzzed and I had to run down to the lobby. Oh, I ran. I ran to say yes. And when I heard his voice, I said nothing. Nothing at all. Then I managed to delay him again and hung up before he could go on. I went back out onto the streets – to avoid being there if he telephoned again. I was out for most of the night. At six I came back, packed my bags, made the Romanian woman wake the owner, paid and left by taxi for the Gare d'Austerlitz. There I had to wait an hour before taking a train to Saint Florent, near Bourges, two hundred kilometres from Paris. I telephoned a painter friend from the small station. My friend had a big house surrounded by flat sunflower fields and a studio in a farm building. I knew that he would have room for me.

Two pages of photocopy remained in my hand.

20 NOVEMBER

At 10 A.M. this morning I telephoned. They said he had checked out. They said he has taken his belongings with him, that he is gone. He left no forwarding address. So I was wrong. He is far cleverer than I thought. He is going to play harder than I expected. Perhaps I was too fast with my threats. So it is not over. How much more does he want? Or is that it? I begin to feel he wants to hang on to me, to milk me. If only it were just a case of more. But there is within him more than greed. There is an evil quality. I saw it in his eyes yesterday. I saw it and pretended to see only greed. I reassured myself. There is a seeping air about him. He wants to infiltrate my life, to take everything and to destroy me. How I want it over with. Over. I don't want to play it out and he has sensed this. It must have been in my eyes. In my voice. I must find the strength.

I stayed in my flat most of the day. B called, wanting to come around, to get something from me I imagine. I said I was on the point of leaving. And to make it true, I left. Went back to London to my office. Everyone had gone home. I telephoned Sarah to say I was back and would be working late. I have tried to work but cannot concentrate.

I sat in my chair, unable to move. I looked out the bow window onto St. James's. People walked by. Some of them looked much the way Williams – the English Williams – had looked when I first saw him in the square. Not a great deal had changed in fifteen years. Ties had been wide. Now they were narrow. In any case, Williams's type had stuck with the narrow sort from the fifties on. The heads which these narrow strips of silk choked had certainly not changed, nor their contents. I went to the bar and drank a whisky. Then I phoned Williams's bank. They said he had gone for the day. Too bad, I thought. I'm leaving tomorrow morning.

The next morning I tried to phone again, just before leaving the hotel. I gave my name. There was a long pause, followed by a secretary who said he wasn't available. I don't know what I felt. He was playing with me, feeding a few pages at a time. Anger began to cloud my consciousness. Was he trying to do to me what he thought I had tried to do to his father? I gave the secretary my hotel and room number. Then I changed my plane to the late afternoon and told the hotel I'd keep the room for the day. I telephoned Williams every hour. He was unavailable. About four I told the girl it was urgent. I told her I'd come down there unless she put me through. She said that in any case Mr. Williams had just left for the day. She didn't know where he'd gone, except that it wasn't home.

He was obviously on his way to the club. I went downstairs and walked there as fast as I could. The porter hadn't seen him. I waited in the drawing room for two hours, but he didn't show. By then I was meant to be in another city and instead was at loose ends in London. I went to see a West End farce which wasn't funny; at least, I didn't laugh. The next morning at 7 A.M. there was insistent knocking at my door. It was a bellboy with an envelope which had been delivered to the hotel, marked "URGENT." I was to be woken immediately. I tied my dressing gown tighter, ripped open the envelope and let it drop to the carpet. I began to read the pages where I stood, in the centre of the room.

23 NOVEMBER

Cannot get it right. Cannot think clearly. Cannot understand what Blakey is doing. It all seems to be going well, but what good is my judgement when I am in such a state. Still no sign of the American. How long will he make me wait?

24 NOVEMBER

Completed deal on electronics. The only positive thing in my life right now. And what is it? Only a deal. Such a paltry thing.

Audrey has gone away to stay with girlfriends in London. The atmosphere around me must be unbearable.

25 NOVEMBER

The American called this afternoon to my office. It was a very bad line. Not from Paris. I think he was drunk. I could make no sense of it. He went on and on, only bits of it intelligible.

He seemed to want the money. That was the heart of it. That and "no need to threaten." He hung up in the midst of this. I think I heard laughter in the background. I could think of nothing to do except sit very still behind my desk.

An hour later the lawyer for NewWays appeared at my door. He had a commission. The management of the company were pleased with the deal but had understood that Blakey would be chairman of the controlling corporation. That I was resigning. They were surprised that I had not done so. If I do not, then they will themselves resign. Apparently they have alternative backers. So they will have freed themselves of NewWays's debt – which is all I would retain – and have kept their real assets: experience and personnel. Now I understand. I understand but can think of nothing to do. I thanked the lawyer for his message and showed him out.

27 NOVEMBER

The officers of NewWays today resigned. The shares, of course, have plummeted. They will carry our own company with them if I don't pull myself together. All I need is time. With time I'll find a way.

1 DECEMBER

Sarah found this book in the conservatory. I know I drank a lot last night. She said she found me there asleep, half-carried me to bed and only this morning discovered the book. Of course, she read it all. That is her character.

She has understood nothing. She thinks I have girlfriends

in Paris. Old-fashioned mistresses. I will not repeat the
conversation between us. There was no conversation. Two
snails in their shells. She left before lunch to stay with friends
in Yorkshire. It was a tactful protest. How much she is hurt
I cannot tell, she has so many veils to hide behind and yet I
love those veils. How many lies am I living? Now at least I am
free to deal with everything. Do I feel nothing? It is buried so
deep? When will it explode?

4 DECEMBER

I have been once to London. It is a disaster. I prefer to take
refuge here.

5 DECEMBER

Where is the poetry in my heart. Why is the song not sung.
Why is the air so empty of sound, so flat upon the earth.

6 DECEMBER

The American telephoned a moment ago. Hearing his voice
in this empty house, it seemed to echo from the phone out
around the rooms. He said he was coming to London soon
and would telephone again. When I hung up I could still hear
his voice in the drawing room, in the kitchen, everywhere.
He has infested me. I can no longer think because I can
no longer escape him. I came into the conservatory to try to
consider this development. There were so many dead flowers
on the oleanders that I felt obliged to pick them off. Perhaps
there is no explosion.

There was no more. I remembered the first telephone call. I had been drunk, just as he suspected. I had told the whole story to my friends, but they wouldn't believe me. It became a great joke – how I was going to become rich. Reality is such a tenuous thing. Williams became a joke even for me. My call was a prank, nothing more. Silly. Stupid. But the second call I did not make. I have no memory of it. I did not go to England. I'm certain of that.

At 10 A.M. I went to the club. Williams was sitting in the bow window. He did not greet me, but when I was seated next to him he turned and handed me two photocopies. The first was an internal memo written under a solicitor's letterhead. It was dated December 8. The handwriting seemed to be the solicitor's notes for a client file.

RE: CHARLES WILLIAMS
Police called this afternoon (1500 hrs.): Williams's secretary gave them my name. His body was found by a cleaning woman this morning. Dead 2 days. In conservatory. Something about soup. Police found remains of this substance in kitchen. He had boiled oleander leaves? Police say 80 leaves in pot.

Apparently oleander contains oil equivalent to strong sleeping pills. Released by boiling.

They're convinced suicide although Sarah W. missing. I encouraged discretion.

<u>TO DO:</u>

- will

- Sarah

- family doctor?

- notify children?

The second photocopy was a letter from a doctor to Sarah Williams. It was full of good sentiments and the certainty that he had died a painless death.

Williams took back the two pages with a flick of disgust for the doctor's letter. "I disbelieve that kind of sop. We were left with very little money once the mess had been cleared up. I was not able to go to university as my father intended. It is only through very hard work that I have managed to do so well."

I asked without hearing my own voice, "What about your mother?"

Distaste came over Williams's face. "She died a few years ago. She was never able to deal with what happened. She knew that he had killed himself and that it was because of you. She spent the rest of her life waiting for someone to appear. That was always my impression. My sister and I were told nothing. We believed he had died of a heart attack. I do not intend to tell my sister anything to the contrary. The details of his death I learned from these solicitor's notes. They were in the same file as his diary. However, I now understand. My mother was waiting for you."

"Look here, Mr. Williams, I know you don't want my explanations and I know I am in part to blame. I wish you could understand to what extent it was all a tragedy of misunderstandings." He did not seem to hear me but I pressed on. "And of his time. Today his homosexuality would not have seemed such a scandalous thing. It wouldn't have weighed on him in the same way."

Astonishment came over his face. "My father was not a homosexual! Don't you think you have done enough damage. You are such a degenerate people, you Americans. Always preaching, preaching to everyone, but your own lives are a cesspool. My father's only weakness was that he had an American side to him."

"You needn't worry," I said, leaning forward, "I'll resign from the club." It was an idiotic thing to say, but the man brought out the worst in me.

"You needn't bother," he cut in. "I delivered my own resignation this morning, accompanied by a letter stating that I could not belong to a club that admitted black-mailers." He paused to see my reaction. I don't believe I allowed much to show. "I did not name you. You may do as you wish. That is your affair." He stood up as if to leave, but paused to look down at me. "My guess is you will not do a thing." He turned and left the room.

I didn't move for a while. Looked over my shoulder out the window without really seeing anything. Got up to get a newspaper. Sat back down and stared at it. Put it down.

I SLOUCHED IN THE CHAIR, the preconceived ideas of the eighteenth century cutting my back and cramping my arms. My eyes wandered up to the garlands moulded onto the ceiling and down to the parquet de Versailles. Paint peeled off the former and the latter needed a good waxing. These Enlightenment remains were disrupted by Doctor Bicauld, stiff behind a marquetry desk where he read my report. And behind him, a large window opened onto the geometric garden and the Normandy countryside.

"So you have told your Paris physician that you are not an habitual drinker."

My eyes rolled back up to the ceiling. "This place needs a paint job."

There was a short silence – a gap in time.

"We are a clinique, sir. Not a chateau tour. Only your liver is of interest here."

"Good." I met his stare. "That being so, doctor, you will see from the report that my bilirubin is elevated – severely,

I understand – in spite of the fact that I rarely drink more than average amounts of alcohol. In Paris they suggested I come here to rest and to be away from the temptations of drink while I wait for the results of further tests. I didn't realize that I was also paying three hundred dollars a day to be called a liar."

He nodded – it might have meant anything – then pulled a file from his desk drawer and pushed it across. Inside I found photographs of gigantic swollen stomachs lying on top of pale patients lying on hospital beds.

"Cirrhosis of the liver. Terminal stage." He added, with a sentiment bordering on satisfaction, "I knew them all. Rich patients rarely arrive here carrying reports that deal with their drinking. But then you, sir, are not an habitual drinker. On the other hand, you may have cirrhosis of the liver."

"I'd like to see my room."

The doctor picked up a little gilded bell from his desk and tinkled it fastidiously. A nurse came to lead me away. It was a perfectly rational small chateau with large salons running right and left off the central hall, from which an elegant central staircase rose. I turned to climb it, my hand grasping the carved marble balustrade.

"This way, please."

Behind me the nurse was holding open a door towards the rear. I followed her out into the garden, where twenty or so gardeners were hard at work. I looked again. There was a certain style to their gardening clothes; something about the stitching on the gloves, the casual flow of the plaid shirts.

"You leave those bluebells alone, Janet." This came in Massachusetts tones from an older woman wearing a Hermès scarf. "I know a lot more about them than you."

"Who are they?" I asked the nurse.

"Guests."

"What are they doing out here?"

"Exercise."

I stared again. Half of them looked American. The others were probably French. "Exercise?"

"Doctor Bicauld believes in fresh air and natural exercise. Most of our guests are here for a rest or to lose weight. A cure. Few of them are very sick like you. Doctor Bicauld does not believe in sitting in mud or sulphur springs. All of these can do bad things to you. As can jumping up and down on exercise machinery. He forbids his guests to run. These runners will all need to replace their hip joints one day. And difficult knee operations. Oh yes, Doctor Bicauld has revolutionized the cure." She made him sound like a Jacobin.

"Robespierre or Saint Just?"

She liked that. "The doctor is a man of rigour, but sometimes he releases the poetry that is within him." By that I guess she meant they were sleeping together. Well, that was her problem. "Here we are, then. This is your room."

We were at the stables. A row of doors had been fixed onto the facade. Inside was a slit of a room with a simple bed and plastered walls. Little else. I guess my restrained elation was obvious, because she began to explain,

"Some guests come once, even twice, a year. They reserve the grand bedrooms in the chateau." She held open the door. "Welcome!"

I unpacked, then took a book out into the garden. There wasn't a chair in sight. Apparently the flowerbeds were to be worked on, not looked at. I dropped to the ground beneath a wall where the shade was generous. What a miserable few months. The business around Eleanor was far from over. And I was still trying to reconstruct or understand my memory of Williams. When I next looked up, a number of the guest gardeners were staring at me with disapproval. Really I should have just jumped on a plane back to New York when this problem appeared, but my French friends quite rightly pointed out that they belonged to a nation which drank itself to death faster and in greater numbers than any other. Therefore, they concluded with a hint of patriotism, it followed that the world's greatest experts on the liver should be French, rather in the way the English were experts in gout and the Americans in obesity. I opened my book, but the doctor's photographs kept floating into my mind and I closed my eyes in depression. Generally I think of life as being very short. A friend of mine in Bangkok has always argued that it is long. Terribly long. With only a few moments that count. All the rest is just waiting for the end. The trouble is, those key moments are never marked out. You can slide through them, failing to respond, without even realizing that this is it. For once, I was in agreement with him. Perhaps that was the real reason for my depression. Perhaps Charles Williams had taken up my few moments. And I had failed. All the rest, the years that came after, was made up of what? Of succeeding? The most over-rated human activity. The lynchpin to our temporary delusion of immortality. Of what, then? Of passing time? Of stealing other people's moments? Of observing? Or was it voyeurism? Of words? No lack of words out there. Well, then, this sickness might be a good thing. Now, perhaps, the wait would not be so long.

There were sixty of us at dinner, most of whom had "dressed." Certainly the room warranted an effort. It was painted in the Pompeian style with two fluted pillars at each end. The china was decent Limoges. The silver was silver and crested. The downside came in two parts. First, I was placed at the end of the table where they dumped the new or one-time patients – i.e., the sick people, not the cure seekers. And most of us were patients, not guests. The sick stood out because few had thought to bring evening dress. And we were subdued compared to the laughter in the middle and at the other end. Second, there was no compensation on the handsome plates. A thin yet granular soup made of unidentifiable vegetables came first. Slices of grey meat with large carrots and floury potatoes followed on its heels. Everyone was served the same fare. Everyone picked at it.

While I scratched away at the plate, a lady from Washington on my right discussed weeds with her neighbour. She was not a patient, but a novice guest. She revealed herself to be a fanatic of the twenty-minutes-per-side school. The moment the first twenty minutes ran out – I had been watching the time from boredom – she turned to me without finishing her last sentence on the other side. Her husband – dead – had bought an ambassadorship to a small Middle European country. Not too big. Not too expensive. I suppose twenty minutes per side had been emphasized in the spousal program on the ambassadorial training course. That would have been decades ago. But the lesson stuck.

"You don't look sick. And you don't need to lose weight. So?"

I replied a bit defensively. "A rest."

"Like me. A friend told me about this place. I kind of like it. You know, I get so bored sitting around in those saltwater baths every year. You can't finish a magazine page before it curls."

"Curls?"

"Curls. You know, the humidity."

"Right."

"Do you like the country?"

"Depends."

"Normally I hate it. There's no one to talk to. Nothing to do. No one to play Scrabble with. I've got to admit they're pretty smart here. They give you lots of food but you don't want to eat it. Now, there's a psychological diet. And it is a lovely home. Don't you think so?"

I nodded.

"Those people down there. They're regular comers. I was working with them this afternoon. Tomorrow we're going to attack the ornamental pool. They were saying it's gotten weedy since last year. You can hardly row across it." When this didn't draw my interest, she leaned closer. "Have you seen the marquis yet?"

"The marquis?"

"De Mazarine." She stretched it out into a brand of margarine. "He still lives here. I met him today. A real gentleman. He told me his family built this place."

"Where is he?"

"Oh, he eats alone. He's a big guy. Big like that one."

She pointed down the table. I leaned forward to follow her finger. It was aimed at a large fat man who sat on our side. He was entertaining the half-dozen people around him. His dinner jacket enclosed fold upon fold of pink flesh, an effect magnified by his bald head and the hairless quality of his skin.

It was Darius Resphanturi. I hadn't seen him in years, not since my last trip to Tehran six months before the Shahenshah fell. So he had survived the tumble. I suppose he was one of the many who had placed money outside well in advance.

On my first visit to Tehran – it was a cold January – I had received a gold-engraved invitation, on the large side, to a soirée at Darius's house. That was what the card said. "Une Soirée." Who he was, how he knew I was in Tehran, why he had invited me, I didn't know. I showed the card to a friend, who laughed and said, "Go! Don't miss it."

The sky was black long before seven, when the taxi began wallowing up the slush towards the top of the hill on which he lived. Other drivers had chains or were in Land Rovers with wonderful tires. We slid around, missing things by miraculous inches, and crawled up into deeper and deeper snow.

The gate was near the top. Two armed guards blocked it and high walls with shards of glass on top stretched off to either side. They looked dubiously at the old Mercedes, but I flashed my invitation. Within was a landscaped forest, half of pines. The road wound romantically over a wooden bridge beneath which a small river was rushing by and on to a house fused somewhere between China, the Middle East and Japan. Two Land Rovers were stopped before us depositing a bevy of girls in high leather boots and fur coats. I waded up the steps behind them to where a row of servants took their coats and offered them seats on which to exchange their boots for their high heels.

All before me was white and silver. Marble, mirrors, rows of chandeliers. It was a Californian dream of grandeur. Small rooms – by comparison – ran off a large central hall where a white piano encrusted with diamonds – not real, but real paste – was centred to dominate. Behind it were a half-dozen musicians playing "San Francisco."

I asked a guest which of the three, perhaps four hundred people was my host. He pointed at a mountain of a man – in those days Darius had been even fatter – floating around the floor, literally floating, as if off the ground, carrying a sparrow of a girl with him. Champagne was pressed into my fingers. I wandered among the dancing and eating crowd until a soft hand touched my shoulder. It was the floating giant.

"You are the scribbler. I feel it. You make me glad you came. I love you, you Americans! You make me so rich! You make me have a good time possible. Hey! You must dance!" He pulled a dark, lithe girl towards me. "Dance!" He pushed us off to sea.

At first I thought the girl was Iranian, but Kattey turned out to be from Cincinnati and was in Tehran running a construction company. After a while she dragged me towards the caviar.

"This is your first time?"

The question surprised me. "Does he do this often?"

"Wednesdays. He calls them gratitude parties."

"What for? What does he do?"

"Nothing. He has three cousins. They can make things happen. So you go to Darius, give him some money, lots of it, and he puts you together with the right cousin. Darius doesn't do a thing beyond a phone call or a dinner. He just dances a lot. Really well."

"He certainly gets a selection of women here." They outnumbered the men two to one.

"Dancing only. Darius is too fat for sex. Or whatever. He just likes having a good time."

"Like a Neapolitan eunuch."

She looked at me doubtfully, as if unsure whether I was talking ice cream or politics. "Lots of fun," Kattey insisted. "Not much use to a girl, that's all."

We danced some more, then I took her downtown, bought her dinner.

I was in Tehran for three weeks, so twice I went back to Darius's. The first time he sang with his band. Despite his gratitude to Americans he had a weakness for "April in Paris." With his accent and cadence, a common phrase like "chestnuts in blossom" took on a sexual connotation.

"Now I sing you a song from my Paris days," he had announced.

"Not again!" someone shouted. "'Singing in the Rain'!"

Darius laughed and went ahead with "April in Paris," through which he lightly scraped. Only then did he give us "Singing in the Rain," while he danced around the floor with a cordless microphone. Partway through he pranced into a little room and came out with an open umbrella that became his partner and won him great applause. At the end he came to rest on my shoulder, his great weight heaving in search of breath. Only then, at close quarters, did I realize that he was a good seventy.

He sensed what was going through my mind and laughed like a child.

"I am dancing into the sunset. Hey, scribbler. A good way to go, eh?"

To my mind he was right and he danced so well. In those heady days of arms deals and oil deals and road contracts and palaces and money pouring out to Switzerland and the Antilles, Darius was a sign of the city's corruption and yet he, unlike so many others, was never perceived that way. Perhaps because he was so pure in his indolence and marginal in his corrupt acts; and also because he was nice. As power brokers and percentage men go, Darius didn't count. He just happened to be well placed.

When we got up from dinner at the Chateau de Mazarine – after rice pudding with some sort of instant custard on top – I headed towards him. Before I could get there he had dashed out into the hall. I followed, but he had disappeared. And though I waited around in the salon, he didn't reappear for coffee. It was lunch the next day before I caught him.

"Hey, scribbler. Hey, my friend. So I find you again!"

He was with a New York couple – owners of a munitions company – and their daughter, Claire. She was of age and of shape and had an olive warmth that Darius seemed to like in girls. Her parents were there for a cure. She had been dragged along. They had known Darius in Tehran, where of course they had gone to his soirées.

"Why don't we give a party tonight?" I suggested.

"Darius is such a bore." Claire's mother leaned her face into our conversation. "Every night he says he's tired and goes to bed after dinner."

I whispered to him, "What about dancing into the sunset?" He smiled good-naturedly. "Okay. Tonight. Just once."

"I can't stand that hallway another day," Claire's mother half-shouted in a take-charge voice. "The doctor tells me they have the paint. Now, who is going to help me and we'll get it done this afternoon?"

A group volunteered. Darius melted away. But that night, after turkey steaks and canned fruit, we all crowded into the big salon, where a record player had been set up – an object from the fifties. Darius produced a small suitcase of "my favourites." He carried them everywhere "just in case."

And he danced around the floor, Claire in his arms, accompanying Gene Kelly with the same old skill. It was a great success. Then we all joined in. When Darius tired, I took Claire from him for a few songs. There was a hint of raspberries on the breath from her lips and suddenly I felt my liver would never begin to swell.

The next day I saw Darius sneaking off into a field – no doubt to sleep – and followed him.

"Why are you, of all people, wasting your money in a place like this?" I called out.

Darius looked around and laughed and waited for me

to catch up. "Not my money, scribbler. It is Mr. Bluestad's money." That was Claire's father. "He is paying my ticket." He saw I didn't understand. "The Shahenshah is gone. My money is gone."

"You didn't get any out before?"

"Before?"

"Everyone else did. That's one of the reasons he fell."

"Did they?" He seemed confused. "That's what my friends tell me. I like to dance, scribbler. I like to have fun. I don't understand politics. Now I have a nice room in New York. You know, the West Side. Up at 115th Street. I fold up the bed to make space. I put on my records and we dance. All my friends come. The Bluestads come. Sometimes fifty people. If we don't have room we dance in the hallway. My friends bring champagne, sometimes caviar. I sing and dance. You will come and see, scribbler."

"Does Claire come?"

He paused to glance more carefully at me. "Yes, she comes. Not always."

We found a plane tree, just big enough to give us shade, and lay on opposite sides beneath it.

"So, scribbler, what have you been up to?" I sensed that his eyelids were already halfway down.

"Me. Oh, little things." I tried to describe my own life, but that isn't my specialty.

After a while he interrupted, almost in a grunt, "Sounds shitty to me."

I sat up. "What do you mean?"

He pulled a chocolate from his pocket and when he saw me start at the sight of it, took a bite before throwing the rest over. It was black and bitter with buttercream and slivers of orange inside. I swallowed it.

"All those bits and pieces, scribbler, of other people's lives. You peep at them. You write down their secrets. 'Shitty' I think is the word." With his accent, the double t's took on a special significance.

"I'm a writer, Darius. I don't see it like that."

"So why do you look so bad?"

"I'm supposed to be sick."

"You don't look sick. You look unhappy. Examine yourself. If you don't like what you see in the mirror, don't break the mirror, break your face."

"What?"

"Persian saying."

"For Christ's sake. Look at it this way. What I have is a sort of ad hoc vision in which I am the alchemist's conductor. See? So the sum of the parts, contrary to cliché, magically adds up to some kind of whole."

He made a noise which I at first took to be an insult. I leaned around the tree. He was merely snoring.

That evening Darius disappeared the moment dinner ended, as did Claire. Mrs. Bluestad took it upon herself to explain that they brought Darius along every year to keep them cheered up. In fact it was he who had first told them about the place.

"We moved back to New York two years ago," she

volunteered. "Coming for a cure every year was my husband's idea. Before New York, we were in Nigeria, which we loved, though the people are pretty poor. That was after Tehran. We like New York very much, too, but I can't figure out why the mail service is so slow."

"You find it slow?"

"Very slow. Nigeria was much faster."

"The mail?"

"People delivered things very fast."

"People?"

"There are a lot of people in Nigeria."

"I suppose that's true."

I spent as much of the next few days with Claire as I could trap her into. The evenings were my great failure. She usually disappeared to her room. But during the day we had all our time. She wasn't drawn into the gardening/painting syndrome, which left myself and Darius as her only possible entertainment. I think the likelihood that I might be very sick, even dying, and unjustly at that – without showing any external signs such as smell, swelling or peeling – made her automatically feel a certain sympathy for me. I resembled a Thomas Mann hero. I was someone for her to worry about. We took long walks. Sometimes Darius came along.

On one of these walks I learned that he had known the Marquis de Mazarine since his student days in Paris. And when Darius had come out of Tehran as a penniless refugee via Paris, he had gone down to stay with his friend and had promised to encourage anyone he might still know, now that he was poor, to come to Mazarine la Clinique. It turned out there were a lot, and now they all came and they paid Darius's way to keep them amused.

"I don't know why you accept."

"Friendship, scribbler. It is good to see my friend Mazarine. Sometimes after dinner I go off to see him in his wing and we ... well, we, you know, we talk about good times."

"I'd say he's on to pretty good times now. Is that where Claire goes after dinner?"

He sensed the jealousy.

"Mazarine is my age. And he has no children. So sometimes she does come with me." He glanced over kindly. "You are very much on edge. When do your results come from Paris?"

I shrugged off the question, though he had seized upon precisely what was driving me. "Soon enough. Take me along to meet your friend tonight. I can't stand all these thinning people."

"Sure, scribbler. You would like him. Not tonight. Maybe another night."

Three more days of vegetable soup and grey meat went by without my being taken to meet his friend. Nor did I catch a glimpse of this elusive Mazarine coming in or out or inspecting his grounds. Periodically I would overhear one of the guests, with excitement in their voice, describe a chance encounter with the marquis under some specific tree or near a compost heap. On the third afternoon I was eating lunch and wondering where Darius and Claire had got to when the nurse came up behind me. Doctor Bicauld had sent her.

I went down the corridor to his office feeling very much worse than I had on arrival. For one thing, I had lost just enough weight to feel my trousers dragging. That limp, loose feeling around the waist is in itself depressing. So is bad food. Not simple food. Bad. As for alcohol, I could do without it, but didn't particularly want to. And so I slunk into his office like a prisoner to hear a sentence. Bicauld was rigid behind his marquetry desk. He fingered an envelope.

"Your results have arrived."

I knew the mail was delivered by 10 A.M. So he had hesitated four hours before calling me in. I could feel my willpower being dragged down beneath a long slow wave. The news could only be bad. My hand went out to take the papers, but he withdrew them and dropped the whole envelope into his drawer where he kept the photos of swollen livers.

"Now. Here is the situation. I am afraid that you suffer from a congenital condition known as Gilbert's disease. The result of this disease is a permanently elevated bilirubin. This also accounts for the jaundiced colour of your eyes."

"My eyes?"

"The whites, they are yellow."

I resisted the urge to look around for a mirror. "A congenital disease? What are you trying to tell me, Doctor Bicauld?" I wondered whether he heard the tremble in my voice.

"Is that not clear." It was a statement.

"Well, what are the implications ...," I wanted to say, for my life, "... for my liver?"

"None."

"Well ... what other implications are there?"

"None. It is a condition. Disease is only a technical word in this case. You have an elevated bilirubin. That is all. It means nothing."

"You mean I'm perfectly healthy?" I felt air rushing into my lungs, buoying me up.

"Reasonably."

"Why? What else is the matter?"

"I mean for a man of your age."

"You mean like most habitual drinkers?" It is amazing how fast the tongue recovers when fear recedes. There lies the most resilient part of the human body. Just like fishing, only the opposite. Up bobs the float the moment you get death off the hook. "When can I get a train to Paris?"

"They leave in the morning at eleven thirty-five."

So that was why he had waited to call me in. One more night. An extra three hundred dollars. I left his office with dignity, but once out of his sight rushed to find Darius and Claire. I felt alive and yet not really. How can you be alive until someone else knows and cares? They had disappeared.

Just before dinner an old Peugeot came up the drive. I was watching from a salon window. A woman was driving. Claire. And Darius was beside her. I ran down the hall and out onto the raked gravel, filled as I was with my news and yet furious with them.

"Where were you?"

Darius smiled softly. "Mazarine lent me his car ... We couldn't find you."

I smelled wine on his breath. "It doesn't matter. My results came in."

Claire jumped forward to take my arm.

"I'm innocent. Alive and well."

She threw herself on me in a hug and there was that hint of raspberry on her breath. Once I had her, I didn't let go for a time.

"We must celebrate!" Darius shouted somewhere in the background. "We must dance. After dinner."

Dinner was carrot soup, filets of sole reduced to cotton wool in béchamel. And canned peaches. As we got up, Darius drew me out of the room. Claire followed. In the central hall he unlocked a door with a large key he kept in the depths of his trousers. The mass of Darius in black evening clothes was like part of the night detached. He lit a hallway beyond the door and relocked the door behind us. Twenty yards brought us into a large office, which had obviously once been the library. There was a wooden ceiling painted with muses. From the files and typewriters scattered around I guessed it was now the clinic's office. The walls were covered in old photographs. I fell behind to look at them. Some showed the chateau and its garden in a rundown state with, in the foreground, various groupings of what I took to be the Mazarine family. Others concentrated on a young man, sometimes on a tractor, sometimes on horseback about to set off on a hunt. Whether in farm gear or hunting colours, he looked hungry and shabby. Darius pushed open a door in the far corner of the room.

A voice boomed through, "Viens. Vite! Ça va tomber!"

Darius rushed ahead into what turned out to be a delightful little dining room, all eighteenth-century carved panelling, an intimate ceiling painted with symbols of the arts, a Neopolitan marble fireplace, its warm colours dancing with the flames of a big fire. I suppose it had been a cozy reading room when the library was next door. There, an enormously fat old man sat behind a suitably enormous soufflé. He didn't look up from it, but shouted again, "Sit down! Vite!"

There were two empty places. Only then did the man notice that we were one too many. He showed momentary surprise, then swung towards a young servant girl hanging back. "Vite! Une autre place!" He could not wait. While silver and plates were being produced he began to serve the others. "Présentations later." He filled

Claire's plate. Standing behind her I could smell the crab and cream and cognac wafting out.

We ate in virtual silence. Mazarine stopped long enough to grab up a bottle of Corton Charlemagne and fill our glasses very full.

"Aghh!" he murmured. "Voilà des bonnes choses. N'est-ce pas, Darius?"

Darius was too busy eating to reply. Even Claire was caught up in the compulsive atmosphere of consumption. As for myself, well, I was the released prisoner seeking balm.

The plates were whisked away as we emptied them. Between burps, Darius found enough time to explain who I was. Other plates rushed forward, as if self-impelled, and an extraordinary object followed behind. It had the shape of a round, high cake but was made entirely of sliced duck separated into layers by green beans, leeks and mange-tout. There was a rich essence to pour over it. With no more than another "aghh," Mazarine filled new glasses with Cheval Blanc.

"For this man who finds life!" He raised his glass to me, then emptied it. Then refilled it. "Aghh."

The salad and cheese were attacked with less violence. But after them came slivers of flaky pastry separated by peaches and cream. A strawberry puree was poured over it and a sweet Bordeaux helped us to get everything down.

Darius rolled to his feet. "Now we dance!" He led us

into the next room – a small, square salon where the carpet had been taken away. On a sophisticated machine that looked as if it could fly, he placed a Frank Sinatra record and led Claire to the floor. "'Strangers in the night,'" I could hear him crooning over her shoulder, "'exchanging glances ...'"

Mazarine had her next and I was third. The order might have been by age or weight or dancing skill. I held her tight and moved very slowly, very happily.

While Darius danced his next turn, I took a Calvados from Mazarine.

"Who," I asked, "is the man in all the photographs in the next room?"

"What man?"

"The thin one."

"Me! You see. Me!"

"Pas possible!"

"Oui, oui, c'est moi, c'est bien moi."

Mazarine put his arm around my shoulder in a reassuring way. He had a warm, comfortable smell about him.

"It is the fault of Darius. I was your typical French artisto with a beautiful house falling apart, a vast maze of standards to keep up and no cash. So I farmed my own land. Like a paysan. That was how I worked. A slave to my house and my property and my class. Oh, my class. We are all slaving away for a dead past. I kept up a little bit of garden – just enough for the appearance, you know, when people came down the drive to see me. So they could not say, 'Mazarine, he is going under.' Having standards; that means what your neighbours think of you. I painted. I plastered. I did everything. And I ate that filthy food you all eat in the clinique. Just the way my parents had. Just the way all the aristos eat. Part of it is because there is no money. But no money does not cook meat too long or make potatoes floury or forget the salt. And they are not all poor. Some have lots of money. I think it is a hair shirt we put on to remember that we lost our power, our whole meaning for existence, to the bourgeois. So now we are just names and farmers' fields and standards. Fluff in the wind. To learn to cook ourselves would be bourgeois. So we eat like peasants in penitence for our great failure. The bourgeois are the ones who eat well.

"Twenty years ago, Darius came to visit me from Perse. I had not seen him since school in Paris. He was horrified to see the way I lived. I had not thought when I came home from university. I did not consider the meaning of all this. I did the way I knew. 'You live like a domestique, Mazarine,' he said to me. 'You are a victim of your class obsession.' I think he was perhaps ashamed, because he had brought with him two American friends. They all stayed a week. They kept saying, these Americans, 'Monsieur le marquis, we would just love to be thin like you.' I went out to farm every day and when I came back I would find they had been cleaning and gardening. They said they 'just loved to look after my chateau.' I understood. They could pretend they were aristos. Now that is the American dream. The immigrant comes back to Europe and discovers he was not an Irish potato farmer. He was Monsieur le Marquis de Mazarine. Americans are all revolutionaries who would prefer to be aristocrats. Well, they did not like the food, but you know, after a week they had lost a lot of pounds. 'It is your filthy food,' Darius said. 'No wonder you look like a scarecrow.'

"These Americans, they asked if they could come again. So they came and they brought two friends. That was the next year. Then I had my idea. I had read about in the magazines these cliniques – sulphur, seawater, mud, special diet this, special diet that, salt-free. We never put salt anyway. Taste is too bourgeois. So I thought, I have the perfect diet, the perfect exercise, the perfect social *train, train*. We say that. '*Train, train.*' You understand?"

"I understand."

"So I went to Paris. I found the most unpleasant docteur in the world, I think. That is good. That is authoritative. I give him carte blanche and I hide myself away in my wing.

"Now all the patients they live and eat like I used to. And I live and eat like they do when they are not here. Now I am fat and happy and they are fat and unhappy. Only for two weeks they come here to be a little bit thin and a short time happy because they eat so bad and pretend they are Monsieur le Marquis de Mazarine."

I took his turn on the dance floor with Claire. After a

few minutes I whispered to her, "Would you come away for a few days. I know a little place –"

"As they say."

I laughed. "As they say. It's on the coast. They have wonderful –"

"Beds."

"Big, anyway."

She said nothing.

"We'll borrow Mazarine's car. Darius will explain something to your parents. Let's go now. Tonight."

"Tonight?"

"Right now."

She turned us towards the door and danced us that way. In the corridor she ran ahead to collect a few things.